RUNNING into LOVE

Shooting Stars Series

Fighting to Breathe
Wide-Open Spaces

Alpha Law CA ROSE

Justified
Liability
Verdict (Coming Soon)

RUNNING
into LOVE

Aurora Rose Reynolds

Montlake
Romance

Text copyright © 2017 Aurora Rose Reynolds
All rights reserved.

Published by Montlake Romance, Seattle

www.apub.com

Amazon, the Amazon logo, and Montlake Romance are trademarks of Amazon.com, Inc., or its affiliates.

ISBN-13: 9781542046800
ISBN-10: 1542046807

Cover design by Letitia Hasser

Printed in the United States of America

To my son and husband.

Chapter 1

TROUBLE!

LEVI

Lifting my eyes off the pavement below my feet, I frown when I see a woman running toward me with her eyes closed and her hands in the air, waving from side to side. Jesus, what the fuck is she doing? I don't even have a chance to get out of her way, and before I can prepare, she's running into me at full speed and we're both tumbling toward the ground. Attempting to keep my weight from crushing her, I try to spin us at the last second, but I only manage to turn us to our sides before we land and skid across the ground.

Groaning from the impact, I roll over and move to my knees, rising above the woman, and scan her from head to toe. She's tiny, so much smaller than me that I know I could crush her without trying. I just hope I didn't. "Babe." I wait for her eyes to open, and when they do I'm stunned. She's beautiful in an unusual sort of way that reminds me of a fairy. Her blonde hair is a mass of wild curls. Her face is soft; her nose, tiny; and her lips are a shape I wouldn't mind studying more, but her eyes aren't like any I have ever seen before. The color reminds me of an old beat-up green pickup truck I used to have—the green had faded and peeled away, leaving layers of silver and blue. I loved that truck. Feeling her eyes on me, I shake my head and force myself out of whatever spell she has me under. "Are you okay?" I ask her. Her eyes move to my lips, and she frowns. "Christ, do we need to get you to a doctor?" I question, watching as her hand lifts and her finger covers my lips, her brows pulling together. "Do you think you can move, or should I call an ambulance?"

"Are you talking to me?" At her question I frown, then move my eyes over her head and down her neck, and then I see the cord to her earphones. Realizing her music is still blasting and she can't hear me, I move my hand to her neck to take hold of the cord, then let out a grunt as she hits me in the stomach and her knee comes up, barely missing my nuts.

"What the fuck?" I bark.

She starts to go wild, yelling, "Help! Fire!" at the top of her lungs, causing the people walking by to slow to see what's happening.

"Jesus!" I finally get a grip on the cord and pull, which tugs the earphones out of her ears, and her body stills. "Are you crazy?" I grit out, and her eyes move over me, then to the cord in my hand.

"Oh shit. Oops!" she pants, covering her face with her hands. Oops? Is this chick for real?

"What the fuck is wrong with you?" I ask, and she uncovers her face, moving her eyes to my abs as I sit back on my knees.

"Tinker Bell, can you get a fucking clue for a minute?" I snap, ready to wring her pretty little neck, and she pulls her eyes off my torso, then looks around, and her cheeks fill with color.

"Everything's okay. Show's over, folks." While she sits up, she waves her hands out toward the crowd that has gathered around us; then she looks at me and points at my chest. "And, you, don't call me Tinker Bell!"

"You're bleeding," I inform her as I stand, and her eyes drop to her knees, and her face scrunches up. I don't want to think that she looks cute with her face like that, but I do.

"Gross." She stands, not noticing the hand I'm holding out to help her to her feet. Stepping back, I open my mouth to again ask her what the fuck is wrong with her, but my mouth dries up as she rips her shirt off over her head, leaving herself in nothing but a sports bra. As my eyes scan over her tight little body, my cock twitches. Then I realize I'm not the only one checking her out; a couple of other men have stopped to stare. At that, my anger irrationally spikes.

"Are you kidding me? Put your shirt back on! What the hell is wrong with you?" I step close and pull my tee from my back pocket, where I'd shoved it at the start of my run. "Put this on," I demand, holding the shirt out toward her, and she shakes her head.

"No, thanks."

"You seriously must be crazy. What the hell kind of woman runs with her eyes closed?" I ask, and her head starts to lift, but her gaze pauses on my abs before she lifts her eyes slowly to meet mine.

"If you knew my eyes were closed, why didn't you get out of my way?" she asks before moving her eyes back to her knee, which pisses me off. It shouldn't matter, but I fucking hate that she keeps taking her eyes from me.

"You must be a natural blonde," I grit out, but she doesn't give me the reaction I want.

Her eyes stay on her knee as she mutters, "And you must be a natural asshole."

Standing there staring at her, I realize I must have hit my head, because I seriously want to get this woman's attention. What the fuck is wrong with *me*? Without knowing this chick, I can tell she's a whole different kind of trouble. "Just run with your eyes open from now on," I bark, pissed off at myself. I need to get away from her before I do something stupid.

Like kiss the crazy woman.

"Run with your eyes open," I hear in a mocking voice behind me. My head swings around, and I find her rolling her eyes at me.

3

"I saw that," I inform her like a fucking five-year-old.

"Good." She shrugs, and frustration fills my chest. I have never been more turned on and annoyed in my fucking life. "I thought you were leaving." She raises a brow, and my jaw ticks.

"I am." I turn and jog off before I do something crazy like toss the woman over my shoulder and run home with her crazy ass and fuck her until neither of us can move. Reaching the park exit, I feel something hit my thigh, and I realize then that I still have her headphones. With a shake of my head, I shove them into my pocket and look at my watch. The movers will be at my place in just a few minutes, which means even if I wanted to go find her to return her headphones, I don't have time.

FAWN

"Why are the hot ones always jerks?" I shake my head in disgust, pulling my eyes from the hot shirtless guy's retreating back. When I first opened my eyes after crashing to the ground and saw him above me, I thought I was seeing things. The light from the sun had caused a halo to appear around him, making him look like the gods themselves had cast him down to Earth. Luxurious dark hair had fallen across his forehead, and golden eyes with thick dark lashes had scanned me from head to toe, making something inside me feel warm and dizzy. Then I saw his lips move like I was in some kind of strange dream, and I asked him if he was talking to me. I probably shouldn't have assumed he was trying to attack me when he was only pulling out my earbuds, but how was I supposed to know he wasn't? On that thought, I shake my head and limp over to one of the benches lining the path and take a seat. Pulling out my beloved iPhone from the pocket in my sports bra, I sigh, realizing that my headphones are gone. Getting up, I look around to see if he dropped them on the ground, then look toward where Mr. Hot Guy ran off and debate whether I should try to catch up with him. Deciding that I don't want another confrontation—since my ego can't handle it—I head home, walking slowly through the city.

Once I reach my block, I notice a large moving truck parked in front of my building with the back flap open and two guys sitting on boxes inside. Diva, who lived in the apartment across the hall from me, moved out of the building and in with her fiancé a month ago, so it's a good bet that I'm finally getting a new neighbor. Walking up the stairs, I stop dead in my tracks. There is no way my luck could be this bad.

Mr. Hot Shirtless Guy from the park is standing in front of Diva's empty apartment door talking to two guys who are carrying a large leather couch. Ducking my head, I try to get past his open door without being noticed, but I know I'm too late when I hear him ask, "Are you stalking me?"

"You wish." I glare at him as I pull a key out of my sports bra and walk across the hall to open the door to my apartment.

"You have got to be kidding me." He narrows his eyes, which makes me smile and his eyes narrow further.

"See you around, neighbor."

I laugh, shutting the door with my heart pounding as a voice in the hall says something about a hot neighbor before a different voice booms, "Shut the fuck up." Smiling at that, I look around. I am quite proud of my little nest. My apartment is considered large by New York standards, because in addition to my bedroom I have a small office space with a door that could be considered a second bedroom. The kitchen is to the right and has a bar that stretches the length of the kitchen, separating it from the living room. Four heavy metal bar stools with high backs line the bar, each in a different color—one rusty red, one dusty blue, one burnt yellow, and the last a weathered green. The living room, where I spend most of my time, has a suede sofa with throw pillows of different colors, which tie into the bar stools, and a painting that hangs above the couch of a pot of flowers sitting on an old table. The bedroom has the same furniture I had growing up: a double bed with an elegant wrought-iron frame, a tall white dresser, and one glass-top metal-framed side table that I found at a flea market. Above my bed hangs a picture I took of the ocean when I was around fifteen that my mom had blown up a few years ago as a Christmas gift. It reminds me of home but also complements the bedside lamp filled with sand from that exact beach and some shells I have collected over the years. The blue-green duvet and sheets make my room look like it belongs near the sea, a place I love.

Pulling myself from the front door, I head to the couch and lie down, closing my eyes for a few much-needed minutes of shut-eye.

Feeling a wet, rough tongue run over the side of my face, I smile.

"Hey, baby." I greet my girl, running a hand through her fur while opening my eyes. You would never know that Muffin is only ten months old judging by her size. My Irish wolfhound pup once weighed eight pounds, but now she weighs a hundred and fifteen. "You missed out on the run today, girl," I say, sitting up to make room for her when she climbs up next to me on the couch. "Mama biffed it in the park and had some tango time with a shirtless hot guy," I inform her, and she licks my cheek again. Grabbing both sides of her face, I look into her brown eyes. "Next time I'm dragging you along whether you want to go or not."

"Ruff."

"Too bad, because next time you're coming along," I reply to her bark, which I'm guessing means no. This morning when I left for my run, she refused to budge from the bed, and I wasn't about to fight with her about going out. She's stubborn as hell when she wants to be. The one time I attempted to take her for a walk against her will ended badly for both of us. As in I had to carry my seventy-pound puppy home two blocks in the rain.

"Coming," I yell when someone starts pounding on my door. Pushing myself up off the couch, I head across the room, knowing who it is without even looking through the peephole. Putting my hand on Muffin's head to hold her back, I look down at her. "Be nice," I

6

command, and she huffs, taking a seat. She doesn't like men at all. One of my boyfriends was cornered in the kitchen when he got up to get some water in the middle of the night. I found him there the next day asleep on top of the counter. After that he refused to come over, which in turn ended our relationship, since there was no way I was going to get busy with him at his place while his mom was in the next room.

I swing the door open, taking in my new neighbor, who looks like he's had a shower in the last ten minutes. "Can I help you?" His hair is still damp on the ends, and he smells like soap and some kind of dark, intriguing cologne. I can't help but notice he's just as hot in a white tee, almost-black jeans, and black boots as he was shirtless and sweaty.

"Did you even check the damn peephole?" he barks, and my eyes fly up to meet his.

The corners of his eyes have small lines forming around them, and I wonder if I should tell him something my mom always tells me. *"Honey, stop frowning. You know it causes premature wrinkling. You don't want to look like your aunt Lizbeth, do you?"*

"I knew it was you." I shrug, leaving out the information about wrinkles, figuring he probably wouldn't care.

"How?"

"How what?"

"How did you know it was me?"

"For starters, no one I know would ever pound on the door like they're the police. Secondly, I'm not expecting any company, so I risked it all and took a wild guess. Are you here to return my headphones?" I ask, holding out my hand toward him.

"What the hell is that thing?" he asks as his eyes drop to Muffin, who is trying to push past me to get to him.

"It's a chicken. Now do you have my headphones or not?"

"Are you always a pain in the ass?"

"Are you always an ass?" He shakes his head, dropping the headphones into my open palm. "Thanks." I smile as he runs a hand over his head, looking at me, then looking around. "Did you need something else? Flour, sugar, my firstborn child?"

"You are so strange," he informs me as his eyes roam down my chest and stomach, causing my skin to tingle, my stomach to dip, and me to realize that I'm still shirtless.

"Thanks." I smile—or try to—before my dog shoves me out of the way. "Muffin, *no!*" I cry as she runs right past my new neighbor, across the hall, and into his apartment. Running after her through his open door, I find Muffin sprawled out on his couch like it already belongs to her.

"Muffin, come here," I growl pointing to the floor at my feet. Her head lifts for a second before she lowers it back down and closes her eyes. "Muffin, do you want a treat?" I ask, and she opens one eye but still doesn't move.

"She's very well trained," my new neighbor chuckles as my face heats.

"I'm really sorry about this," I say, trying to hide my now scarlet face.

"Levi."

"Pardon?" I ask turning my head toward him.

"My name's Levi."

"Oh." I mutter, thinking Mr. Hot Shirtless Guy fits him better, but I guess Levi is okay, too.

"And this would be the time you tell me your name." He raises one brow expectantly.

"Fawn," I say under my breath.

"What?" He frowns, moving closer.

"My name's Fawn—like a baby deer." I sigh, hating that my parents named me after an animal that has a history of getting hit by cars or shot by hunters.

"Fawn," he rumbles while his eyes slide over me once more, making me suddenly aware of how close we are and how very attracted I am to him when I totally shouldn't be. I know men like him, and I know they always lead to one thing—heartache.

Wow, okay, time to go. I slap myself mentally while moving toward Muffin, ready to carry her out of here if I have to.

"Her name's Muffin?" he asks as I pull on her legs in an attempt to drag her off the couch.

"Yes," I confirm, glaring at her when she tucks her long doggy legs under her body and turns her face away from me.

"Muffin, come," he says with a snap of his fingers, and she instantly lifts her head and bounds off the couch to stand in front of him. "Sit," he orders, and she backs up, taking a seat.

"Traitor."

"You're a good girl," he coos, walking toward her, and I know this is when she's going to show her true colors and try to attack him. But of course it's just my luck that she stays still and allows him to pet her. "You just need to be the alpha," he tells me with a devastatingly smug smile while my girl rubs against him with her tail wagging. So much for dogs knowing anything about girl code!

Okay, I'm officially jealous of my dog.

"She likes you," I whisper in shock as she licks his palm.

"Most women do." He grins, and I roll my eyes even though I'm sure it's true. Most women are attracted to assholes—it's human nature.

"Let's go, Muffin." I clap my hands against my thighs, and she looks at me, then back at Levi.

"Come on, girl, let's go," he commands as he turns for the door.

"Yeah, the alpha thing is totally working. You should write that down for me." I snicker as she climbs back onto his couch and lies back down.

Sighing, he looks at Muffin, then runs his hand through his hair. "Why don't you go get her a treat and I'll wait here for you to come back." With a nod, I head across the hall to my apartment and grab a treat from the large jar on the kitchen counter, then rush back over to his place.

"Muffin! Treat!" I sing as I walk through the door, then cross my arms over my chest and stare. Levi's standing over Muffin rubbing her belly and cooing at her like she's a small child. "She's not going to want to leave if you're doing that."

"If I didn't have to work I would say she could stay, but I need to leave soon." He gives her one last rub as he looks at his watch.

"What kind of work do you do?" I hold the treat close to Muffin's mouth, then pull it away when she tries to snatch it, hoping she will follow the treat—but she doesn't.

"I'm a detective with the NYPD."

"Well, thank you for your service." I smile, then continue softly, "My dad's a detective out on Long Island, so I know how difficult your job can be."

"It's a lot of work, but it's also very fulfilling," he agrees. "Where do you work?" he asks after a moment of watching me try to tempt Muffin off the couch with the treat.

"Hustler on West Fifty-Fourth Street," I say with a straight face.

"Thanks for your service." He winks, and laughter bubbles up the back of my throat and my head tilts back as I laugh loudly. "What do you really do?" he asks softly when my laughter has died down and I've wiped the tears from under my eyes.

"I'm a fifth-grade teacher." I smile, then let out a frustrated breath as Muffin grabs the treat from between my fingers and swallows it in one gulp.

"Do you like it?" He laughs at Muffin as she scoots over just enough to shove her head under his hand so that he'll pet her again.

"Love it," I respond immediately. "I know it's cheesy, but there is no better feeling than seeing a kid's face when they learn something new." His eyes change and fill with a softness that makes my stomach flutter.

Seeing that look, I know I need to get out of here, because the level of hotness is enough to make me question my recent decision to join a convent. I enjoy dating about as much as I enjoy getting my monthly Brazilian.

The whole dating scene has changed so much during the last few years. Now instead of just telling someone that you like them and you would like to spend time with them, you're left competing for—I don't know what. The whole swipe left, swipe right, call, don't call, text, don't text, interested, not interested, have sex, don't have sex scene has left me a little confused and a lot overwhelmed. On my last date, the guy openly compared me to another woman he was seeing. I think he was drawing up an Excel spreadsheet in his head while I sat across from him. He actually asked me my jeans and shoe size. I was surprised he didn't ask me my SAT scores or bank balance. When I got home from that date, I knew I was done. I decided that I would rather spend my days alone than be made to feel inadequate.

Looking at Muffin, I pray she takes me up on my next offer so I can get out of here. "Do you want to go for a walk?" Barking excitedly, she jumps off the couch and leaves through the crack in the door. "Finally," I mumble, then turn to face Levi again. "Thanks for being so cool about this."

"No problem." He smiles gently, and my stomach flutters again.

"It was nice meeting you."

"See you around, Fawn," he rumbles, making my girlie bits sit up and take notice.

"See you around, neighbor." I give him a dorky salute, then head across the hall to my apartment, grabbing a hoodie from the coat closet and Muffin's leash. Leading her down the two flights of stairs, I smile when Levi greets us with a smirk from the bottom landing.

"Are you sure you're not following me?" he questions as we descend the last three steps.

"Positive." I roll my eyes, before remembering my manners. "Thank you." I smile as he opens the door, letting us exit before him. I guess chivalry isn't totally dead—yet.

Looking both ways, I try to figure out where he's going to go so Muffin and I can head in the opposite direction. "Which way are you going?" I ask, giving up trying to figure out his path. There are two subway stations close to our building, and depending on what precinct he's working at, he could take either train.

"This way." He nods to the right.

"Bummer, we're going the other way." I tilt my head to the left, then smile. "Be safe at work."

A slow smile spreads across his face, like he finds something entertaining, and he rubs Muffin's head briefly before meeting my eyes again. "See you girls around."

"See ya around." I wave as I drag Muffin down the sidewalk away from him. Halfway down the block, I can't help myself, and I look over my shoulder, then bite the inside of my cheek to keep my emotions in check when I see that he's still standing where I left him. Crossing his arms over his wide chest, he lifts his chin ever so slightly and his eyes bore into mine.

Pulling my gaze from him I whisper, "I'm in so much trouble," earning an unsolicited bark from Muffin.

Chapter 2

Totally Read That Wrong

Fawn

"I think we should get dressed up for Halloween and go out tonight. We never go out on Halloween anymore," my sister Mackenzie complains as she flops down onto the couch next to Muffin, who then takes an opportunity to lick her face.

"We went out last year," my little sister, Libby, mumbles while frowning at her cell phone.

"Yeah, we went to one of your stupid snooty clubs. The whole night was a complete bore," Mac says, glaring at Libby, who lowers her phone to glare right back.

If I didn't know for a fact that we were sisters, I would think we were switched at birth because we are all so different. Mackenzie, better known as Mac, is the oldest and a complete tomboy. Okay, a tomboy who looks like a model when she dresses up. Mac has long, natural red hair and big green eyes, just like our dad. Our baby sister, Libby, is the beauty queen of the three of us, with dark-brown hair that ends at the middle of her back and crystal-blue eyes—she looks just like our mom's high school prom picture. Then there's me, the classic middle child and the nerd, with untamable curly blonde hair and odd blue eyes that look more like river gray than Libby's ocean blue. Our parents still question where I got the blonde hair, and there's a running joke that my features match the postman's, which would be funny if it wasn't true.

"I wanted to order Chinese, watch *Hocus Pocus*, and hand out candy," I say, knowing neither of them will likely listen to me or what I want to do, even though they both chose to come to my house for the night. Where my sisters love to go out, I enjoy hanging at home. I would much rather spend an evening in my pajamas than get dressed up to go anywhere.

"You always want to stay in," Libby mutters, gaining a nod of agreement from Mac.

"There is nothing wrong with staying home," I grumble under my breath, defending myself.

"No, there is nothing wrong with staying home . . . occasionally . . . but you would never leave the house if you didn't have to," Libby says, tossing her phone onto the coffee table, then looking me over and barely concealing her obvious disappointment in the fact I'm not like her and could really care less about my appearance. Those crystal blues travel from my hair—tied up in a ponytail—to a tee stating I went to Hogwarts School of Witchcraft and Wizardry to my ripped jeans that I've had forever before resting on the grubby red Toms that I refuse to part with. "When was the last time you went on a date?"

I sit back in my chair and put my hands up to my scrubbed-clean face. "Nope, not happening. I'm not going to let you hook me up with someone *again*." I shout the last word, and her nose scrunches up like I'm being dramatic. The first and last time I let her set me up was a disaster. The guy was an actor who thought he was god's gift to women.

"You didn't even give Phil a chance."

"In Fawn's defense, Phil is high maintenance," Mac chimes in, gaining a disapproving glare from Libby.

"He's a nice guy," Libby defends her friend.

"He asked to use my compact during dinner," I growl at her.

"So what's wrong with that? Maybe he had something in his teeth." She waves her hands around dismissively.

"Yeah, I thought so, too, until he used my powder, saying that the lighting was making him look shiny." Mac starts giggling, and Muffin stands above her, wagging her tail happily thinking that she wants to play.

"He's an *act-or*," Libby states, like that fact alone should make it okay for a man to use a woman's makeup, when in all actuality, it's not okay for a woman to use someone's makeup without asking for permission.

"Well, then, cross actors off my list," I grumble.

"What kind of men are you interested in?" Libby asks, and for some stupid reason the hot detective next door comes to mind, but I push that thought aside, since for the last two weeks I have avoided any contact with him—going so far as to hide in my room when he's knocked on my door.

"I'm focusing on work right now, so I don't really have time to date," I lie, watching her eyes narrow.

"You're not still stuck on Jayson, right?" Mac asks, and my stomach turns.

"God, no," I practically yell. Jayson was my last serious boyfriend, and he was also a serious dick. I don't know what I saw in him, but I do know that because of him I've decided to be more cautious when dating and warier of attractive men.

"You know what, Mac? I think you're right. I think we should go out," Libby says, looking at me.

Rolling my eyes, I look at Mac, who is grinning ear to ear. "Fine, let's go out. What's the worst that could happen?" I shrug, knowing they won't give up, so I might as well go and, hopefully, be home early enough to at least watch *Hocus Pocus*.

"Great. I just happened to bring a few costumes." Mac jumps up and heads to the front door, picking up her duffel bag she dropped there when she came in.

"You just so happened to bring costumes with you?" I ask, and she grins, carrying her bag to my room. Following her, Libby and I sit on the edge of the bed as she starts to pull the costumes out of her bag.

"This dress is yours." She smiles, handing Libby a piece of red fabric that looks more like a tube top than a dress. "And this one is yours." Taking it from her, I notice that it is the same style as Libby's, only it's dark blue. "And this one is mine." She grins, holding up a piece of white fabric in front of her.

"This is a dress?" I question, holding out the supposed dress. I can't imagine that the thing can cover more than one of my vital parts at a time, and I will have to choose between the twins or my vajayjay.

"Exactly what are we dressing up as?" Libby asks, stretching out the material.

"Hoes." Mac smiles proudly.

"Hoes?" I repeat.

"There's a pimps and hoes party tonight at Jack's, so we're going as hoes."

"Can I be a pimp instead?" I ask, stepping on the dress and pulling it up, trying to make it longer, but it ends up snapping back and hitting me in the face.

"You're not going to get a man if you're dressed like a pimp." Libby rolls her eyes like I'm ridiculous for not wanting to wear a dress that wouldn't fit one of my fifth graders.

"I don't want a man, and if I did, I wouldn't want one that wanted me because I'm dressed like a prostitute." I sigh, flopping back on my bed and looking at the ceiling.

Why didn't god give me brothers?

"I'll do our makeup," Libby chirps happily, and I groan against the palms of my hands as I cover my face.

"Come on, it will be fun," Mac says, tugging my hands away from my face. Glaring at her one last time, I give up and let her pull me out of bed and into the bathroom. Looking at myself in the mirror, I sigh and tug at the hair tie just barely containing my blonde mop. Unleashed, my hair looks how I imagine a lion's mane does on a bad hair day.

"That is the perfect look." Libby smiles in the mirror behind me as I frown and look at myself. Setting her makeup bag down on the counter, she aims a can of hair spray in my direction.

"No more." I cough as she sprays and sprays until I wrestle the can from her evil grasp. I now look like I have a fro and am in major need of a deep conditioner.

"Now let's do your makeup."

Looking at my sister in the mirror, I shake my head no. "I'll just do my own makeup."

"When was the last time you wore makeup?"

"I wear makeup every day."

"You wear mascara."

"Mascara is makeup," I defend as she closes the lid on the toilet and pushes me down to take a seat.

"Close your eyes." Letting out a huff, I shut my eyes and allow her to do my makeup, which I realize is a huge mistake a few minutes later when I stand to look at myself.

"Could you at least make me look like a high-class hoe?" I pout at my reflection; the blue eye shadow wouldn't be so bad alone, but the black liner, the bright-pink lipstick, and my hair, combined, make me look like a twenty-dollar hooker from 1989.

"What can I say? I'm good at what I do." Libby smiles, happily adding a touch of pink shadow to her eyes.

"This is going to be a disaster," I tell her, and Mac elbows me in the ribs.

"Oh, stop. It's going to be fun—you'll see." She grins, shimmying into her so-called dress.

"Is Edward going to be there, by any chance?" I question, and her cheeks get pink, giving me my answer.

"He had a baseball game tonight, but the guys usually show up after." She shrugs like it's all the same to her, but I know that's a lie. Edward is my sister's sometime physical therapy client and full-time crush. He treats her like one of the guys, which drives her crazy. Really, I don't even think he knows that she's a woman, which means he's an idiot and must be completely blind.

"So you're going to dress like a hooker to see if he'll notice that you are, in fact, a girl?"

She chews on the inside of her cheek and shrugs again.

"Leave her alone. At least she's trying," Libby snips, meeting my eyes in the mirror.

"I just want to know what kind of night I'm in for," I defend myself, snipping right back at her.

"Just go put on your dress." She pushes me out the door, then takes Mac's hand and pulls her to take a seat on the toilet. Rolling my eyes, I go to my room and pick the dress up off the bed. I have tank tops that look longer, I think as I kick off my red Toms and jeans, then take off my shirt and tug the dress over my head. Pulling the dress down as far as it will go, I sigh when it snaps back right below my ass. Giving in to the whole look, I go to my closet and find a pair of heels and a long coat to cover the whole embarrassing ensemble.

"Are you guys America?" our cabbie asks in a thick Hispanic accent as the three of us pile into the backseat twenty minutes later.

"We're actually hookers," I tell him with a straight face, gaining an elbow in the ribs from Libby, whom I elbow right back.

"American hookers?" he asks, looking at us over his shoulder.

"Yep, American hookers." Mac laughs, and Libby sighs.

"Two of my favorite things," he says, then turns to look at the dash and starts the meter. Struggling into my coat, which I didn't have time to put on before we left, I sink down low in the seat and pray the night ends quickly.

The ride to the bar doesn't take long. When we arrive, I pull out a twenty-dollar bill, and in a fit of generosity/humiliation, I tell the driver to keep the change. Once I'm on my feet, I attempt, with little success, to pull down the skirt of my dress again.

"Let's go," Libby says, grabbing my arm and dragging me with her.

"Hey, darlin'." A giant of a man with tan skin, dark blond hair, and blue eyes greets Mac with a southern accent as soon as we reach the door.

"Hey, Tex, how's it going tonight?" She smiles, tipping her head back as he leans down to press a kiss to her cheek. If his accent didn't give away that he wasn't from around here, his plaid button-up shirt, worn blue jeans, and cowboy boots would. Not many men in Manhattan could wear what he was wearing and look hot doing it.

"Been busy." He smiles at her; then his eyes come to Libby and me and he asks, "These your sisters?"

"Yep. Libby and Fawn, meet Big Tex." Mac waves her hand toward him, and he smiles.

"Nice to meet you," Libby and I greet him in unison, and his smile turns into a grin, taking his look from hot to over-the-top hot.

"You, too, ladies." He looks at Mac again and asks, "Have you been saving your money for the next home game?"

"No, but I already know where I'm going to spend yours." She smiles, making him chuckle.

"Wanna raise the odds?" he questions, and her face lights up. Mac loves a good bet, and it seems this guy knows it.

"Name your price."

"Dinner. I win, you cook, you win, I'll pay," he states, and she tilts her head back toward the night sky, then looks back at him.

"I look forward to eating on your dime." She grins, and suddenly I feel bad for Tex, because clearly my sister has no idea that he is into her.

"We'll see, darlin'. Now, go on in—it's cold out," he tells her, opening the door to the bar.

"Thanks, Tex," she replies, heading inside, followed by Libby.

Getting up on my tiptoes, I press my hand to the hard wall of Tex's chest so I don't tip over in my heels, and his startled gaze comes to me. "Keep at her. She never sees what's right in front of her," I tell him, and his eyes narrow in a way that looks almost dangerous.

"I'm married," he growls.

Blinking, I fall back on my heels and ask, "You're married?"

"Very fucking married. To her friend." He lifts his chin toward the door.

Oh shit. Whelp, I totally read that wrong.

"Oh," I mumble under my breath, then nod and smile through my embarrassment, because what else can I do. "Keep up the good work, and congrats." I pat his chest, then scurry inside, only to stop dead when I clear the door.

There are a lot of men and women inside, so many that the entire room is packed, but absolutely none of them are dressed up.

Not one.

"Well, this is awkward," I mutter to myself, watching Mac and Libby head toward the back of the bar. Catching up with them, I press my lips together as they set their coats in an empty booth. "I think I'm just gonna leave my coat on," I say when Mac turns toward me and holds out her hand, wiggling her fingers.

"You're not leaving the coat on."

"Did either of you happen to look around? No one is dressed up— not one person," I cry, batting Libby's hands away when she tries to untie the belt of my coat.

"It's still early," Libby informs me.

I look at her, then back to Mac, and ask, "Are you sure this costume party was scheduled for tonight?"

"Tonight's Halloween. When else would it be?" She looks around. Following her gaze around the room, I stop on a poster behind the bar announcing the pimps and hoes party has been rescheduled for tomorrow night.

"We're a day early," I point out, and she looks around again and bites her bottom lip.

"So we'll make the best of it and have a good time tonight," Libby says, and I hope she knows that if it were possible she would be dead by now, lit on fire with the lasers I'm trying to shoot from my eyes. Unfortunately, she doesn't read the threat.

"Do you know how ridiculous we look right now?" I ask, looking between the two. Mac, at least, has the decency to look apprehensive, but apparently Libby has set her mind on doing this, because she just raises a brow and wiggles her fingers in a silent command for me to give up my coat. "Well, then, you both are in for it, because I'm now going to drink away my embarrassment, which means you will both be responsible for making sure I get home safely or you can face Mom and Dad and explain to them why their favorite daughter was found dead dressed like a prostitute."

Mac's eyes narrow, and she yell-whispers, "I'm Mom and Dad's favorite."

Snorting, I shake my head no, then give in and slip off the coat.

"You both know I'm their favorite. I'm the baby," Libby chimes in, tossing my coat onto hers and Mac's in the booth.

"You wish," I mutter, and she glares at me.

"Come on, let's just go get a drink, and next time we see Mom and Dad, they can tell us who their real favorite is," Mac says, stepping between us.

"Fine," I agree as Libby curls her lip up and repeats.

"Fine."

"I see this is going to be a tequila kind of night." Mac sighs, dragging us toward the bar.

~

"I can't bewieve someone stole our jackets," Libby slurs four hours later, stumbling into me and causing me to stumble into Mac as the three of us huddle together in an attempt to keep warm as we rush down the street toward the train station.

"At least we have a MetroCard." Mac giggles, stumbling into my other side and making me bounce against Libby.

"You guys are good sisters," I tell them, happily ducking my face down into the huddle to ward off the cold I feel biting my cheeks.

"The best," Mac agrees, and I frown, wondering who put a disco ball outside as red-and-blue lights flash around us. Then my body freezes when I hear the all too familiar *bweep, bweep.*

"Oh no," Libby whispers, voicing my fear as we turn to look over our shoulders and watch two officers get out of a squad car that has pulled up behind us.

"Ladies, if you could walk back toward us, that would be appreciated," one of the officers says, placing his hand on the butt of his gun as he stops beside the hood of the squad car.

"Just play it cool," Libby says, straightening her spine and shoving her shoulders back before sauntering toward the cops, which I realize a little too late is a bad, bad idea. "What can we do for you, Officers? Is there a problem?" she purrs, but the words are slurred and she stumbles in her heels, taking her from sex kitten to klutzy drunk in two seconds flat.

"Is this your normal track?" the cop on the driver's side asks, and Libby stops and tilts her head to the side, flipping her hair over her shoulder.

"Pardon?"

"Is this your normal track?" the cop on the passenger side repeats, and Libby looks at Mac and me, frowning.

"Do either of you know what they are asking?"

"They think we're prostitutes," I chime in blandly, not surprised. That old saying if it walks like a duck and talks like a duck comes to mind, and seeing how we look like prostitutes, are dressed like prostitutes, and have no coats in the dead of night when it's freezing out, I'm sure the cops are putting two and two together and coming up with ten.

"We're not prostitutes. We just dressed up like them," Mac says, and both the officers look at her.

"Do you ladies have IDs?"

"Someone stole our coats, and our IDs were in the pockets," I explain. The cops look at the three of us, and I know they don't believe us at all—not that I can blame them, because I wouldn't believe us, either.

"A prostitute was murdered two blocks over. Do you know anything about that?"

"No." I shake my head, wrapping my arms around myself, feeling a chill that has nothing to do with the cold creeping over me.

"Can we go? It's kind of cold," Libby whispers, and the officers look at her, then me and Mac.

"We're gonna have to ask you ladies to come down to the station to answer a few questions."

"We're really not prostitutes," I tell them, and they nod, like, *yeah, sure you're not* as they open the back door to the squad car.

"At least we're not out in the cold anymore," Mac says once we are all tucked into the backseat, and I turn my head and look at her in disbelief. "What, just saying." She shrugs. Closing my eyes, I lean my head against the window, thinking this can't get any worse.

I really should know better.

Chapter 3

FLUSTERED

FAWN

"It will be fun, they told me. Live a little, they said," I huff, staring at my sisters through our reflection in the mirror in front of us—and ignoring how horrifying I look right now. My makeup has melted off, and my hair is now a hundred times bigger than when we left the house. I look like something the cat spit up before dragging home.

"It was fun." Mac yawns, and I turn my head to glare at her. She shrugs. "What? Even you have to admit you had fun tonight."

"No part of being arrested is fun."

"We technically weren't arrested," Libby puts in, and I transfer my glare to her. She rolls her eyes. "Well, we weren't—they didn't even read us our Miranda rights."

"We're sitting in an interrogation room at a police station," I point out.

She looks around, muttering, "This is true." She bites her bottom lip like she just realized where we are.

"God save me." I drop my head to the top of the table with a thud, then lift it quickly and sit up straight in my chair when the knob starts to turn. As soon as the door opens, my eyes widen and the color drains from my face. "This cannot be happening," I breathe, watching Levi step into the room. His head is down; he's looking at a stack of papers in his hand, so I can't see his beautiful face, but I have no doubt it's him. I'd know his broad shoulders and thick head of hair anywhere. Scooting as low as I can in my seat without crawling under the table, I lower my face toward my chest and try to hide, praying he doesn't recognize me.

"Aren't we supposed to get a phone call?" Mac asks, and I scoot even lower, swearing I feel his eyes burning into the side of my head as I study the top of the table like it's the most fascinating thing I've ever seen in my entire life.

"Fawn?" Pretending I have no idea who Fawn is, I tuck my chin closer to my chest.

"How do you know my sister?" Libby asks, blowing my cover and leaving me with no choice but to lift my head and look at him.

"Oh, hi, Levi." I wave like the idiot I am, and his brows pull together tightly over his beautiful golden eyes in confusion. "These are my sisters, Libby and Mac," I introduce them, and his gaze narrows.

"What the fuck are you doing here?"

"It's a long story." I smile, then watch him turn back toward the door and stick his head out.

"Jinks, come in here," he shouts, then turns back to face me, crossing his arms over his chest.

"What's up?" one of the officers who brought us in asks, poking his head in through the crack in the door before coming into the room completely.

"I thought you and Van said you brought in three prostitutes."

"We did. We picked them up two blocks over from the murder."

"These women are not prostitutes."

"They looked like prostitutes and were in a known area for prostitution," Jinks says.

Glaring at him, I grit out, "I told you we were walking to the train to go home."

"You also had no IDs." He shrugs his broad shoulders, and my hands ball in my lap.

"This is my neighbor," Levi states with a shake of his head at Jinks before looking at me once more. "What were you doing over there? And why the hell are you dressed like that?" he questions, raking his eyes over me, causing my skin to tingle and heat the same way it did last time I was around him.

"We were at a bar—"

"You were at a bar dressed like that?" he cuts me off, and there is no mistaking that he's angry, judging by the tick of his jaw and the growl in his tone. I just don't get why. It's Halloween. Most women I know use Halloween as an excuse to dress like they are streetwalkers. Okay, some go as zombies, but even then, they are typically slutty zombies.

"It was a pimps and hoes party," Libby says unhelpfully, and I shove my elbow in her side, only to have her do the same back to me, making me wince and cover the abused spot with my hand.

"Pimps and hoes," he repeats, looking directly at me, and I shift in my seat.

"Yes, a pimps and hoes party at Jack's. You know, the bar near the stadium," Mac tosses in, and I close my eyes briefly, wishing my sisters would just be quiet.

"So why were you three walking in the cold without coats?" Jinks asks.

"Like we told you on the ride to the station, our coats were stolen from the bar, but I still had my MetroCard in my bra, so we were walking to the train, which now I realize was a giant damn mistake," Libby grumbles, glaring at Officer Jinks.

"Ya think?" Jinks asks with a grin, and we all glare at him—including Levi. "Just sayin'." He holds out a hand in front of himself. "You could have called a cab and paid the fare when you got to your place."

God, we are seriously so damn stupid, because not one of us thought of that.

"I'll take you home," Levi mutters, and my stomach drops to my toes as panic fills my chest.

"That's not necessary. You're working—we can take a cab, you know, and pay him when we reach my apartment," I say hopefully, wringing my hands together in my lap, but he shakes his head, not uncrossing his arms.

"I'm heading home anyways, so I'll take you."

"Perfect." Mac stands along with Libby, leaving me no choice but to do the same, since it would look really strange if I refused to go with them. Silently cursing myself for being such a pushover with my sisters, I stand and attempt to pull my dress down enough to cover my ass. After a few seconds of tugging and pulling, I give up the fight and start toward the door, watching Levi's jaw clench the closer I get to him.

"Here." He slips off his suit jacket and swings it around my shoulders before I have a chance to refuse. I feel the weight and warmth settle around my body and the scent of soap and musk seep into my lungs. My gaze locks with his, and my head gets dizzy while my legs feel weak, and it takes everything in me to keep standing.

"Thanks," I murmur, getting lost in his eyes.

"What about us? Do we get jackets?" Libby asks, breaking into the moment, and Levi's hand that had been resting lightly on my shoulder drops away, making me want to growl from the loss. Jealousy fills my chest as his eyes go to her, and I wait for the inevitable to happen. I know men think Libby is beautiful—because she is—and I know she can get pretty much any man she wants, so I expect to see some kind of flare of desire when he looks at her. But there is nothing, not even a hint of something. Which is surprising, since every guy I've ever been even a little interested in has looked at her with interest, even if they try to hide it.

"Sorry, only got one," he says with a shrug, holding the door open for us. When we step into the hall, my stomach knots as we wait for him to move ahead of us. I don't know what just happened, but my heart is pounding so hard I can feel its relentless *thump, thump, thump* in my throat.

"I can't believe you never mentioned living next to a hottie who knows how to use a set of cuffs," Libby whispers loudly, leaning into me as we follow Levi and Officer Jinks down a long hall while they talk quietly.

"Shut up, Libby," I hiss, trying to keep up with Levi's mile-long legs in my heels that are now killing me.

"Just saying, I totally understand now why you didn't want me to hook you up with anyone."

"Libby," I warn, watching Levi's shoulders tense as my sister continues talking.

"What? I'm just saying, if I had a guy like him living next door to me, I wouldn't look elsewhere, either."

"Please." I look at her and jerk my chin toward Levi's back, hoping she will realize he can totally hear every single word she's saying.

"Oh yeah, sorry," she mumbles, having the audacity to look contrite. "You probably don't want him to know that you want him." My teeth snap together, and I glare at her, letting her know silently that if we weren't in the middle of a police station I would take her to the ground and force her to be quiet like I've been doing my whole life.

"Libby, stop being a pain." Mac laughs, tucking Libby into her side, forcing her to walk next to her a few feet ahead of me. Thankful for the reprieve, I drop my eyes to the ground and wrap my arms around my middle as I walk behind them.

"Fawn," Levi calls, and I stop walking and lift my eyes to his staring back at me.

"Levi?" I prompt when he does nothing more than scan my face.

"I'll be right back."

"Uh, sure." I nod, gaining his chin lift in reply before he and Jinks disappear behind a closed door at the entrance of the station.

Feeling Mac and Libby get close, I pull my eyes from the door to look at them. "Someone's been holding out on us," Mac says, and I shrug.

"He's my new neighbor. I don't really know him." Her eyes search mine, and a slow smile spreads across her face like she knows something I don't. "I've only talked to him once before today," I continue, and her smile broadens.

"Sure," she says, like she doesn't believe me, and I bite my tongue, refusing to let her bait me into an argument, which is something she does often.

"Ready?" Levi asks a few minutes later, and I let out the breath I've been holding.

"Yep." I start for the door behind my sisters, who have already stepped outside ahead of us.

"Hold up." His voice slides over me as his long, warm fingers wrap around my wrist and tighten when I try to tug free.

"What?" I look up at him, hating how breathless I sound.

"Paper."

"What?" I repeat, getting lost in his gaze and touch as the fingers on his other hand slide up my temple and through my hair.

"You have paper in your hair," he says, gently flicking his fingers out, causing a small scrap of white paper to float to the floor.

"Oh." I drop my eyes from his and shake my head, trying to get rid of the dizziness and the feeling in the pit of my stomach.

"Come on, let's get you home." He drops my wrist and moves his hand to my lower back, where it burns a hole straight through his jacket and my dress into my skin, until he finally drops it away so he can help me into the front seat of his SUV. He makes sure I'm settled before he slams the door.

"So are you going to tell us who this guy is to you?" Libby asks from the backseat as I put on my seat belt.

"Leave her alone, Lib," Mac says quietly, and I watch in fascination as Levi moves around the hood to the driver's side. I've never really noticed the way a man walks before, but his walk is confident and sure.

"I'm just curious," Libby grumbles right as Levi opens his door.

"Are you all going to the same place?" Levi questions, sliding in behind the steering wheel, putting the key in the ignition, and starting up the engine.

"Yes, and thank you for giving us a ride. We really appreciate it," Mac says from the backseat as we pull out into traffic.

"It's not a big deal. I was heading home anyway," he replies as we stop at a red light.

"What are you doing?" I tense as he reaches across the middle console between us.

"No need to yell fire, babe," he jokes, reminding me of our first encounter, and my cheeks heat as something in my stomach twists on the word *babe*. Holding my breath, I watch him adjust the heater vents on my side to blow directly on me before turning up the warm air.

"I thought you were going to kill me," I defend myself, hearing him chuckle as the light turns green and he presses the gas.

"I thought about it."

"You did?"

"Yeah, I also thought about a couple other things," he says, and I wonder what those things were, but I don't have enough guts to ask him.

"Did you have a good night at work?" I ask instead, then wish I hadn't, because he's obviously a homicide detective and I can't imagine any part of that being good. "Sorry, that was a stupid question. Ignore me."

"It's all right." He turns his head toward me and smiles. "Can't say it was a good night, but there is always a little bit of satisfaction involved when I bring someone to justice."

"Did you . . . I mean, did you bring someone to justice tonight?"

"Yeah, but now I have a new case to solve."

"The guy who killed the prostitute?" I ask softly, watching his expression change in the green lights coming off the dash.

"Yeah." He nods once, and his fist tightens on the steering wheel.

"It must be difficult witnessing firsthand the worst parts of humanity, day after day."

"It's not easy," he agrees, and I wrap my hands together in my lap to keep from reaching over and touching him in some way. To assure him that what he's doing is important and appreciated. "I'll drop you girls off out front, then go find parking," he says, and I pull my eyes from him and realize we have already reached our block.

"Sure, thanks again." I give him a small smile as he pulls up in front of our apartment building and I unhook my seat belt.

"Yeah, thanks for the ride," Libby and Mac say.

I open my door and hop down, slamming my door as he says, "No problem."

Heading to the building, I punch in the code for the door and let my sisters in ahead of me. "Um, how are we going to get into your apartment?" Mac asks as we head up the stairs to my place.

"My hidden key," I tell her, walking across the open space between Levi's apartment and mine. Bending, I lift the corner of the mat in front of my door and pull off the spare key I taped there when I moved in.

"That's not very safe." Libby eyes the key as I peel it off the tape.

"The building's safe, and only tenants have the code for the front door."

"Still, Dad would kill you if he knew you had a key hidden under your mat."

"Dad will never know." I shove the key in the lock and push the door open. "Hey, baby, did you miss us?" I smile at Muffin, who greets us with her tail wagging a hundred miles an hour. Giving her some love, I pat her head, then walk around her. "Let Mama change; then I'll take you out to potty."

"Yeah, and when you come back, you can tell us about Levi," Mac says, dropping to the couch. Muffin climbs up next to her, pushing her head under Mac's hand.

"There's nothing to tell," I mutter to myself, kicking off my heels before taking Levi's jacket off and laying it across the end of my bed carefully. Pulling the dress off over my head, I roll it into a ball, then head for the bathroom, where I toss the stupid thing in the trash.

"There is some serious chemistry going on between you and Mr. Officer," Libby informs me as she leans against the bathroom door while I grab a makeup removal wipe and start to scrub my face clean.

"He's just a nice guy." Shrugging off the look she gives me, I pick up my hairbrush, then drop it back to the top of the counter and grab a hair tie instead and tie my hair into a ponytail. As soon as I'm done, I look at her in the mirror. "I'm not interested."

"Sure, you're not," she says sarcastically, stepping out of my way so I can leave the bathroom.

"It's the truth," I grumble, opening my closet and grabbing a pair of my favorite sweats off the top shelf, then a tank top from my drawer. I put both on quickly before slipping on my Toms.

"If you say so." She turns and leaves the room. Biting my tongue to keep from replying, I head for the living room behind her and watch as she flops down on the couch next to Mac.

"I think he likes you," Mac says, and Libby agrees as she kicks off her heels.

Ignoring both of them, I open the closet next to the front door and grab my windbreaker and Muffin's leash.

"Ready?" I ask my girl, who is already waiting at the door, looking at me like I need to hurry up. As she wags her tail in reply, I attach her leash, then look toward the couch. "I'll be right back."

"We'll be here," Mac says, flipping on the television.

Swinging open the door, I groan when I find Levi on the other side with his hand ready to knock.

When will this night end?

"Hey, hold this." I shove Muffin's leash at him before he has a chance to say anything and turn back to my apartment. Going to my bedroom, I quickly grab his jacket and head right back to the door without looking at the couch, where I can feel two sets of eyes watching me. I have no doubt both my sisters are smiling.

"Night, Levi," Libby calls, and I shut the door quickly, cutting off the sound of her and Mac laughing.

Feeling my face heat in embarrassment, I shove his jacket into his chest without looking at him, muttering, "Here's your jacket. Thanks for letting me borrow it," while attempting to take Muffin's leash from his tight grasp with my free hand.

"Are you taking her out?" he asks, placing his fingers under my chin and forcing me to look at him.

"Yeah."

"I'll go with you." His hand drops away, and he finally takes his jacket from me. At a loss for words, I watch him as he walks the four steps to his apartment—still holding Muffin's leash—opens his door, and tosses the jacket in carelessly before slamming the door.

"You don't have to come with us. We're just going across the street to the park."

"I don't mind." Okay, what the hell do I say to that? *I don't want you to go with me because you make me dizzy and I don't know how to act when you're close?*

"All righty then," I murmur instead, catching his lips twitch before I drop my gaze to the top of Muffin's head so I can avoid looking at him.

Heading down the stairs with Muffin leading the way, we leave the building and walk in silence across the street to the park. I expect Muffin to do what she always does as soon as we make it to the grass— which is take care of business quickly before dragging me back home— but tonight is apparently not that kind of night. No, tonight my dog has decided she needs to sniff every single blade of grass and stop at every tree as we walk slowly down the tree-lined path.

"Your sisters seem nice," he says, breaking the silence, and I turn to him and find his beautiful eyes on me.

"They are, but they are also crazy." I kick a pebble, watching it fly through the air and bounce a few feet away before rolling into the grass.

"I doubt they have anything on my brothers."

"You have brothers?" I tilt my head back toward him, again watching him smile.

"Yep, three. All younger." Studying him with the dim light coming from the streetlamps above us, I try to guess how old he is.

"I'm thirty." He nudges my shoulder with his, and I duck my head, wondering how he knew what I was thinking.

"How old are you?" he asks, stopping to let Muffin sniff another tree.

"Twenty-seven in three days."

"You're still a baby."

"I guess if I were an old man I'd think twenty-seven was young, too." I smile, enjoying the sound of his deep laugh as it rumbles through the quiet night. "So, do your brothers live in the city?"

"No, they all live in Connecticut near my parents, in the town we grew up in." He stops and pulls me close to him as a man jogs by, then lets me go once he's passed, and we resume walking. "Our mom would lose her mind if any one of them left with her grandkids."

"Do all of your brothers have kids?"

"Yep."

"But you live here in the city."

"I do."

"So you don't have kids?" I surmise, watching a slow grin spread across his face.

"Nah, no kids. Not yet anyway."

"Cool," I mumble like an idiot, silently begging Muffin to hurry up so I can get home before I make an even bigger fool of myself.

"Are you cold?" he questions, and I realize I've half disappeared into my windbreaker, trying to escape the freezing wind that has suddenly picked up.

"A little. It's been so warm during the day, I keep forgetting how cold the nights are."

"Come here." He wraps his arm around my shoulders, and my body stiffens. "Relax, I'm just keeping you warm." Relax? Is he crazy? How the hell am I supposed to relax when he's touching me? It's bad enough being around him, let alone feeling his warmth against my side and his smell of clean soap and musk suffocating me. "What are your plans for your birthday?"

"I . . . um . . ." Oh god, he's short-circuiting my brain. I can't even get a full sentence out.

"That sounds fun." He chuckles, and I smack his abs without thinking.

"Don't make fun of me."

"Gorgeous, I'm not making fun of you. I think you're adorable when you get all flustered."

"I'm not flustered," I lie, trying with everything in me to ignore the butterflies in my stomach that have taken flight and the fact that he's once again making me dizzy.

"It's cute."

"Whatever." I pull my eyes from his, thanking the good lord above when Muffin starts to do her business, then curse under my breath when she looks at me, stops, and walks to another spot to start her search all over again.

"So what are your plans for your birthday?"

"My parents are coming into the city on Friday to take me to see *The Lion King*. Every year for my birthday we see a show—it's a tradition."

"That's nice, but your birthday's Tuesday, right?"

"Yeah."

"So what are you doing on your birthday?"

"I don't know. I have work the next day, so I'll probably just order a pizza from Caminos and watch a movie or something." God, that sounds lame, even to me.

"No boyfriend taking you out?" he asks, and his arm tightens around me ever so slightly on the word *boyfriend*.

"No . . . um, no boyfriend." I pull my bottom lip between my teeth and bite hard to keep from asking why he wants to know.

"And your sisters aren't taking you out?"

"After tonight, I think I need a break from them," I mutter drily; his arm tightens, and his body shakes with laughter.

"That bad, huh?"

"I told you they're crazy."

"Well, if you want some company, I'm off Tuesday. Just knock on my door—we can hang out and order pizza."

"Okay." I nod, knowing I'd be more inclined to run naked through Times Square than knock on his door for any reason, let alone ask him to hang out with me on my birthday.

"She'll never knock," he says to himself, and I look up at him.

"Pardon?"

"You won't knock. Hell, if I see you after tonight, I'll be surprised."

"What does that mean?" I frown, and his eyes scan my face.

"Since I moved in, you've been avoiding me. I don't see that changing."

"I haven't been avoiding you," I lie, wondering how the hell he knows I've been avoiding him. Have I been that obvious? I don't think I have been.

"Babe, I've knocked on your door and heard you on the other side turn off the TV and play possum."

Oh my god, how the hell did he hear that? "I don't know what you're talking about."

"I bet you don't." He sighs, and I can't tell if it's a sigh of annoyance or something else as his arm tightens again, forcing me deeper into his side as we stop at another tree.

"Good girl," I call to Muffin when she finally takes care of business and turns her head toward the sound of my voice. Her ears perk up, and her tail wags, shaking her whole body as she gallops back toward us and bumps her nose into Levi's thigh.

"Are you ready to head back?" he asks me while rubbing the top of her head.

"Sure." I let out the breath I've been holding as he turns us around and leads us back through the park and across the street to the apartment building. Once we are both inside our building, I expect him to give me Muffin's leash and remove his arm from around my shoulders, but he doesn't. Instead he keeps us locked together side by side as we take the stairs with Muffin ahead of us. I want to dislike the way it feels being tucked almost protectively under his arm, but I don't. Instead I'm wondering what kind of excuse I can make up to spend more time right where I am without actually having to admit to myself that I like him.

"If I don't see you on your birthday, I hope you have a good time," he says, letting me go once we reach the landing between his apartment and mine. Turning to face him, I take Muffin's leash as he holds it out, then look up into his golden eyes.

"Thanks."

"My pleasure." His fingers touch the underside of my chin; then his thumb sweeps just below my bottom lip. Getting lost in the way he's looking at me, I lean into his touch and hold my breath as his face starts to descend toward mine.

"Oh good, you're back. I was just coming to check on you." Mac breaks into the moment. I jump back a mile like I've been caught with my hand in the cookie jar, and I hear Levi curse quietly behind me. "Oh sorry, I thought you were out here alone," Mac says, and I don't even have to look at her to know she's smirking.

"It's fine, I was just coming in . . . um, night, Levi." I wave in his direction without looking at him, then growl under my breath when Muffin tugs on her leash, preventing me from making my escape.

Feeling my face heat, I turn around and find *my dog* sitting at Levi's side with his hand on the top of her head. "Go on in, girl," he commands with a pat to her head, and Muffin looks up at him, then looks at me, but what she doesn't do is move an inch.

"Come on, Muffin," I urge, giving her leash a gentle tug as my face grows hotter.

"I think Muffin wants to stay with Levi." Mac laughs, and I glare at her. "Just sayin'." She smiles.

"Come on," Levi rumbles, and I watch him lead Muffin to my apartment door, where Mac steps back to let him inside. Feeling the leash in my hand pull, I know I don't have a choice but to follow behind them.

"Oh, hey, Levi," Libby calls from the couch as I release Muffin so she can get to Libby. "We're getting ready to watch a movie. Do you want to join us?" she asks, and I peek up to find him already halfway out the door.

"Sorry, it's been a long day." He pauses to look over his shoulder. "Maybe next time," he says, then his eyes find mine and I hold my breath. "Night, Fawn. See you soon." The promise in those words and the look in his eyes has goose bumps breaking out across my skin.

"Night, Levi." I watch him close the door behind him as he leaves.

Shrugging off my windbreaker, I avoid looking at either one of my sisters as I hang it in the closet along with Muffin's leash.

"So Levi went with you to walk Muff—"

"Don't." I hold up my hand, cutting Mac off, because I know what's coming. I don't want to answer a million questions, and I don't want to listen to her and Libby tease me about Levi, especially when I'm feeling so conflicted.

"I was just going to say that was nice of him," she grumbles, walking to the kitchen to get a bottle of water from the fridge.

"Sorry, I'm just tired." I sigh, rubbing my face. I'm actually not tired anymore, even though I should be, since it's almost three in the morning. Instead I feel wired, like I've just drunk three cups of coffee and taken a trip on a roller coaster.

"Come watch a movie with us," Libby pleads, and I look to the couch, where she and Muffin are curled up under one of my blankets.

"I think I'm just going to go to bed."

"We won't talk about Levi anymore if you watch a movie with us," Mac pouts, taking a seat on the couch and pulling a separate blanket from the back.

"Fine," I give in, feeling guilty for being so short with her moments ago. Kicking off my Toms, I go to the couch and take a seat next to Mac. As soon as I sit, she drapes part of her blanket over my lap, then picks up the remote. "What are we watching?"

"*Nightmare on Elm Street.*" Libby smiles while Muffin stands, only to lie down across Mac's lap so she can rest her head on my thighs.

"God, I haven't seen this in forever," I say, absently running my fingers through Muffin's thick fur.

"Me neither. I wonder if it will be as scary now as it was when we were kids."

"I doubt it. Most movies I thought were scary back then aren't as scary now," I say as the movie starts to play. Not even thirty minutes later, I yawn for the fourth time in a row and look over at Mac and Libby, finding them both asleep. I think about waking them and helping them set up the pullout, but they honestly look comfortable enough. Flipping off the television, I climb carefully off the couch and head to my bedroom as Muffin follows me. Shutting my bedroom door, I turn out the light, take off my sweats, and climb into bed, feeling Muffin jump up a second later. She groans as she flops down next to me. Lying there in the dark, it takes forever to find sleep as my mind spins with thoughts of Levi.

Chapter 4

It's My Birthday—I'll Cry If I Want To

FAWN

"Time to pack up, guys," I call from the front of the class, seeing that it's two minutes until the bell will ring. "Remember, your permission slips need to be turned in tomorrow, so make sure you have your parents sign them tonight if you haven't already," I shout over the sudden eruption of talking, books slamming, and coats being put on. "Also, don't forget that your book reports are due tomorrow, so bring your books with you to class," I say, watching my students look restlessly from the clock to me, ready to escape as soon as the clock strikes three fifteen. I can't blame them—I love what I do, but after being surrounded by four walls all day long, I'm just as antsy to get outside. Hearing the bell ring, I smile. "'Bye, guys."

"'Bye, Miss Reed," they say one after another as they pass me on the way out of the room. Giving them all smiles or pats on the back, I wait until the last student passes, then turn around and grin when I see Tamara, one of my favorite students, with her head buried in a book.

"Honey, class is over," I say, and her chin flies up, causing the curly ringlets covering her head to bounce. As she looks around, her mocha cheeks get pink just a bit, and she shakes her head.

"I did it again?" she grumbles, and I smile.

"Don't worry, the bell just rang," I reassure her as she stands and pushes her cute little blue glasses up the bridge of her nose and slips on her three-sizes-too-big jacket. "What book are you reading now?" I ask, knowing it will probably be something that will surprise me. Tamara reminds me a lot of myself at her age. I loved reading and could easily get lost in a book for hours on end if left alone.

"*To Kill a Mockingbird,*" she says softly as she unzips her backpack, shoving the book inside.

"That's one of my favorites," I say after a moment, and she nods without looking at me. "If you ever want to talk about it, I'd love to hear what you think of the story," I say, knowing this book isn't something an eleven-year-old girl would necessarily be reading, but her mother explained during our last parent-teacher meeting that she allows Tamara to read pretty much whatever she wants. If I'm honest, Tamara is far too smart for the books we read in class.

"Thank you, Miss Reed."

"You're welcome, honey. Is your mom picking you up today?"

"I don't know, her or her boyfriend will be here." She shrugs, looking uncomfortable, and I bite my bottom lip. I have no issue at all with the fact that Tamara's mom is a stripper. I actually think it's admirable that she puts food on the table, a roof over her girl's head, and clothes on her back. The problem I have with her is she constantly has men in and out of Tamara's life, and none of them are ever any good.

"If no one's here by four, come back in and let me know. I'll make sure you get home," I say, sliding off my desk to stand.

"Okay." She chews the inside of her cheek, twisting her backpack in her hands.

"Is everything okay?"

"Yeah, um . . . I got you something."

"You got me something?" I say, not able to hide the surprise in my tone. Nodding, she opens her backpack and pulls out a crushed pink gift bag with darker pink polka dots on it.

"It's nothing big," she says quickly, looking nervous, but she's very wrong. I know that whatever she has gotten me she most likely paid for with her own money and got on her own time, making it huge.

"Honey, you didn't have to get me anything at all." I pull her in, giving her a hug before leaning back and taking the bag from her. Opening it up, I pull out a simple purple candle and hold it to my chest. "I love candles." I smile, giving her another tight hug. "Thank you, honey."

"Happy birthday," she whispers, then her body stiffens against mine, and I turn to see what's causing her distress.

"Your mom said you'd be waiting out front. Come on, I'm going to be late." Tamara's mom's new boyfriend, Juan, says from the doorway. He sounds annoyed and his eyes are narrowed. My spine stiffens. Moving closer to Tamara, I rest my hand on her shoulder, giving it a gentle squeeze.

"Sorry, Mr. Varges. I asked Tamara to wait after class so she could help me put away a few things," I lie, not wanting her to be in trouble with him.

"Well, we have places to be, so if you're done, we need to go," he says, keeping his eyes locked on Tamara. I step slightly in front of her, and his eyes finally come to me.

"Sorry about keeping her, and thank you for being understanding."

"Sure." He lifts his chin, and Tamara quickly heads toward him without a backward glance. Watching them go, I feel like I always do. Torn. There is nothing I can do, and there is nothing I despise more than feeling helpless when it comes to my kids. Taking a seat at my desk I put the candle back in the bag and carefully place it with my stuff to take home before pulling out the spelling tests I need to correct before I leave for the evening.

An hour later, I circle the huge A in red ink on the last spelling test and smile. My kids are all smart, and I feel like a proud mom who knows she's done a good job. None of the kids got lower than a B, and by New York City public school standards, that is amazing. Tucking the now-graded tests away in the top drawer of my desk, I pick up my bags and head for the door. I'm starving—I didn't get a chance to eat lunch, since we had a teacher meeting during my lunch hour, so the pizza I plan on ordering for dinner is sounding better by the minute.

Pulling out my cell phone once I'm out of the building, I send thank-you texts to Libby and Mac, who both messaged to say happy birthday, then one to my mom and dad telling them how excited I am to see them in a few days. Even though it's my birthday, tonight is going to be a very low-key night; all I want to do is go home, put on a pair of yoga pants and a sweatshirt, walk my girl, order a pizza, and go to bed. Okay, I kind of want to add seeing Levi in there somewhere, but I still don't know if that's smart. I can't figure out if he's different or just like every other gorgeous man I've ever met.

Hopping on the subway, I take the train uptown and get off at my stop, then walk the two blocks to my building. As soon as I'm home, I take care of parts one and two of my plans for the night. I put on my yoga pants and hoodie as soon as I get home, then take out Muffin, who wasn't at all happy about having to go out in the cold on a short walk—or drag—through the park. By the time I make it back to my apartment, it's almost six, and my hunger has turned into starvation.

Pacing back and forth in my apartment, I groan. Levi said that if I wanted company on my birthday to just knock on his door, but the idea of actually doing that is making me feel sick. I wanted to just order pizza, then maybe go over and see if he wanted some, but then I thought, what if he doesn't like the kind of pizza I like? What if he's allergic to pineapples and he ends up going into shock from eating them, or what if he was just being nice and he didn't actually mean for me take him up on his offer? "Stop being stupid," I say out loud, putting my hand to the knob. I release it just as quickly and resume pacing. "This is getting ridiculous." Shoving my shoulders back and lifting my chin, I put my hand on the knob.

The moment I swing my door open, my empty stomach turns with nausea, along with something else that I'm not willing to acknowledge, as I stare at the woman standing just outside Levi's closed door. She's gorgeous, model gorgeous, with thick, dark hair; tan skin; and a willowy figure that would make even Libby jealous.

Turning her head toward me, she smiles a beautiful, blinding-white, perfectly straight-toothed smile. "Hi," she chirps, and a muscle in my chest constricts.

"Uh . . . hi. Sorry, I thought you were my pizza," I lie, and she tilts her head to the side and giggles. Even her giggle is beautiful, I think with disgust, then panic when I see Levi's door start to open.

"'Bye." I slam my door quickly and drop my face to my hands.

Oh my god, I'm an idiot. Why did I think for one moment that he wouldn't have a girlfriend? Why the hell didn't I ask him when he asked me if I had a boyfriend?

This is why I don't date. I don't know how to date—I have no clue when a guy is actually interested or when he's just being nice. "God, you are a loser." Tears burn my eyes, and I curse the fact that my period is due any day now. I'm not a wuss unless it's that time of the month—then I cry and blubber about everything under the sun, even stupid laundry detergent commercials with cute little bears in them.

Feeling Muffin press into my side, I fall to the floor and pull her down to my lap so I can cry ugly, fat tears into her fur. "It's just going to be me and you forever," I moan into her coat as she consoles me with a lick up my cheek. "I'm going to end up old and alone like Aunt Margret," I wail, feeling completely sorry for myself. "One day when I'm still single at fifty, I'm going to think that some hot twenty-year-old who's only after my money wants me because I'm so desperate for love." I sniff, burying my face deeper into Muffin's wiry fur, hearing her whine, then feel her press her cold nose against my neck. With a hiccup I give her one last squeeze and pull myself up off the floor.

As much as I want to sit around and feel sorry for myself, my stomach won't let me. I know if I don't eat I will likely pass out from hunger. Wandering over to the kitchen, I search through the cupboards for something to fill the void in my stomach, since there is no way I will be ordering pizza—the idea alone has my stomach turning. Finally, in the last cupboard, I find a can of chicken and stars soup and some crackers my mom brought me when I had the flu last year. Looking at the expiration dates on both, I know I will be testing fate if I eat them, but desperate times call for desperate measures. Dumping the soup into a bowl, I place it in the microwave, setting the timer for three minutes, then open the package of crackers. Taking a small bite out of one, I sigh in relief when it's not as hard and stale as it should be.

Needing something to wash the dry cracker down, I open the fridge and dig all the way to the back behind the dozens of takeout food containers I've collected and pull out the bottle of moscato my sisters brought over a few weeks ago. I don't normally drink alone, but tonight seems like the kind of night when someone—a loser—such as myself would drink by herself. Twisting the cork out of the top, I dump the almost full bottle into one of my giant plastic tumblers and take a huge gulp, feeling it cool my dry throat on the way down, then burn my empty stomach. Shoving another cracker into my mouth, I chew and swallow while I grab my bowl of soup from the microwave, practically burning my hands off as I put it down on the counter. With one more large gulp of wine, I find the tray my mom also brought over when I was sick, put everything on it, and carry it over to the couch. The moment I sit, Muffin hops up next to me.

"Happy birthday to me," I mutter, picking up a handful of crackers and dumping them into my soup.

"Ruff."

"Thanks, girl. I love you, too." I pat Muffin's head, then toss her a cracker that she catches, then spits immediately on the floor. Looking at the cracker, then her, I shake my head, find the remote, turn on the television, and flip through for something to watch.

"Oh god . . ." I breathe through my tears, resting my fingers against my lips as Hilary Swank reads another message from Gerard Butler. "Why did he have to die?" I sob right along with Hilary not for the first time since starting this movie, then my head flies up as someone knocks on the door. Wiping my face with the sleeve of my sweatshirt, I hop off the couch and press "Pause" on *P.S. I Love You* as I step over the dishes I set on the floor, along with the pile of Kleenex. Knowing my sisters probably ignored me and decided to show up anyway, I open the door without checking who it is—regretting the lapse in judgment when I find Levi on the other side.

"Uh, hi . . ." I move my eyes past his shoulder toward the hall to see if his girlfriend is with him.

"Hey," he says softly, then lifts up my chin, and his eyes scan mine. "What the hell is wrong?"

"Nothing." I tug my face away from his fingers when his touch practically burns me.

"Something's wrong, you've been crying."

"I was watching a movie."

"You were watching a movie?"

"Yes, I was watching a movie," I huff, dropping my eyes to glare at Muffin when she whines and paws the door to get to him. *Traitor.*

"What movie are you watching?"

"It doesn't matter, did you need something?" I ask, looking in the vicinity of his chin, not having the willpower to look him in his beautiful eyes.

"You didn't knock."

"Pardon?" I frown, trying to keep up, but the wine sloshing around in my system is making it difficult.

"Can you look at me?" Reluctantly my eyes meet his, and I hold on to the doorjamb to keep standing as my head grows dizzy from the wine I've drunk.

"Why does he have to be gorgeous?" I think—or think I think it, but his lips curve into a very sexy smirk, letting me know I'm drunker than I think I am.

"You think I'm gorgeous?"

"I . . . um . . ." I shake my head.

"Have you been drinking?" he asks suddenly, and I pull myself up to stand at my full height, then tip slightly to the side.

"I had a cup of wine."

"A cup of wine?"

"Yes, a cup of wine. Are you going to repeat everything I say?"

"Okay . . . What the fuck is really going on?" he growls, and I automatically lean back.

"Nothing is going on. It's my birthday, I—"

"I know it's your birthday. That's why I brought you a cake," he cuts me off, and I blink. Um, what? Did he just say he brought me a cake? He holds a pink box up between us that I didn't notice before. I look at it, then him. "My sister-in-law owns a bakery. She was coming into the city today, so I had her bring a cake for you."

"What?" I breathe.

"Jesus." He rubs the bridge of his nose, muttering something under his breath, then puts his hand to my belly. When he pushes me back into my apartment I almost fall, but I stumble into him as his hand grabs onto the front of my hoodie and he pulls me roughly into his hard chest . . . Unfortunately he does it with the box holding the cake, so it's flattened between us.

"Oh no," I whisper, looking from the box to his somewhat amused and slightly pissed, very handsome face.

"Will everything with you always be difficult?"

"I ruined your cake," I shout, attempting to push away from him, but he doesn't let me go.

"Actually, you ruined your cake," he mutters, and I feel it coming on—I know I'm about to cry again. Only this time it's worse, because I'm going to ugly cry in front of him.

"I'm sorry." I squeeze my eyes closed and duck my head, trying to fight back the inevitable tears I feel building behind my closed eyelids.

"It's just a cake." He holds me up against him as he leads me across the room. "Have you been crying all night?" he asks, and I open my eyes and catch him studying the mound of Kleenex on the floor. The cracker Muffin spit out crunches under my bare foot as he helps me sit.

"Yes . . . no . . . maybe . . . I was watching *P.S. I Love You*," I whisper, lifting my foot to dust off the cracker bits stuck there. I need to do something so I don't just blurt things out anymore.

"Are you not feeling well?"

"Pardon?"

"You ate soup and crackers for dinner. Are you feeling okay?"

"I always eat expired soup and crackers on my birthday," I mutter under my breath, and his eyes narrow. Shaking his head he pulls out his phone, and I sit up. "What are you doing?"

"I'm ordering a pizza. What kind do you like?"

"Why are you ordering pizza? I already ate soup."

"The bowl's still full." He points at the tray with my still almost full bowl of soup and stale crackers, then picks up my mound of Kleenex, placing them on the tray before he carries it all to the kitchen while putting the phone to his ear. "Are you good with half Hawaiian, half pepperoni?"

"Uh yeah," I agree as my stomach growls and my mouth waters.

With a nod, he gives the person on the phone the order and the address, then shoves the phone into his back pocket. Needing to look at anything but him, my eyes go to the box sitting on the coffee table. It's ruined—so smashed that cake is squeezing out of the open edges. Untying the string around the box, I open the lid and feel my stomach dip. The cake was decorated with a fawn colored with light-orange icing. Or at least I think it's a fawn—now that it's squished, it looks like a chubby bear playing in grass.

"You had your sister-in-law make this cake?" I whisper.

"Yeah."

"That was nice," I say absently, wondering why he would ask her to make me a cake for my birthday when we don't even really know each other. Swallowing through the strange feeling in my chest, I finally work up the courage to look at him. "I was going to knock on your door earlier, but . . ." I look away, wondering if I should just come out with it, then figure, what the hell. "I thought your girlfriend was over and I . . . I thought that you were just being nice when you told me I should knock on your door on my birthday," I say, looking back at him and noticing his eyes have changed ever so slightly.

"I'm not that nice, and I don't say things I don't mean. Ever," he says, petting Muffin, who is currently leaning into his side with her full weight. "And I don't have a girlfriend. You probably saw my brother's wife, Ruby, since she's the only woman who's been to my place since I moved in."

God, I'm really bad at this stuff. I assumed he had a girlfriend, cried about it like an idiot, then ruined the cake he had made for me, because once again, *I'm an idiot.* Covering my face with my hands, I hiccup as the tears I've been holding back start to fall. *Stupid fricking period.* Feeling the couch dip as he takes a seat next to me, I startle when his arm wraps around my shoulders and he guides me to rest against his chest. "I'm not normally this lame," I cry, and I'd swear I hear him laugh, but I ignore it since I know it will piss me off if I think he's making fun of me.

"It's okay, birthdays are hard."

"It's not that. I'm a girl and the red bitch is due any day and she ruins my life every month when she comes into town." I sniffle, feeling his chest shake. "Oh god, I said that out loud, didn't I?"

"Take a breath. It's all good." It's not all good—I'm blubbering against his chest like a baby on my birthday when we don't even know each other, and to top it off, I told him I'm getting my period.

"I'm sorry, you probably think I'm a weirdo now."

"Actually, I think you're cute," he says quietly, rubbing my arm. *Cute, he thinks I'm cute?* I take a chance and peek up at him, and he softly rubs his thumb under my eye, then down the bridge of my nose, tapping the end. My eyes cross. "Definitely cute." Swallowing, I lean away from him, needing to put some space between us. This is too much, whatever this is. It's way too intense for me right now. "And . . . the walls are back up."

"Um . . ."

"It's all good. I'm patient." *What does that mean?* Before I can ask that exact question, the buzzer in my kitchen goes off, telling me that someone's at the door downstairs. "That's the pizza. I'll be back."

"Sure." I nod, and then watch him unfold his tall, lean frame from my couch and stand. I continue to watch his ass as he walks across the apartment and out the door. "I think I'm in over my head."

"Ruff."

"I know, girl. Trust me, I know," I whisper to Muffin as she plops to her bottom and stares at the door.

When the door opens a couple of minutes later, I hurry to the kitchen and grab plates and napkins, along with two bottles of water from the fridge as Levi heads to the couch with the pizza. "Are you okay with us finding something else to watch?" he asks as I walk toward him.

"You don't want to watch *P.S. I Love You?*" I joke as he takes a seat.

"If we watch it, will you cry?"

"Probably," I say truthfully. I always cry watching it, which is part of the reason I was watching it earlier. I figured I could use the movie as an excuse for shedding a few tears.

"I think you've had enough crying for the day."

"True," I mutter as he takes the stuff in my hands from me, setting it all on the coffee table. "Pick whatever you like." I hand him the remote, and he flips through the channels so quickly that I can't keep up. He lands on a true crime detective show I actually watch all the time. "I love this show."

"It's good," he agrees, opening the lid on the pizza box. The second the scent hits my nose, my stomach growls, and he grins. "Hungry?"

"A little . . ." He raises a brow. "Okay, a lot." I sigh, watching him laugh. Picking up one of the plates, he slides a slice of each kind of pizza onto it, then hands it over to me before doing the same with his own plate. "So have you caught your bad guy yet?" I ask quietly after a minute, and his eyes come to me and soften.

"Not yet, but I have a few more leads now, so I'm making progress."

"That's good."

"It is." He leans back on the couch, getting comfortable. Doing the same, I tuck my feet under me, rest my plate on my lap, and try to focus on the TV and not the fact that he's sitting next to me on my couch, in my apartment, while we are alone. "Do you have plans for Thanksgiving?"

"My sisters and I always go out to Long Island to my parents' for the holidays. What about you?"

"I'm on call that night. I'll probably head to Connecticut a couple days after and pray that my brothers haven't eaten all the leftovers by then."

"So you're going to be alone on Thanksgiving?" I question, feeling a ping of sadness at the idea of him sitting alone in his apartment while everyone else is enjoying time with their families.

"I'll probably be working, so it's not a big deal."

"But still, that's sad," I say quietly before taking a bite of pizza.

"It comes with the territory." He shrugs, taking a bite of his own pizza.

"I guess you're right; my dad missed a lot of holidays, so I know it's a sacrifice you have to make."

"Most women don't get that," he says, and I look at him.

"Pardon?"

"Most women don't get that my job is important. I don't have a nine to five where I'm home in the evenings, and things happen that mean I may get a call during dinner or a date that can pull me away."

"Oh." I nod, not quite understanding why he's telling me that. Clearing my throat, I take another bite of pizza, then look at Muffin when she whines and drops her head to her paws while staring at Levi with wide puppy-dog eyes.

"Can she have a piece?"

"Sure." I shrug expecting him to give her a small piece from one of his slices. Instead I watch with wide eyes as he gives her a whole slice of her own. "Um . . ." I press my lips together as she takes it from his hand and carries it, half hanging out of her mouth, to the kitchen.

"You said she could have some."

"I thought . . . Never mind." I laugh, shaking my head, and he grins. Finishing off both my pieces of pizza, I'm thankful that I have on my yoga pants, since there is no way I would be able to breathe if I didn't. Groaning, I lean forward to set my plate on the coffee table and hear him laugh.

"You okay?"

"Stuffed." I lean back as he picks up another slice.

"I used to think Chicago had the best pizza until I moved to New York," he says, folding his new slice in half and taking a huge bite.

"I've never had Chicago-style pizza."

"You haven't?"

"No, I'm a New Yorker. In New York you only eat one kind of pizza."

"Have you traveled?"

"Some, but not much."

"What about family vacations when you were younger?"

"Like you said, your job means you have to make sacrifices. My mom and dad are glued to each other. My mom would never take us on a vacation unless my dad could go along, and since that was rarely possible, we didn't do much traveling." I shrug and watch his eyes fill with something close to regret. "I had an amazing childhood," I say, feeling like I need to reassure him for some strange reason. "We lived a few blocks from the beach, so during the summer that's where we would spend our days. I never missed traveling because I was always happy right where I was."

"That's a good way to look at it."

"Have you traveled a lot?" I ask, watching him chew and swallow the bite he just took.

"Some. I've got family in Chicago and Georgia, so at least every couple of years we make it a point to go see them."

"All my family is in Long Island. My mom and dad grew up there, along with their brothers and sisters. No one ever moved away, so we never had to travel to see anyone since we all lived on the same block."

"Are you all close?"

"If you're asking are they constantly in my business and annoying me, the answer is yes," I say. He throws back his head, and a deep rumbling laugh comes out that makes my insides turn liquid.

"I get that, my family's the same way."

"Family is awesome," I say sarcastically, and he chuckles as he finishes off his last bite of pizza.

"You done?" He nods to my plate on the table, and I smile.

"Yes, it was so good. Thank you." I sit up quickly and try to take the plate from him when he starts to pick it up. "I'll get it."

"I've got it—relax." He nudges me back down to the couch, and I sit back watching him take both our plates to the kitchen along with the pizza box.

"What the hell is happening?"

"What?" he asks, and I feel my eyes widen.

"Oh no, I was talking out loud to the TV. You know, asking what's happening on the show, since we've missed most of it," I blabber as he comes back toward me and looks at the screen—where a cell phone commercial is playing. Feeling my face heat in embarrassment, I bite my bottom lip and look away from him.

"Hmm." He takes a seat next to me, this time closer than before. Muffin, who isn't one to miss an opportunity to be petted, jumps up next to him, forcing him even closer as she lays her paws and head in his lap.

"You know she's never really liked men before you."

"Pardon?"

Clearing my throat I look at him, then Muffin, who is now in dog heaven as Levi's big hand and strong-looking fingers run through her fur. "Um . . . she's never liked a guy before you. I mean, she likes my dad, but she hates my uncles and cousins. I have to board her whenever I go to my parents for a few days."

"Are you planning on having her boarded when you go away for Thanksgiving?"

"Yeah, she goes to Prestigious Paws downtown when I have to leave her."

"Is that the place with the dog spa?" he asks with a smirk, and I smile.

"Yeah, she gets massages and manicures and she has her own TV in her room, plus I get to watch her on live video whenever I want."

"Christ, that sounds better than some of the hotels I've stayed at."

"It probably is better—then again, it's not cheap to board her with them, but I know my baby is taken care of, so that's all that matters to me."

"Well, if I'm around when you're out of town, I'll keep her. I may not give her pedicures, but she'll be taken care of."

"That's nice, but—"

"No buts," he cuts me off before I can disagree.

"If you're working . . ."

"I can always stop by," he interrupts again. "My job's close by, so I can always get away for a few minutes here or there to take her out."

"That's nice, thanks."

"No problem," he says as he rests his arm over the back of the couch behind me. I wait to see what he will do, if he will wrap his arm around my shoulders like he did earlier, but he doesn't make a move, so once again I'm left confused and conflicted.

"Come on, girl." Hearing that, my eyes blink open. I don't remember falling asleep, but I must have been so comfortable that I did. Hearing Muffin's dog tag jingle, I get up on my elbow and watch through the dim light of the living room as Levi leads Muffin out the door.

"Levi?" I call, sitting up, and his eyes come to me over his shoulder and soften.

"Just taking her out, we'll be back."

"Um . . . give me a second and I'll come," I say, starting to stand, but he shakes his head no.

"I got her—it's cold out, stay," he says, then closes the door behind him. Pulling in a breath, I bite the inside of my cheek and look at the open cake box on the table. We ate my birthday cake right from the box with one fork that we both shared. It was sweet—he's sweet, funny, and easy to talk to, but I still have absolutely no idea if he's interested in me as anything more than a friend.

Chapter 5

A Kiss Is Just a Kiss, Right?

Fawn

Each breath I exhale as I run causes a huge puff of fog to appear out of my mouth. It's cold; actually it's freezing, but after last night I needed to get a run in before work so I didn't spend my morning sitting around thinking about Levi. When he came back with Muffin after taking her out last night, he didn't stay. He wished me a happy birthday once more, then left with nothing more than a tap to the end of my nose like I was a little kid he found cute. I was so confused by that gesture that I stood at the door for a good ten minutes with my hand on the knob debating whether to go over to his apartment and demand he tell me what the hell was going on. Instead I went to bed, where I tossed and turned most of the night tormented by thoughts of him once again until I gave up on sleep altogether, got up, put on my jogging gear, and went on a run. I need to talk to someone about him. I could call my sisters and ask them what they think it all means, but I know if I do I will never hear the end of it.

Plus, with our parents coming into the city Friday, I can't trust my sisters not to bring Levi up in front of Mom and Dad. Our parents are not like most parents nowadays who want their kids to wait to get into a serious relationship. No, our parents want the complete opposite—they want their girls settled with babies, the sooner the better. They want us to find love at a young age, like they did. My mom and dad met and started dating when they were in high school. My dad was two years older than my mom, and she was only sixteen, but that didn't stop him from pursuing her. He says he fell in love with her at first sight, and she says the same thing. They were inseparable from the day they met, and she literally moved in with my dad the day she graduated high school. Six months later they got married at the courthouse, and two months after that, they found out they were pregnant with Mac. I can't say things didn't work out for them; our mom and dad are crazy about each other. They have a love that most only dream of finding, but it's that love that has made them delusional. They don't understand dating nowadays, and they definitely don't get that most people are lucky if they find someone they like enough to start a family with, let alone love. So there is no way I want them to catch wind of Levi—I do not want them to do what they did to me when I was with Jayson, which was basically to try to convince me that he was perfect for me when he was anything but.

Feeling Muffin tug the leash in my hand, I slow my jog to match her pace, then squeak when she veers off the running path and takes off at a full sprint across the grass, dragging me behind her. "Muffin, stop," I scream, stumbling on the uneven ground as my earbuds fall out of my ears and my hand burns from my tight grasp on her leash.

Hearing a deep, rumbled "fuck," then "halt," I trip over a tree root protruding from the ground and fall facedown, barely catching myself with my hands before I do a face-plant in the dirt.

"Ugh," I moan, rolling to my back, trying to pull in a full breath from my overworked lungs and crushed chest.

"Muffin, sit." *Oh god.* I close my eyes, hoping I'm wrong, hoping that voice I know so well isn't the one I just heard. "Baby." My stomach melts at the endearment as a large, warm hand spreads across my forehead while another very large, very warm hand rests against my stomach, where my running jacket has ridden up. "Are you okay?" Hell, no, my dog almost killed me trying to get to the man she's obviously in love with.

"I'm okay." I look up at him and immediately feel a sense of déjà vu as sunlight casts a halo behind him that accentuates his too-gorgeous face.

"We really need to get your dog trained." He grins as Muffin sniffs my face, then licks up my cheek.

"She must have seen you," I grumble, glaring at my dog.

"Yeah, I gathered that." He smiles, patting Muffin's head as I attempt to push her freezing nose away from my neck, where she is trying to bury it. "Are you sure you're okay?" he asks tenderly, studying me from head to toe and making those stupid butterflies take flight.

"I'm fine." I sit up, avoiding his gaze as I dust the dried dirt and leaves off the front of my jacket and yoga pants. With the way I keep making a fool out of myself in front of Levi, it's really no wonder he doesn't think of me as anything more than a cute, clumsy kid.

"Are you heading home now?" he asks, and I nod, keeping my head down, using retying my shoe as an excuse not to look at him.

"Yeah, I need to get ready for work soon." Putting my hands behind me to heft myself up off the ground, I hold my breath as he scoops me up and carefully sets me on my feet.

"If I knew you were running this morning, I would have run with you." I want to ask why, but then I realize he's my neighbor and he wants to be my friend. Friends do things like run together, hang out with each other, and bring each other cakes on their birthdays. God . . . I have been friend zoned by the first guy I'm actually really interested in in what seems like forever. *I'm officially an idiot.*

"I go running most mornings, so if you—"

"I don't run often," I lie, cutting him off quickly before he can say more. I actually run almost every day, but I don't want to spend more time with him. Okay, I do want to spend time with him, but I don't want this small crush I have on him to turn into me suddenly stalking him, because that would be awkward, so it's best we keep our time together to a minimum. "I was up early today, so I figured why not," I say, and his eyes narrow, then relax and sparkle with something I don't understand. Something that makes my stomach dip and my head grow dizzy.

Looking down at Muffin, he takes the leash close to her neck, then attempts to take the end I'm holding out of my hand as he mutters, "I'll walk you girls home."

"That's not necessary." I hold the leash tighter, wanting this encounter to be over. "You should finish your run." I wave him off as Muffin barks in disagreement, like she knows what I'm saying.

"I was finished when I saw Muffin dragging you across the park to me."

"Oh . . ." I glare at my dog once more, not that she notices. No, she's too entranced by all that is Levi as he rubs the top of her head.

"Come on." He takes my other hand and I feel his warm fingers twine with mine as he pulls me along with him. When I try to tug my hand free, he holds it tighter, so like the idiot I am, I soak in the moment and pretend we're just another couple out walking our dog in the morning before work. "Are you hungry?" he asks once we reach our block and my eyes find his looking down at me.

"Yeah, but I'll probably just grab something on the way to work and eat before class starts."

"What time do you have to leave for work?" he asks.

I shrug. "Seven the latest. What time is it now?"

Reaching into the front pocket of his track pants, he pulls out his cell phone, clicking on the screen. "It's six," he says, bringing us to a stop in front of our building. Letting go of my hand, he punches in the code for the door, which he then holds open for me.

"Well, thanks," I mutter without looking at him once we reach our landing, but he doesn't respond, and Muffin's leash once again tightens as I head for my apartment. Growling under my breath, I pray that for once Muffin shows some kind of loyalty to the person who feeds her and puts a roof over her head. Opening my mouth to call her name as I turn around, I blink as Levi unhooks her leash from her collar, lets it drop to the floor, then walks into his apartment with Muffin following him. "Um . . ." I wind the leash up as I walk to his door, then stand at the threshold, not knowing what the hell to do.

"Levi?" I call into his apartment, not seeing anything but a large black-and-white photo of Mets' stadium hanging behind his black leather couch. A low, shiny coffee table sits in front of the couch on top of a fluffy gray rug that I would love to have for myself.

"Come on in, baby." What the hell is going on, and why does he keep calling me *baby*? Walking through the door, I frown as I watch him set a large bowl full of water on the ground in the kitchen for Muffin, who looks like she's been at his place every day of her life. "Are eggs and toast good with you?" he asks, and I look to where he's standing in front of his open fridge.

"Eggs . . ."

"If not, I got a few bagels."

"Bagels?"

"Babe, are you here with me?" Am I? I don't even know what's happening here. "Do you want eggs and toast or a bagel for breakfast?"

"Eggs are good," I finally get out, and he nods, pulls out a dozen eggs, and sets them on the counter before looking at me once more with his lips twitching.

"Can you shut the door for me?" Feeling awkwardly for the door behind me, I swing it closed, then walk toward the kitchen, not sure what to do with myself. Looking around his place, I notice it's the complete opposite of mine. Where I have bright colors everywhere, all of his stuff is different shades of blacks mixed with grays and white. His bar stools are chrome with black leather tops; the canisters and things on the counters are all black, including his coffeemaker and toaster. His place is definitely a guy's place.

Taking a few more steps toward the kitchen, I set Muffin's leash down on top of the island, then watch him pull out a pan and start up the stove. "How do you like your eggs?"

"Scrambled, if that's okay."

"You want ham and cheese in them?"

"Sure." I nod, watching him in confused silence as he starts to crack enough eggs to feed an army.

"You mind making the toast?"

"Okay." I slide off my jacket, setting it on one of his bar stools, which leaves me in a formfitting long-sleeved top. Going around to the inside of the kitchen, I take the loaf of bread he hands me and put four slices in his toaster while he rips up pieces of ham and cheese, adding them to the bowl with the eggs.

"Would you like coffee?" he asks, dumping the bowl of egg mixture into the pan.

"Yeah, thanks." I give him a small smile as he pulls down two cups and hands them to me. "Coffee's there. Milk's in the fridge. Sugar's in the tall black thing." He nods to the counter and sets down both cups. I fill them both, then go to the fridge; when I open it, I notice there's not even one fast food container, which is also the complete opposite of mine.

"Would you like some?" I hold up the half gallon of milk after dumping a few drops in my coffee.

"Nah, I take my coffee black." Of course he does—he's obviously a man's man, so no way would he put something in coffee to take out the bite that's supposed to put hair on your chest. "What's funny?"

"Hmm?" I turn and set his cup of black coffee next to the stove.

"You were smiling."

"I was?"

"Yeah."

"I don't know," I lie, picking up my cup and taking a sip of delicious warm coffee.

"Hmm." He shakes his head, then goes back to flipping and turning the eggs over in the pan.

"Is butter in the fridge?" I ask when the toast pops up, and he looks at me over his shoulder.

"Yep, and plates are above the sink. Knives in the drawer next to it."

"Cool," I mutter, then go about getting plates and buttering the toast. Once I'm done, he pulls the pan off the hot stove and scoops out some eggs for himself and me, then pulls down another plate and dumps the rest of the pan onto it. I don't know what I expect, but when he sets the plate on the ground for Muffin, I'm dumbfounded and tongue-tied.

"Come, eat before it gets cold," he urges, ushering me around to one of the bar stools and pulling it out for me to sit.

"You just made my dog breakfast," I blurt once I'm seated, and he chuckles.

"I made you breakfast. I just made enough for her to get some, too," he mutters, setting a plate in front of me.

"It's no wonder she's in love with you," I grumble as he heads back into the kitchen to get his own plate.

"She just knows a good thing when she sees it," he says. I watch his mouth move and would swear he adds, *unlike her oblivious owner.* But I can't be sure, and no way will I ask him.

Coming back a second later, he takes a seat next to me and digs into his food, so I do the same. "This is really good. Thank you."

"You're welcome." Sitting there next to him, I shovel food in my mouth to avoid talking. I don't need to embarrass myself any more than I have today, and I don't want to accidentally blurt out the thousands of questions currently pinging around in my skull. I keep reminding myself that he's just a nice guy and a nice neighbor who wants to be my friend.

Finishing off as much food as I can, I take a sip of coffee and use it as an excuse to study Levi over the rim of my mug. He's as gorgeous as always, maybe even more so with the little bit of morning scruff shadowing his jaw, accentuating his full lips and strong profile. My hand actually itches to reach out and touch him. To see for myself what the stubble would feel like against my fingers and how smooth his lips would be against my skin. Feeling my cheeks heat in embarrassment when he looks over at me, I duck my head and set my coffee cup down. "I should go get ready for work." I stand, gather up my plate and cup, and take them both to the sink, where I wash them quickly. "Thanks for breakfast. Next time it's my treat," I say, putting everything in the dish drainer without looking at him.

"Fawn."

"Hmm?" I pick up Muffin's leash and look to where she is sprawled out on the floor, asleep. "Up, girl, it's time to go," I tell her, and she opens one eye, then closes it. *Seriously, not this again* . . .

"Fawn."

"Yeah?" I bend over and lift Muffin off the ground with my arms around her middle, then huff when she falls back to her belly after I have her on her feet. "Stubborn dog."

"Fawn." Oh god, the sound of his deep voice behind me and the feel of his large hand sliding around my hip to my stomach and his groin pressing into my ass cause a flood of heat to spread between my legs.

I don't even think about what I'm doing. One second I'm feeling his very large, very evident erection poking me in the ass, and the next I'm spinning around to face him, up on my tiptoes, pressing my mouth to his.

"Christ," he breathes against my lips before nipping the bottom one. On my gasp his tongue slides between my parted lips, and the taste of him and coffee exploding across my taste buds makes me moan. Feeling his hands roam up the back of my shirt across my skin, I press deeper into him, needing more, wanting more. I cling to him with all my strength while his hand cups the back of my skull and he takes over the kiss and my mind. Sliding my own hands around his back and up under his shirt, I press deeper into him and whimper down his throat. Getting lost in his mouth against mine, I allow him to lead me across the room. As the couch bumps the backs of my legs, my nails dig into his back.

"Fuck." He stops suddenly, pulling away, leaving me off balance and completely mortified.

"I . . ." I press my fingers to my tingling lips while my chest heaves in sync with his. "I gotta go." I bolt for the door, and by some act of god Muffin follows me out of his apartment and across the hall.

"Fawn . . . stop," he shouts as I make it to my door. Before he can say more or make it across the hall to me, I get inside, slam the door, and bolt it with the lock. I've messed up. I've messed up big-time, and now I need to find a new place to live. "Fawn . . . we need to talk," he shouts through the door with a pound of his fist, and I close my eyes.

"It's okay, no talking necessary . . . I'll see you around," I shout back, then shake my head to myself, burying my face in my hands. I don't know what came over me—I've never been aggressive before, but it's like I couldn't help myself.

Hearing a thump, I wonder what it is; then I hear his quietly growled words through the wood. "This isn't over, baby, not by a long shot. I'll see you tonight."

He will not be seeing me tonight or ever for that matter. Tonight I'm going to my sisters', where I plan on staying until I can find a new place to live . . . preferably in another country. I've always wanted to teach abroad, so this is the perfect excuse to finally move to Paris and put those eight years of French I took to good use. While I'm there I will spend my days working and my nights trying to forget about Levi and the fact that he gave me the most devastatingly beautiful kiss of my life. With that plan in my mind, I head for my room to get ready for work.

∽

Sitting on the corner of my desk when the bell rings, I study Tamara as she slips on her jacket and puts away her things. Today, like every day this week, she's been quiet and withdrawn, whereas normally she's outspoken and fully involved in class. I'm worried about her. Smiling at each kid as they leave the room, I look back at Tamara, who's for once ready to go when everyone else is. "Tamara, can I speak to you for a minute?" I ask as she starts to pass in front of my desk; her eyes move to the clock on the wall before coming back to me.

"I have to be out front. My mom's boyfriend is picking me up." She swallows, looking nervous.

"It will just take a second," I reassure her. There is no way that I will allow her to get into trouble by keeping her too long, but I need to make sure she's okay before I can in good conscience let her leave for the day.

"Okay," she agrees before turning to smile at Addie, one of her friends in class, as she passes.

"'Bye, Miss Reed." Addie smiles.

"'Bye, Addie. Have a good day." I know the girls in class talk to one another, so I have no doubt Tamara probably opened up to her friends about whatever's going on. I just hope she will trust me enough to do the same with me.

Keeping my place perched on the edge of my desk, I look at Tamara as soon as the room is empty. "I noticed that you seem a little off this week. Is everything okay?"

Her immediate yes sets off warning bells, but I don't let it show. I know better than to make it seem like I don't believe her.

"If you ever want to talk to me about anything at all, I'm here, or if you would rather talk to Mrs. Jenkins, her door is always open," I say, referring to the school counselor, whom all the kids love.

"I know." She shrugs her shoulders, licking her bottom lip. "I'm fine."

"Okay, honey," I say softly, giving her a small smile. "Go on. I'll see you tomorrow."

"'Bye, Miss Reed."

"'Bye, Tamara." I watch her go, wishing that I didn't have to. My gut tells me that something is happening, but I also know that without her talking to me, there is nothing I can do to help her. With a helpless sigh, I stand up and gather my bags and coat, then head for the front office.

"Hey, Sammy," I greet the principal's receptionist as soon as I walk through the door; her head flies up, causing her unruly hair to fall in front of her face.

"Hi, Fawn." She smiles, blowing her hair out of her eyes and looking completely rattled—then again, she always looks rattled.

"Is Mrs. Thompson available?"

"Yep, go on in." She nods toward the door behind her with a smile, and I head across the office and open the door, finding Mrs. Thompson sitting behind her computer, looking as polished as ever in a dusty-blue suit with her dark hair pinned back away from her very pretty face.

"Hi, Miss Reed, how can I help you?" She smiles at me as I move into the room and take a seat across from her.

"I'm a little worried," I admit, setting my bags on the ground next to my chair.

"Worried?" she asks, sitting back and resting her hands in her lap as she studies me.

"Yes, Tamara Albergastey hasn't seemed like herself in class the last few days."

"What do you mean?" she asks quietly.

"It may be nothing, but she hasn't been participating in class like she normally does, and she's seemed really withdrawn." I rub my hands together, wishing I had something more to go on. "I asked her after class if she wanted to talk and if she was okay, but she said she was fine."

"Oh dear." She sits forward, resting her hands on her desk. "Have there been any changes at home that you are aware of?"

"Her mom has a new boyfriend and I don't think they get along, but I don't know that for sure."

"Hmm." She smiles a soft, sad smile knowing Tamara's mother's history better than I do, since she's been one of her students for the last few years.

"I understand how difficult this situation is, but unfortunately there is nothing we can do about the men Tamara's mother chooses to spend her time with."

"I know," I agree quietly.

"I will see if I can find out what's going on, but in the meantime, keep your chin up. Your students adore you, and Tamara is likely to speak to you about what's happening before anyone else."

"Thank you."

Studying me for a long moment, the principal's eyes search mine, and her face softens. "You're a great teacher, Fawn, and I know these kids mean a lot to you. It shows in your work and their grades. We're lucky to have you here in this school, but those kids are also very lucky to have someone who cares about them and their futures. Please know that Tamara's situation is one that you do not have a lot of control over, regardless of how badly you wish differently."

"I know, I just want to make sure she's okay."

"I know you do," she says gently, moving her eyes past my shoulder briefly. "I wish more teachers cared as much as you do. I know what it's like to see the potential in a child and want more for them. When I first started teaching, I had a student named Michel who was my favorite kid. He was good at everything but especially good in science, which was also my favorite subject to teach. I wanted him to get into a few different after-school science programs, but his family couldn't afford for him to stay after school. He was the oldest and the one responsible for making sure his younger siblings made it home and had dinner. I hated that he had to make that sacrifice, but eventually I found a weekend science program for him to be a part of, so in the end everyone was happy."

"That's amazing."

"No, what's amazing is that he shared his love of science with his siblings and now they are all in college—and all of them are doing something in the field of science." Sheesh. I pull in a breath and hold it to fight back the tears. "Keep doing what you're doing, not only with Tamara but with all of your students."

"I will." I nod, picking up my bags and coat from the floor. "Thank you again."

"You're welcome, and you know my door is always open."

"I do," I agree. When I was interviewing for teaching positions, Mrs. Thompson was the reason I wanted to work at PS 189. From the very moment I met her, I could tell she cared deeply about the students—she wasn't jaded like some of the other principals I interviewed with. She didn't just see her job as a job, she saw it as a way to make a difference in the world, which is the exact reason I wanted to be a teacher.

Shutting her office door, I say a quiet goodbye to Sammy as I pass her desk, seeing her nose buried in a folder she's looking through.

"You, too, Fawn," she mumbles back absently. Slipping on my coat, I button it up, then put on my hat and gloves before leaving the office, placing one earbud in so I can listen to my newest audiobook. Walking out of the school, I head up the block for the subway, where I fight for a place to stand on the train during the rush-hour commute. I don't want to go home, but I still need to pick up Muffin so I can take her with me to my sisters'. My sisters think my apartment is being fumigated, which is why I need to stay with them. Yes, I lied to them, but there is no way in hell I could tell them the truth—that I'm hiding from Levi because like the idiot I am, I kissed him and made a fool out of myself.

As the train comes to a stop, I get off with the crowd, then make my way up the steps with everyone else to street level, where the air is at least twenty degrees cooler. Adjusting my bag on my shoulder, I tuck my hands into my coat pockets and walk with my head down to ward off the cold that's nipping my cheeks. I growl under my breath as I watch a single snowflake fall onto the sleeve of my coat and melt. I hate when it snows in New York. I hate trudging through the slush and ice on the way to work. I know a lot of people love snow, and I agree it's pretty to look at when it first falls, but after a couple of days on New York City sidewalks, it's a disgusting mess.

Reaching my block, I breathe a sigh of relief when I don't see Levi—not that I thought he would be waiting for me, but with the way my luck has been going lately, I wouldn't have been surprised if I ran into him. Yes, I know eventually I will have to face him, since moving is about as realistic an option as teaching abroad, but truthfully, I'm hoping if I avoid him long enough he'll forget I even exist.

Punching in the code for the building, I swing the door open, close it behind me, then take the stairs as quietly and quickly as I can. I duck as I pass Levi's door with my key out. As soon as I'm inside my apartment, I lock the door and head for my room with Muffin in tow.

"We need to pack, girl. We're going to go stay with Mac and Libby for a couple days," I explain as she presses her head under my hand, forcing me to pet her. Taking a seat on the side of the bed, I give her a rub, then grab both sides of her face. "I know you're going to be mad at me, but I don't think you'll be seeing Levi much anymore." Huffing, she falls to her bottom and tips her head to the side. "Sorry, girl, but it's for the best," I say, softly kissing the top of her head before I stand. Going to my closet, I pull down a bag, then shove a couple of outfits in it along with a pair of pajamas and my bathroom stuff. As soon as I'm packed, I grab Muffin's leash from the closet, attach it to her collar, and head for the door, cursing myself stupid when I see Levi standing in the hall with his eyes on me. *Why the hell didn't I check the peephole?* As much as I want to run back into my apartment and hide, I know I can't, so I might as well just get this over with now. With a resonating sigh, I head in his direction.

"Hey," he says, studying me with a soft look in his eyes that makes me even more upset about this whole thing.

"Hi," I grumble, gritting my teeth as he takes my bags from me without asking.

"Are you taking her out?" he questions, looking at Muffin.

"Yes."

"Are you leaving town?" he asks, holding up my bag.

"No, I'm staying with Mac and Libby for a couple days."

"We need to talk," he murmurs, heading for his door, but I refuse to budge—unlike Muffin, who is attached to Levi's side, willing to follow him anywhere.

"No talk necessary," I say, quickly stomping toward him. With an annoyed tug, I pull my bag from his grasp. "I'm sorry about this morning. I don't know what I was thinking, but believe me, I regret it and it will never happen again." Okay, that was easier than I thought it would be.

"That's too bad." I hear the smile in his voice, and my eyes fly up to meet his. "I sure as fuck don't regret what happened this morning, and I definitely want more of that, but, babe, seriously, we were two feet from my couch, where in my head I had already stripped us down. Neither of us had time for what I wanted to do to you, and you are not even close to ready to go there with me."

"Ex . . . excuse me?" I stammer, staring at him with wide eyes.

"I like you, I like that you're a little bit crazy and a whole lot blind, but until I know you understand exactly what's happening between us, there is no way I'll take you to my bed." Blinking at him, I try to understand exactly what the hell he's saying, but all I can focus on is the fact that he called me crazy and blind. "I'm not crazy or blind."

"Gorgeous, you're so fucking stuck in your own head, you can't see straight."

"I am not," I growl, resting my hands on my hips as his eyes move over me and his lips twitch.

"I'm not going to argue with you about this."

"Well, it's not even true," I huff, then step back when he takes a step toward me.

"Oh, it's true, but that's okay. I'm enjoying this game we're playing," he murmurs, taking another step closer.

"Game?" I breathe as he reaches out, rubbing his thumb over my bottom lip.

"You're cute when you get flustered, and I like that you don't know how much you affect me and my self-control." *Okay, what the hell is going on?*

"What are you doing?" I whisper, pressing my hands to his chest when his head lowers toward mine.

"Kissing you."

"Why?"

"To prove a point." His lips brush over mine, and I know instantly that I wasn't in trouble before, but I'm in so much trouble now.

Chapter 6

Just Add That to the List

Fawn

"Hey, mamacita," I greet my mom as soon as I open the door to my apartment. Throwing my arms around her, I hug her tightly while she rocks me back and forth. Pushing me away while holding my arms, she searches my face and smiles, then pulls me close again.

"I've missed you, honey," she whispers, petting my head the way she always does.

"I missed you, too." I breathe in her scent that hasn't changed since I was little, taking comfort in its familiarity before she lets me go.

Hearing my dad clear his throat behind me, I turn to find him with his arms open wide. "Daddio." I grin, his laughter deep as he tugs me into him.

"Kiddo," he mutters, kissing the side of my head. "It's been too long."

"I know," and it really has been too long. I haven't seen my parents since school started back up, and I miss them both like crazy. Talking on the phone every couple of days is not even close to the same as seeing them in person. Letting Dad go after a few seconds, I step back, bumping into something, and look behind me to see two small suitcases side by side. My dad must have brought them inside when I was hugging my mom.

"Um . . ." I look between my parents, who haven't changed much over the years. My mom still has the same short bob she's always had, which fits her round pixielike face and small stature. And my dad is still intimidating looking, with wide shoulders, red hair, and a scruffy beard. "Do you still need to check in to your hotel room?" I ask, and my dad looks at my mom, who grins at me.

"We're staying with you. Won't that be fun?" she asks excitedly.

Um, what? Did she just say they were staying with me and the word *fun* in the same sentence? Yes, I love my mom and dad, and yes, I miss them, but I moved out of their house for a reason. The first one being that they do not understand the meaning of personal space or boundaries.

"All the hotels we looked into were a little too expensive, so we figured we'd save a few bucks and stay with you," Dad says, and I press my lips together. My parents are not broke—no, they're not rich, either—but they can definitely afford to stay at a hotel. This isn't about them saving a few dollars. I know this is about my stupid sisters opening their big dumb mouths about Levi. Levi, who two nights ago insisted on giving me a ride to my sisters' place after he kissed me stupid in the hall. Levi, who laughed his ass off when they asked him about the building we both reside in being fumigated. I didn't think it was as funny as he did, and my sisters had no clue why he thought it was hilarious, but they did find it very entertaining when he kissed me in front of them before leaving.

"All I have is the couch," I mutter as Muffin finally pulls herself off said couch to come over and greet everyone.

"We figured we'd take your bed and you could have the pullout, unless there is somewhere else you wanted to stay—you know, somewhere close by?" Mom smiles knowingly, and I feel my eye twitch.

Oh.

My.

God.

I'm going to kill them. I'm going to be on the eleven o'clock news tonight, because I'm going to murder both of my sisters.

"I'll sleep on the couch," I grit out, trying to make it look like I'm smiling at the idea.

"Well, good, that's all settled." Dad grins, picking up both suitcases and taking them to my room.

"Are you ready to go?" Mom asks, and I pull my eyes off my dad's retreating back to look at her petting Muffin.

"Yep, all ready," I grumble, walking across the room to grab the black wool coat I laid on the edge of the couch earlier. Putting it on, I do up the four toggle buttons, then slip on my deep-red hat, scarf, and mittens set. Once I'm done, I pat Muffin's head, mumbling, "Be good, girl," as I head past my mom for the door.

The last time Levi sent me a text message, he said he would be working most of the weekend, but I still want to check to make sure the coast is clear. All I need is for my parents to run into him, and god help me if that happens.

"Honey, if we're going to leave, you're going to have to open the door," Mom says from behind me, laughing, and I groan inwardly.

"I know." I open the door and step out into the hall with them following me. As soon as we are all out of my apartment, I watch my dad turn to check the knob to make sure it's locked before we all head toward the stairs.

"So did you get a new neighbor?" Mom asks, sounding far too innocent, as we pass Levi's door.

"Yep." Maybe if I keep my answers short and sweet they will give up.

"Oh, that's nice. What are they like?"

"You know, just a person." Just a person—seriously, like, what could he be, an alien? I'm never going to make it through this weekend at this rate.

"What kind of person?" Dad asks, and my shoulders sag.

Damn with that. I know they are not going to give up until I give them something. "Fine," I sigh. "Let's get this over with." I spin around to face them on the stairs, and they both stop two steps above me. "His name is Levi, he's a detective. Yes, he kissed me, and yes, I may like him, but it's too early to tell if I do or not. So right now he's just a nice guy that I kissed . . . that's all." I pause, then add, "Well, that and he's my neighbor. So, please, can we not talk about him while you guys are here?" I ask, and their eyes are wide, but neither of them is looking at me. No, they are both looking past my shoulder. "There's someone behind me, isn't there?" I whisper, and they both nod. Lowering my head, I shake it from side to side, then turn around hoping it's not who I think it is—but of course it is.

"Please tell me you didn't hear any of that," I plead to Levi, who's standing at the bottom of the stairs near the front door with a smile on his face.

"Baby." He chuckles, and I hear my mom whisper *baby* behind me.

"Great." My eyes slide closed as my cheeks heat. One more thing to add to the ever-growing list of embarrassing things I have done in front of him.

"I'm Levi, Fawn's new neighbor." His heavy boots sound on the wood of the stairs, then his warm hand comes to rest against my lower back. Opening my eyes back up, I find him standing next to me with his free hand held out toward my parents.

"Aiden Reed." Dad shakes Levi's hand, then wraps his arm around my mom's shoulder. "My wife, Fawn's mom, Katie Reed."

"Nice to meet you, Mr. and Mrs. Reed," Levi says as I try to shrink into myself. Where is a sinkhole when you need one?

"You, too," Mom whispers, and I look up, noticing her eyes—glued to Levi—have glazed over. *Great.*

"Are you heading to the show now?" Levi asks, dipping his head toward me and leaving me no choice but to look at him.

"Yes."

"Do you want me to take Muffin out for you while you're gone?" he asks quietly, and I swear I hear my mom swoon and melt into a giant puddle at his feet.

"She should be okay. I took her out not long ago," I murmur as my eyes unconsciously drop to his mouth. Watching a smirk form on his lips, my brows pull together and my eyes narrow.

"Give me your key—I'm home for the evening. I'll take her over to my place, and you can come get her when you get back."

"No—"

"That sounds like a great idea," Dad cuts me off, and my eyes close briefly. Why, oh, why couldn't my dad be like any normal father who would grumble at the idea of a man being inside his daughter's apartment whether she is home or not?

"Yes, I agree that's a great idea," Mom chimes in, sounding far too happy about the idea.

"Fine." Shoving my hand into my pocket angrily for my key, I freeze, then feel in my other pocket, coming up with nothing but a five-year-old ChapStick. *Dammit.* "Um . . . I forgot my key," I say softly.

"Do you want me to call a locksmith?" Levi asks, and I look up at my dad, knowing that he's going to be pissed when I say what I'm about to say. But I don't want to have to pay for a locksmith to come out when I don't really need one.

"There's a key under my doormat," I whisper.

"You've got to be shitting me." It's growled, but not by my dad, whom I'm looking directly at. No, by Levi, who's standing next to me with his hand on the back of my coat, clenched into a fist around the material. "Do you know how unsafe that is?"

"The building is secured," I whisper, and my dad's jaw clenches tight, shifting the beard on his face.

"You know that doesn't matter, kiddo," Dad growls.

Levi mutters, "Damn straight it doesn't." Oh great, now I have both of them growling at me.

"It's been there forever and nothing has happened."

"You know shit can happen, Fawn Grace Reed. My career is based off bad shit happening to people who don't expect it to happen to them." Dad shakes his head, and I know he's really mad, since he didn't just use my name—no, he used my full name.

"I won't put it back after tonight."

"No, you won't," Levi mutters, and I turn to glare at him—not that he notices. His eyes are on my dad's and they are sharing a look that doesn't bode well for me.

"We should go or we are going to be late," Mom says, and all eyes go to her. "We still need to pick up our tickets at the box office."

"Right," Dad mutters, looking from her to Levi. "If you're not working in the morning, come on over for breakfast. Katie's making pancakes, and Fawn's sisters will be over, so there will be plenty." Um . . . what? *No!*

"I'd like that," Levi agrees, loosening his grip on the back of my coat. "Have a good night, Mr. and Mrs. Reed."

"Aiden will do." Dad takes his arm from around my mom to take her hand on the stairs. With his other hand, he pats Levi's shoulder.

"And you can call me Katie," Mom says with a bright smile, and I roll my eyes at both of my parents.

"Okay, Aiden and Katie, I'll see you both in the morning—and Fawn." He dips his face close to mine. "I'll see you tonight when you come to pick up Muffin. Have a good time."

"Thanks," I grumble, watching him smile like he thinks I'm cute. Whatever. I pull my eyes from him and head down the last few stairs, hearing my mom and dad behind me as I open the door to the building. As soon as I'm outside, I inhale a deep breath of cool air. I'm no longer embarrassed about what Levi heard me say. No, I'm annoyed with him for being high-handed as well as pissed that he's going to be coming to my apartment to have breakfast with my parents and sisters tomorrow. I don't want them to get to know him yet, not when I don't even really know him, and I don't want them to try to influence my feelings for him.

"Well, Levi seems very nice," Mom says, taking my arm, and I sigh.

"Yes, he's nice," I agree, because he really is nice.

"I like him."

"Mom, you like everyone," I grumble. My mom has never met a person she hasn't liked; I swear she could find a likable quality in a serial killer if left alone with him long enough.

"I like him, too," Dad says, holding out his arm for a cab.

"Surprise, surprise." I roll my eyes as a cab pulls to a stop in front of us. My dad opens the door for my mom and me to get in the back, and he gets into the front with the driver. Sitting there, I listen absently as my parents chat until my dad asks the driver to pull over so we can walk the last few blocks, since traffic is backed up.

"Are you excited, honey?" Mom questions, leaning into my side as soon as we're out of the cab and on the sidewalk.

"Yes." I smile at her. I don't get to go to shows often, since the tickets are so expensive, but I love getting to pick whatever show I want for my birthday each year. It's always something I look forward to.

"Come on." Dad's arm wraps around my shoulders, pulling me against this bulky chest and holding me there while leading me down the block. Finally getting to the theater, we get in line to pick up our tickets from the box office, then head inside, where we are directed to the first floor. The theater is huge and packed with men, women, and kids from all walks of life, some dressed up to see the show, others wearing jeans and sweaters and pulling luggage along with them.

"We're gonna go find the restrooms." Mom smiles as I head toward the concession stand. "We'll meet you at our seats."

"Okay, do you guys want anything?"

"Wine for me." She grins.

"A rum and Coke and a bag of popcorn," Dad says, wrapping his hand around my mom's.

"Sure," I agree, then watch them disappear in the crowd. Waiting in line for what seems like forever, I finally make it to the front and place my order, making sure to get a magnet since I have one from every show I've ever gone to. With a drink holder, my dad's popcorn, and a bag of peanut M&M's in my pocket, I make my way to the front of the packed theater. Finding my parents already seated, I take the seat next to my mom, unpack the drink carrier, and take off my coat, all the while listening to the quiet hum of excitement around me.

Staring at the red drapes blocking the stage, my mind wanders to what's going on between Levi and me as I nibble my M&M's and sip my wine.

"What?" I ask when I turn to find both my parents smiling at me.

"Nothing," Dad mutters, shoving a handful of popcorn in his mouth as my mom winks and pats my hand. I don't have long to wonder what that's about. The lights dim, and the show starts, pushing all thoughts of Levi out of my head as I watch in wonder as the magic of *The Lion King* on Broadway unfolds in front of my eyes.

"So was it everything you thought it would be?" Mom asks after the show comes to an end and the people start to put on their coats and leave.

"Everything and more. I can't believe how magical it was, how amazing the props were. It was way better than the movie."

"It was cool," my dad agrees, helping my mom into her coat as I put mine on. "I didn't think anything could top *Hamilton*, but this show was very well done."

"It really was," Mom says, touching his cheek with her hand, and he turns his head to kiss her palm. God, my parents are seriously still so in love that it's crazy, and I know without a shadow of a doubt that no matter how long it takes, I will wait for a real love—because I want a love like they have. I want to look at the man I'm with over thirty years later and still feel my face get soft the way my mom's does when she looks at my dad.

"Can we stop and get a hot dog before we head back to the apartment?" Dad asks, and Mom shakes her head.

"You and those darn hot dogs," she grumbles.

"They're good." He smiles, and I laugh. No street-cart food is really good, but my dad likes standing in the middle of Times Square eating a hot dog while looking at the lights.

"If we must," Mom agrees, giving in like she does every year.

"Thanks, darlin'." He kisses the top of her head, then leads us out of the theater with the crowd. As soon as we're outside, we make our way down the block toward the bright lights. Stopping at the first food cart we see, we order two hot dogs and a pretzel covered with cinnamon and sugar, then wander slowly through the crowd of people. There are some truly beautiful places in the world, and Times Square is one of them. It's not full of rare, beautiful history like the Louvre in France, but it's still beautiful in its own way. Standing under the bright lights with people from all over the world around you fills you with an energy that is impossible to describe unless you have experienced it firsthand. I still remember the first time my parents brought us to Manhattan. The first time they bundled us up and took us to see Times Square. That was when I fell in love with the city.

"Thank you guys for tonight," I say softly to my parents as we stop to catch a cab to head home.

"You're welcome, honey," Mom murmurs, wrapping her arm around mine and giving it a squeeze.

"Any time, kiddo." Dad smiles. I love my mom and dad. They have always made it a point to do things with my sisters and me as a family and with each of us separately. Like on our birthdays we get to choose something to do alone with them. Mine has always consisted of a show, Mac's is always a baseball game, and Libby—well, Libby usually asks them to take her shopping. They might not be normal parents in a lot of ways, but where it counts, they are better than most.

Finally getting a cab, we head back across town. As soon as we pull up in front of my building, I get out with my mom and head toward the door while my dad pays the cab driver. Punching in the code, I hold open the door for my parents, then scan the street when I hear my name.

"Oh, it's Levi," Mom says, and I look to where she's pointing. Levi is standing with a woman who's wearing a pair of tight-fitting workout pants and a slim-fitting jacket, and she's petting my dog.

Um, no!

"Baby, come here," he calls, staring at me, and I narrow my eyes.

"I'll meet you guys upstairs in just a minute. I need to get my key from Levi," I tell my parents as I let the door go.

"Sure, honey," Mom murmurs. Stomping to the edge of the sidewalk, I look both ways quickly, then continue my stomping as I cross the street toward Levi and the woman who is now sizing me up.

"Hey, baby," Levi says quietly, and I glare at him, then move my eyes to my girl and take hold of her leash near her neck. No damn way is he going to use my dog to pick up women. Hell, no.

"Levi," I growl, trying to tug Muffin's leash from his grasp, but of course he doesn't let go. No, he uses it to pull me toward him. "Levi," I cry in frustration as his arm slides around my back and I'm dragged into his front.

"Did you have fun?" he asks, brushing his lips over mine and knocking me completely off kilter. I blink, watching him smile. "Never mind. You can tell me about it when we get inside," he mutters, touching his lips to mine once more, then turning me in his arm. "Baby. This is . . . Sorry, what's your name again?" he asks, looking at the woman standing in front of us. Her eyes fill with ice.

"Beth," she huffs as Muffin's head moves under my hand.

"Right, Beth, this is Fawn," he breathes against my ear, making me shiver, and his arm tightens. "We should go in, baby, it's cold." He takes my hand in his as nausea and realization fill my stomach. "Have a good night."

"Yeah, night," she says, looking us over once more before jogging off. Tugging my hand free from Levi's grasp once Beth is out of sight, I move ahead of him across the street to where my parents are still standing in the open door of my building, watching us with varying looks on their faces.

"Hi, Levi." Mom smiles, giving him a hug like she hasn't seen him in forever, and I fight the urge to scream at the top of my lungs.

"Katie, did you enjoy the show?" Levi asks while my dad and I head up the stairs ahead of him and my mom.

"Oh yes, the show was amazing. Wasn't it amazing, honey?" she murmurs.

"It was amazing," I agree through clenched teeth as I head across the open landing toward my apartment. Turning to face Levi outside my door, I move my eyes to his shoulder. "Do you have my key?" I hold out my hand.

"Yep." He digs into the front pocket of his jeans and pulls it out, dropping it into my open palm.

"Thanks," I mutter, turning to open the door for my parents. "I'll be right back." I smile at them—or try to—as they go inside, then shut the door behind them before they can ask me what I'm doing.

Stomping across the wood floors to Levi's door, I cross my arms over my chest and tap my foot as I wait for him to unlock it, feeling anger swell inside my chest when I see him smiling. "You okay, babe?"

Am I okay? *No.* I'm pissed and hurt, but I'm focusing on the pissed part, because that feeling is the safer of the two coursing through me right now. As soon as he unlocks the door, I move in ahead of him and watch him shut the door. "I'm not your woman," I say as soon as he turns to face me. After watching him cross his arms over his chest, my eyes then move to my dog . . . *my dog* as she takes a seat at his side, and he raises a brow. "If you don't want to talk to a woman, just tell her you're not interested. Don't use me to throw her off your scent," I hiss, leaning in, and his eyes narrow. "That is not okay."

"Are you done?" Pressing my lips tightly together in answer, I move toward the door only to stop as he steps in front of me, blocking my path. "You've got me confused with someone else."

"Confused?" I frown, and he grins.

"You think I'm the kind of guy that would do something like make an excuse to a woman so I don't hurt her feelings. That's not me, baby. I'm not that guy. I'm not that nice."

"You're nice." I shake my head, and his fingers run up my jaw, then slide behind my ear, where he tucks a few strands of hair.

"I'm not nice," he says so sincerely that I almost believe him, but I know the Levi who brought me a cake on my birthday, the Levi who offered to watch Muffin when I'm gone, and he's nice, really nice. Maybe even too nice.

"You're always nice to me," I whisper, and the look in his eyes changes ever so slightly.

"Yeah," he agrees, sliding his hands around my waist and turning me until we are face-to-face. "I'm always nice to you."

"Why?"

"Because I like you, because you're different."

"You like me?"

"I think I've made that pretty clear."

"What's going on between us?" I try to keep the vulnerability out of my voice, but it still seeps in. I hate not knowing what I'm doing or where I stand with him. I hate feeling insecure, and I would rather embarrass myself right now and know there is nothing going on than to have one more day go by where I question things.

"Fawn." His face softens, and his fingers tighten. "Can't you see I'm trying to figure it out?"

"Oh." I drop my eyes to his chin and press my lips together. That is not the answer I was looking for.

"Look at me," he urges, resting his fingers under my jaw, and I reluctantly do.

"What I know is that I like the parts of you you've allowed me to see. I enjoy spending time with you and want to do that more. I'm not psychic, I can't see the future, so I don't know what will happen between us, but I'm interested in you enough to want to find out."

"Oh," I repeat, this time swallowing.

"Now, are you on the same page as me?" he asks, and I nod. "Good. Now are you done being pissed?"

"I wasn't pissed."

"Gorgeous." He sighs, shaking his head. "You were pissed when you saw me across the street with Becky."

"Beth," I grumble, and he grins.

"Whatever her name is."

"I thought you were using my dog to pick up chicks."

"I've never needed a dog to pick up a woman. Besides, I've got my hands full with this hot little blonde who lives next door to me and may or may not be crazy."

"I'm not crazy." I feign annoyance while secretly doing flips in my head. *He thinks I'm hot.*

"Crazy people never think they're crazy, gorgeous." He grins, and I slap his chest, then feel my mouth soften when he takes my hand to kiss my palm, just like I watched my dad do to my mom at the theater. "Now, why don't you go on over to your place, make sure your parents are settled, then come back and hang out with me for a while?"

"Sure," I agree as nervous excitement fills my stomach. Muffin has sprawled out on the couch, making herself at home.

"She can stay." He brushes his lips over mine as he opens the door.

"Are you sure?"

"Positive," he agrees. "Now go on and hurry back to me." He taps my ass lightly two times, sending me on my way. Stopping with my hand on the knob to my apartment, I turn to find him watching me. I don't know what he's thinking, but the look in his eyes makes my mouth dry. Pulling my eyes from him, I scoot through and close the door behind me, finding my parents both on the couch in their pajamas.

"Is everything okay?" Dad asks as soon as my eyes meet his.

"Yep. I'm going to go hang out with Levi for a bit. I'll be home in a while," I say as casually as possible, even though my stomach has started to turn with nervous butterflies.

"It's after eleven," he states, and Mom smacks his chest. "What?" he asks looking at her.

"Go on. Have fun, honey." Mom rolls her eyes at him.

"I'm just going to change first," I say, heading to my bedroom and shutting the door. I take off my coat, toss it to the floor of my closet, and dig though my stuff until I find something to wear. Settling on a pair of leggings, an oversize off-the-shoulder sweater over a tank top, and a pair of scrunched, warm socks, I change as fast as I can, almost taking myself out a few times in my rush.

As soon as I'm done, I go to the door and swing it open. "I'll see you guys in the morning," I say, going over to kiss each of my parents' cheeks.

"Night, honey," Mom says, kissing the side of my head.

"Night, kiddo," Dad says, then mutters, "Be smart," giving me a look that I ignore.

"Tell Levi we'll see him for breakfast," Mom says as I slip on my Uggs, and I turn to catch her smiling ear to ear.

"Will do," I agree, opening and shutting the door behind me. After knocking on Levi's door, I don't even have a second to wait before he's pulling me through the door and shutting it behind me. "What are you doing?" I ask his back as he drags me across the living room.

"We're going to make out."

"What?" I squeak as he pulls me into his bedroom and kicks the door closed.

"Your dog's taking up the couch, so we're going to make out in here and watch some TV."

"Oh." He pushes me onto the bed and looms over me, making me feel dizzy once more. "I thought we were going to get to know each other," I breathe as his golden eyes search mine.

"We are." He grins wickedly, then drops his head, covering my mouth with his. After the first touch of his tongue against mine, all I can think is I want to get to know all of him.

Chapter 7

BREAKFAST WITH CRAZY PEOPLE, AKA MY FAMILY

FAWN

Waking slowly, I soak in the feeling of the warm body I'm pressed against and blink my eyes open. Taking in the expanse of Levi's naked chest and the feel of his abs under my palm, I grin, pressing my face closer to his skin, breathing in his scent. Last night after we made out for a while, we got up and took Muffin for a walk. Then we stopped at the Chinese spot on the corner and ordered lo mein to share. Once we got back to his place, we got into bed and ate while watching TV. I planned on getting up and heading over to my place to sleep, but I must have fallen asleep at some point during our second make-out session.

"You awake?" Levi's rough, sleepy voice asks as his fingers tighten around my hip.

"Kind of," I murmur as he pulls me deeper into his side.

"What time do your parents normally wake up?" he asks quietly.

"Maybe eight," I mutter as his fingers slide up my bare side and my eyes close.

"It's nine thirty."

"What?" I practically shout as I sit up quickly with my hands against his abs. I bend half over his body to look at the clock on his bedside table. "Shit," I groan. I never sleep this late. Ever. "I gotta go." I hop off the bed to look for the shirt he took off me last night. My sisters and parents are probably having a field day talking about me. I can practically feel my ears ringing.

"So I'm guessing we can't make out for a while?" he says, and I find him sitting with his back against his black leather headboard, his deep-gray down comforter around his waist, and an amused smile on his face.

"Um . . ." I lick my lips, moving my eyes from his wide chest to his abs, wanting nothing more than to dive back into bed with him.

"Baby." He chuckles, and my eyes fly up to meet his once more. "You keep looking at me like that, and I won't let you leave this room."

"I have to go." I shake my head to rid the sight of him half-naked from my brain. "My sisters are probably already at my apartment, and I have no doubt they are all talking about me not coming home last night," I say while pulling my sweater down over my head.

"I thought about waking you after you passed out, but I didn't want to let you go." He didn't want to let me go . . . Oh my . . . My stomach dips, and my legs get weak. "I'll take Muffin out before I come over for breakfast."

"Um . . ." I chew the inside of my cheek. "About breakfast." I try to sound casual as I sit down on the edge of the bed to put on my socks.

"You don't want me there." God, when he says it like that, I feel like the world's biggest jerk.

"It's not that, exactly, it's just that my family can be a little . . ."

"Crazy?" he asks with a smile.

"Yes." I nod. "They can be a little crazy," I concur as I stand. "And—"

"I'm coming," he states, cutting me off. He throws the blanket off his waist and moves to sit on the side of the bed.

"I . . ." The words I was about to say catch in my throat when his large hands wrap around my hips and I'm pulled between his spread thighs.

"I'm coming," he repeats firmly, the look on his face daring me to argue.

"Okay," I agree quietly, looking into his eyes, which appear darker than their normal gold this morning. I think there is something significant about this moment and him wanting to spend time with my family.

"Good, now kiss me."

"Kiss you?" I blurt like an idiot. Last night he seemed to like being in charge. I didn't have to instigate anything; all I had to do was follow his lead—and he is a damn good leader.

"Yes, kiss me." My eyes drop to his mouth, and I bite my bottom lip, debating how to go about kissing him. "Fawn."

"Hmm?" I hum, studying his mouth.

"Kiss me," he whispers, and I watch his lips move as they form each of those words.

Leaning closer I slide my hands through his thick, dark hair watching his eyelids lower, then press my mouth to his softly. Feeling his warm lips and his breath mingle with mine, I lose myself in him. Sliding my leg over his to straddle his lap, I listen to his groan of approval and shiver when one of his hands slides down to grab ahold of my ass. The other moves up into the back of my hair, where he grips tight in a possessive hold that makes my stomach dip.

"Damn, but I could seriously become addicted to your mouth." He breathes against my lips, and I smile against his.

"Ditto," I whisper, nipping his bottom lip and hearing him growl right before he takes over the kiss, thrusting his tongue into my mouth and making me whimper. Rocking against him I tip my head to the side to deepen the kiss, then mewl in disappointment when he slows the kiss and pulls away, resting his forehead to mine.

"We better stop," he says, sounding like he doesn't want to stop at all, and I nod, closing my eyes and pulling in a much-needed lungful of air.

"Yeah, I need to get home," I agree, opening my eyes to find his on mine.

"I don't want to let you go," he says, and I know in that moment I could get lost in him.

"Then don't." I close my eyes again, not wanting him to see that I really mean *Don't let me go, ever.*

"I don't plan on it." He tips my head down so he can press a sweet kiss to my forehead. "Up you go," he urges, and I reluctantly get off his lap, then watch him stand. "Are you okay?"

No would be the answer to that question. I feel like my life has changed in a huge way. I feel like . . . god, I feel like crying. "I'm good," I lie, and his hand wraps around the back of my neck. He drags me closer so I have no choice but to rest my cheek against his chest.

"You good with me and you?" he asks softly, and I nod, not looking up at him. "That's all that matters." He kisses the top of my hair, letting me go once more. When he turns his back to me, I watch his muscles move under his skin as he opens a drawer and pulls out a long-sleeved navy-blue thermal and puts it on over his head. I want to pout a little that he's covering up, but I don't have time to do that. Instead my eyes drop to his ass, which is covered in a pair of formfitting dark-blue, almost black, boxers as he trades the sleep pants he put on last night when we got back from walking Muffin for a pair of thick gray sweats. Turning back toward me once he's dressed, he smiles. "Come on."

He takes my hand and pulls open his door. Muffin, who is still on the couch, lifts her head to look at us, then slowly pulls herself to stand, placing one paw on the floor at a time. As soon as she's up, she wanders slowly to Levi, bumping him with her nose and not even paying me one bit of attention.

"My dog is seriously in love with you."

"The feeling's mutual, though I'm thinking of giving her a nickname."

"Why?" I ask, watching him pet her before moving to pick up a pair of shoes and carrying them across the room.

"Muffin's not exactly something I like calling her when we are out. I was thinking Brutus would be good."

"She's a girl." I tell him something he should know as he takes a seat on the couch to put on a pair of worn sneakers.

"Why Muffin?" he asks, lifting his head to look at me.

"Do you mean why did I name her Muffin?" He nods. "She was rescued from a breeder out on Long Island," I say, giving Muffin a rub-down when she finally pulls herself away from Levi and comes over to me. "I was visiting my parents over Christmas break last year when a story broke about a breeder out on Long Island who was being charged with animal cruelty. When I saw the news, I went to my dad to ask him about it. He told me that the Humane Society had brought more than a hundred dogs to the local shelter to either be rehomed or put down because they couldn't adjust to life outside the cages they were forced to live in. That day I went to the shelter to see if I could help in some way. I didn't plan on getting a dog, but I needed to do something, so I volunteered my time. That's when I met Muffin. She was the runt of her litter and was scared to death of everyone. No one thought she would make it because she wouldn't eat and she was having a really hard time adjusting. Every day I would spend time with her and the other dogs during breakfast before taking them on a walk or helping with cleanup around the kennel," I say, watching his eyes soften. "Then one day I was doing what I had done the whole week prior. I was sitting on the floor eating while watching the dogs play, and Muffin, who had always stuck to the corner of the room and to herself, ran toward me to get the blueberry muffin I pulled out of my bag. I didn't even have a chance to stop her before she ate almost the whole thing in one bite." I smile, looking down at her. "After that she was glued to my side. If I was there, she was with me, and when I had to come back to New York, I couldn't leave her behind, so I paid a thousand-dollar pet deposit on my apartment and brought her home." I bend down to give my girl a hug around her neck. "So that's why I call her Muffin," I finish quietly, taking a chance to look at him when I feel the vibe in the room shift.

"Jesus." He shakes his head, resting his elbows to his knees, studying us. "You better go before I stand."

"What?" I pull myself from Muffin trying to understand what just happened and why he suddenly looks pissed.

"I want you, Fawn." He pauses, rubbing his hand down the morning scruff covering his jaw. "I want you, and if I get my hands on you right now, there will be no going back, so you need to leave."

"Oh." I lick my lips and look at the door, then back to him, torn between leaving and letting him have me however he wants.

"Go, baby," he growls, so deep that I swear I feel it skim through every single cell in my body.

"Right," I whisper, picking up my Uggs that I took off last night and left next to his door. I pause with them against my chest. "Levi." I turn my head toward him with my hand on the knob to find him still sitting.

"Yeah?"

"Just so you know, I want you, too." I swing the door open and hurry out and across the hall before he can reply. After knocking on my door, since I don't have a key, it only takes a half a second for my dad to answer, and when he does, I swear he's fighting back a grin.

"Well, look who the cat decided to finally drag home." *Here we go.*

"Morning, Daddio," I mutter as he kisses my forehead, and then I scoot past him, dropping my shoes to the floor.

"Where's Levi?" Mom asks, looking behind me without so much as a hello in my direction.

"He's taking Muffin for a walk, he'll be over soon."

"Did you hear that, Libby? Levi's taking Fawn's dog for a walk after she spent the night with him," Mac says and I look to where my sisters are seated on the couch.

"I heard it, sis." Libby smirks, and I roll my eyes at the two of them.

"Could all of you do me a favor, and for once, just try to act normal and not embarrass me?" I plead.

"We would never embarrass you," Mom says, and my head swings to her and I raise a brow. "Well, not on purpose, anyways," she concludes in a mutter.

"Dad," I say, pulling my eyes from my mom to look at him.

"When have I ever embarrassed you?" he asks, and I stare at him in disbelief.

"I don't know, maybe the time Jimmy came over and you asked him if we were having sex."

"That was a serious question." He frowns, scratching his beard.

"I was thirteen," I cry, feeling embarrassed for my teenage self all over again.

"Kids nowadays are having sex young. I wanted you to be safe."

"Just, please, no talking about sex . . ." I pause to look at everyone. "At all."

"I don't know, maybe I should have a talk with him. After all, you did spend the night with the man."

"Oh lord." I cover my face with my hands and rub hard.

"Did you have sex with him?" Mom asks, and I pull my hands from my face to look at her, standing in the kitchen mixing a bowl of pancake batter.

"No, but even if we did, I wouldn't talk to you or Dad about it."

"Why not?" she asks, sounding offended.

"Mom," I sigh.

"Well, I have years of experience. I should be the person you talk to about sex."

"Yeah, Mom's an expert." Libby giggles, and I turn to glare at her as Mac makes a gag face in her direction.

"No one"—I wave my hand around encompassing all of them—"is allowed to even mention the word *sex* once Levi is here," I growl, then stomp toward my bedroom and shut the door. Going straight to my bathroom, I wash my face and brush my teeth, then start up the shower. I know I don't have a lot of time, but I need a few minutes to prepare myself for the torture that I know is coming. My family behaving like normal people is about as likely as winning the lottery.

Stripping out of my clothes, I get in under the warm water and wash my hair, then put in conditioner and leave it in to soak while I scrub head to toe with my berry-scented body wash. Once I'm clean, I comb out my hair, then rinse it with cool water. Shutting off the tap, I wrap myself in a towel and step into my room, sighing when I find my sisters on my bed.

"Levi's here," Mac says, and I look at the door, wondering if I should go out and rescue him before I get dressed. "He's fine. When we came in here, he was helping Mom with breakfast."

"Great," I mutter, grabbing a pair of underwear and slipping them on under my towel.

"So you stayed the night with him—does this mean you're finally going to tell us what's going on between you two?" Libby asks, and I look at her over my shoulder while I put on my bra.

"We're . . ." I pause, not sure what we are exactly. "We're seeing each other." I shrug, figuring that's a safe and true statement. I mean, he didn't say I was his girlfriend or anything, but he did say we were going to see what happened between us.

"So you're dating?" Mac asks.

"Kind of." I pull in a breath and shrug. Turning to grab a shirt, I pull out one with the Goonies on the front and toss it toward the bottom of my closet before proceeding to search through my stack of tees for one that doesn't seem childish. Sadly, all my shirts are basically the same— they all have witty sayings or cartoon characters on them. Giving up on my search and wanting to be more comfortable than fashionable, I settle on a long-sleeved, baby-blue tee with the Muppets on the front.

"Are you going to wear that?" Libby asks as I pull on a pair of black leggings.

"Shut up, Libby," Mac says as I step back into my bathroom to put on deodorant and spray leave-in conditioner in my hair.

"I'm only saying it because Levi doesn't look like the type of guy who would date a girl who dresses like a fourteen-year-old," Libby states when I come back into the room a minute later.

I look down at my shirt, and my stomach twists uncomfortably. She's right—Levi doesn't look like the kind of guy who would date a nerdy, awkward girl with out-of-control hair who prefers wearing leggings and baggy tees. He looks like the kind of guy who only dates models who look like his gorgeous sister-in-law.

"Don't change," Mac says, and my eyes go to her. "If he doesn't like you for you, screw him."

"You're only saying that because of Edward." Libby shakes her head, and I look at Mac.

"What happened with Edward?"

"Nothing." She turns to narrow her eyes on Libby.

"So you want me to tell you what's going on with Levi and me, but you don't want to tell me about you and Edward?"

"There is no me and Edward," she states in a growl, fisting her hands on her lap.

"What happened?" I ask, looking at Libby when I see Mac's lips are sealed.

"He has a girlfriend," Libby says quietly, and my eyes widen.

"What?" I take a seat next to Mac, and her cheeks darken. "Since when?"

"I don't know." Mac shakes her head. "I thought I was finally making progress with him. I thought he was finally noticing me. Then, out of the blue, he calls me three days ago and asks if I want to get a drink with him and a couple of friends. Of course, like an idiot, I agreed. Then the next thing I know, I'm sitting in a booth across from him and his girlfriend while they make out."

"I'm sorry, Mac." I rub her shoulder. She's been crushing on Edward forever, so it had to be devastating for her to watch him with someone else.

"It's for the best," she mutters, moving off the bed to stand. "Lesson learned." She shakes her head, smoothing her hands down her denim-covered thighs. "Never again will I work at trying to make a man notice me."

"You deserve more than a guy like him anyways," I tell her truthfully, and her face softens. "Seriously, he wasn't even that cute."

"True story." Libby smiles, hopping off the bed. "Now, Levi, on the other hand, is beyond hot. You better hold tight to that man."

"He's lucky to have you, not the other way around—don't ever forget that," Mac says, looking at me.

"Mac's right," Libby says softly, wrapping her arm around Mac's shoulders. "Levi is hot, but you are beautiful. If he doesn't want you, someone else will."

"Do not make me cry," I grumble as tears burn the back of my throat. My sisters might drive me nuts most of the time, but I wouldn't trade them for the world.

"Seriously, how lucky will he be if he gets to be a part of this family?" Libby laughs, and Mac and I follow along with her.

"Speaking of Levi, I better get out there before Mom asks him when he plans on marrying me or offers sex advice." I grin.

"Our parents are crazy." Mac shakes her head as I open the door.

As soon as I step out of my room, Levi's eyes come to me and fill with an intimacy that makes my belly melt. "Hey, baby."

"Sorry I wasn't out when you came; I just needed a shower."

"It's all good. Your mom put me to work to keep me busy."

"Did you know Levi can cook, Fawn?" She grabs his biceps and grins, giving it a squeeze as she wiggles her brows suggestively at me from behind his shoulder so he can't see. "Honey, I suggest you get knocked up soon so he doesn't get away."

"What?" Levi chuckles, looking back at her while my jaw drops and lands on the floor with a *thud*.

"Oh . . ." Mom looks around, then looks at my dad, who is sitting across the island from her with his chest moving in a way that shows he's laughing silently. "I . . . never mind." She shakes her head, waving her hand around like a lunatic. Feeling my cheeks getting hotter by the second, I bite my lip. I can't believe she just said that—well, I can believe it, because she is my mom, after all, but seriously, why can't my parents be normal?

"Well, now that you've made things totally awkward," Libby says, moving past me toward the kitchen, "what do you need help with, Mom? Do you want me to find you a turkey baster?" My eyes slide closed. I can't believe I thought for even a second it would be okay for Levi to come over for breakfast. I really should have known better. Opening my eyes back up, I find Levi watching me closely.

"I'm so sorry," I mouth, and his face softens.

"It's all good," he mouths back, then turns when my mom asks him to help with something.

"Come here, kiddo," Dad calls, patting the stool next to him, and I move slowly across the room to slide into the seat. "He's not running for the hills, so I'd say you're okay," he says quietly against the side of my head, placing a kiss there, and I nod.

"So, Levi, you said your family lives in Connecticut. Are you planning on going to see them for Thanksgiving?" Mom asks.

"No." He shakes his head while putting some butter into a pan on the stove. "I'm on call Thanksgiving. So I'll be home."

"You're going to be alone on Thanksgiving?" Mom asks, and he nods, giving her a smile.

"Yeah, it comes with the job."

"Don't I know it," Mom says quietly, looking at my dad with soft eyes filled with understanding.

"So what made you want to move to New York?" Dad asks, and Levi's gaze goes to him.

"I got offered a promotion if I transferred to the NYPD. It was an offer I couldn't turn down, so I packed up my house, put it on the market, and moved."

"How long have you been a detective?" Mac asks, leaning with her elbows on the island next to me.

"Four years now, give or take a few months."

"You're young," Dad states, sounding surprised.

"I'm younger than most of the guys doing my job, but before I was a detective I was working undercover for two years."

"Really?" I question. His eyes come to me, and he nods once.

"That must have been scary," Mom says, patting his shoulder.

"It wasn't scary, but I didn't enjoy living a lie or breathing the same air as the scumbags I was investigating."

"I bet not," Dad says, picking up the cup of coffee in front of him and taking a sip.

"Do you want coffee, honey?" Mom asks me when she sees me eyeing my dad's cup.

"Yes, please." I smile, and she moves to where I keep my cups and grabs one before heading for the coffeepot. When a phone rings, I look at Levi, who pulls his cell out of his back pocket.

"Sorry, I gotta take this," he apologizes, putting it to his ear and walking out of the kitchen to the front door, which he opens and closes behind him.

"Kiddo."

"Yeah." I look at Dad.

"Coffee." He nods to the counter, where a fresh cup of coffee is now sitting in front of me. Nodding back, I pick it up and take a sip, then turn to the door. When it opens, Levi comes in, running a hand through his hair and looking agitated.

"Is everything okay?" I ask, and his eyes come to me.

"I'm sorry, but I gotta go." He shakes his head; then his eyes move to my mom and dad as he walks back toward the kitchen. "It was nice meeting you both."

"You, too, sweetie, and if we don't see you before, have a great Thanksgiving," Mom says, giving him a hug.

"You, too," he mutters as my dad stands and shakes his hand.

"Get my cell number from Fawn. If you ever need anything, just let me know," Dad says, patting his shoulder before stepping back.

"Will do," Levi agrees with a smile as both of my sisters hug him quickly before stepping back. Watching him, I wonder what I should do, then his eyes come back to me and he holds out his hand. "Walk me over to my place."

"Um . . . sure," I agree, sliding off my stool and taking his hand. "I'll be right back," I say over my shoulder as he pulls me toward the door.

"Sure, honey," Mom mutters from the kitchen, but my eyes are locked with my dad's, and I see something there that makes me feel uneasy.

"What happened?" I ask his back as he pulls me across the hall.

"There was a murder downtown," he mutters, pulling me inside his apartment and closing the door behind us.

"I'm so—" My words end as I'm backed against the wall and his mouth crashes down on mine. The second his tongue slides across my bottom lip, my lips part and my fingers fist the fabric of his shirt to hold on. No one has ever kissed me the way he does. No one has ever made me feel the way he does—like he's marking me, claiming me as his. When he pulls his mouth away, I pant, keeping my eyes closed, needing a second to recover.

"I'm sorry about breakfast, baby."

"It . . . it's okay." I blink up at him. "I understand."

"Yeah." He smiles, dragging his thumb down over my lips and chin. "My girl gets me."

His girl. Man, I love the sound of that.

"Go enjoy the rest of your morning with your family."

"Okay," I agree, but he doesn't move to let me go, making my stomach feel warm once more. "You need to get ready," I remind him, wishing he didn't have to. He bends his head; his mouth touches mine once more, this time so tenderly that I almost don't feel it.

He takes a step back, pulling me from the wall, muttering under his breath, "Never hated my job before." My legs get weak, and my heart pounds. "I'm off tomorrow—we'll go out." He opens his door, and I look up at him.

"Tomorrow's Sunday," I say as he surprises me by taking my hand, locking our fingers together for the short few steps to my door.

"Do you have plans?"

"Um . . ." I pause. "No, no plans, just Sundays I always do my laundry and clean."

"All right, we'll hang at your place while you clean, then order in food."

"It will be boring for you to hang around while I clean."

"You have a TV, babe. I'm good with hanging on the couch watching a game. I just want to spend some time with you."

"Are you sure?" I ask as we stop outside my apartment.

"Are you gonna be there with me?" he asks, and I frown.

"Do you mean will I be at my house while you're there?"

"Yeah, babe, that's what I mean." His lips twitch.

"I'll be there," I confirm like a dork.

"Then, yeah, I'm sure I want to be there with you." He leans in, kissing my forehead. "I'll see you tomorrow."

"Okay." I nod, then look across the hall to his door, worrying my bottom lip.

"What's wrong?"

"Can you call and let me know when you get home?" I ask, then immediately drop my eyes from his, because that probably sounded clingy and girlfriendish. "I mean, just so I know you're home safe."

"It might be late when I get back," he says, putting his fingers on my chin, pulling up until my eyes meet his once more.

"You don—"

"You gonna be worried about me?" he questions, searching my face.

"No . . ." His eyes narrow, and I blow out a breath. "Yes," I grumble, and he smiles softly, rubbing my chin with his thumb.

"I'll call."

"Okay." I pull in a breath through my nose, then lean up on my tiptoes, pressing a kiss to his cheek. "Be safe, Levi."

"Always, gorgeous. I'll talk to you later."

"'Kay," I whisper against his mouth when it touches mine. "'Bye." I drop to my flat feet, then turn and open the door, stepping inside. I give him a wave as he steps back.

"Later, baby."

"Later," I agree, watching him head across the hall to his place. He stops to look at me once more before he goes inside.

"Kiddo, breakfast is ready," Dad says behind me, and I shut the door and turn to find all eyes on me.

"What?"

"Oh, you've got it bad." Libby grins.

"Whatever," I mutter, moving toward the kitchen.

"I don't know, I'd say Levi is the one who's got it bad," Mom says, studying me thoughtfully. "I don't think I've ever seen a man more in want than he is."

"I don't like it," Dad says, and I pull my eyes from my mom to look at him and see that same look in his eyes that I saw right before I left a few minutes ago.

"I thought you liked Levi."

"I like him just fine, but—"

"But what?" I cut him off, feeling my face fall.

"I want a different life for my girls than the one I subjected your mom to. Can't you find a nice teacher or a doctor to date?" So that's his sudden problem with Levi.

"Darling," Mom whispers, and he shakes his head at her.

"No, I know how hard my career has been on my family."

"Your career has given us a beautiful life."

"All the holidays I missed, birthdays, anniversaries?" He shakes his head, rubbing his hands down his beard. "I know that was hard on you and the girls."

"Dad, none of us suffered," Mac says softly, and his eyes go to her. "We knew your job was important, and we also knew that you and Mom would find ways to make up for the times we missed out on with you. I don't know about Libby or Fawn, but I never felt like I missed out on anything."

"I never felt like I missed out on anything, Dad. You were always there when it was important," Libby says, and his eyes go to her and soften.

"Dad," I call, and he pulls his eyes from Libby to look at me. "You were out making the world a safer place for Mom, Libby, Mac, and me. There was never a time I resented you for that. Never," I say, meaning that from the bottom of my soul, and he closes his eyes briefly.

"I just . . . I know the life of a detective is a demanding one, and I know that your mom has had to give up a lot for me."

"I didn't give up anything for you," Mom snaps, glaring at him. "I love my life, I love my girls, and I love you, you big lug, and I wouldn't change any part of it even if I could."

"The worry?"

"I'd worry about you if you were a banker, I'd worry about you if you were a fisherman. There isn't a line of work you could do that would erase that worry. I love you; every time you leave the house I worry if you'll come back, but I worry even when you leave to go to the grocery store."

"I just want Fawn to understand what she's getting into with a man like Levi."

"I know, Dad, and I love you for worrying, but let's say I didn't explore things with him. Let's say I let my fear of what could happen win and I missed out on one of the best things in my life because I was scared. Would you be okay with that?"

"You'd be disappointed in her if she did that, Dad," Mac says, and he pulls in a breath, then lets it out slowly.

"You're right, I would be disappointed in Fawn if she let fear rule her life," he says, then looks at me. "Do you really like this guy?"

"I do. I don't know what will happen between us or where our relationship will go, but right now, I like spending time with him. The rest will have to wait—we're just getting to know each other."

"I say he's a keeper. I mean, he did stick around after Mom suggested you get knocked up. I think that says a lot about him," Libby says, and I smile as Mom lets out a huff.

"Just please be careful," Dad says quietly, and I nod, then walk to him when he opens his arms to me.

Giving him a hug, I close my eyes. "I love you. Dad, you are still the best dad in the whole world."

"I love you, too, kiddo, to the moon and back." Giving him one more squeeze, I step back, then smile as my mom engulfs me in a tight embrace.

"I love you, honey, and I have to say I really, really like Levi."

"Mom." I roll my eyes as she lets me go.

"I know, I know, you are just starting to get to know each other, but a mom can pray, can't she?" she asks, patting my cheek.

"Just don't get your hopes up too high."

"If you say so," she mutters, then lets me go with a whimsical smile on her face that says she's already planning a wedding and knitting baby booties. *Lord, save me.*

Chapter 8

THE GOOD PART

LEVI

Hitting "Call" on Fawn's number, I step out of my apartment, pulling the door closed behind me while listening to the phone ring as I head across the hall.

"Levi," her sweet, soft voice answers, causing something in my chest to shift at the sound of my name leaving her mouth.

"Come to the door." I need to see her; I haven't been able to stop thinking about her since I got called out this morning.

"Pardon?" she asks, and through the phone I hear her moving, then realize that her parents might still be staying with her, which would fuck up my plans for the evening unless I can convince her to come sleep at my place.

"Are your parents gone?"

"Yeah, they left this evening around six," she says after a long pause. *Thank fuck.*

"I'm at the door."

"My door?" she asks, sounding adorably confused, and I smile.

"Yeah, baby, at your door."

"Oh." I hear more movement over the phone, and then I hear the sound of her feet on the wood floors getting closer. The sound of the locks clicking sounds right before she swings the door open. "Hey." She smiles her beautiful smile up at me, and that shit in my chest shifts once more. "You showered," she accuses, looking me over as her smile slides into a frown, making me grin. I know I shouldn't get off on her attitude, but she is seriously cute when she's pissed or flustered or aggravated with me.

"I did," I agree, leaving out the fact that I had to shower to wash away the stench of death that had seeped through my clothes and into my pores. Placing my hand against her soft stomach, I nudge her back into the apartment, then turn to close and lock the door.

"I thought you were going to call when you got home." Pulling my eyes from Muffin, who has forced her head under my hand, I lift my head to look at Fawn, feeling my mouth run dry when I finally take her all in. Christ, she's gorgeous. Her blonde hair is in wild curls down around her shoulders, her big blue-gray eyes are soft with sleep, and her cheeks are a sweet shade of pink. Running my eyes down her body, I fight back a groan. She looks like a living wet dream in a pair of plain cotton panties, her nipples visible through a thin tank. *Fucking breathtaking.*

"I was going to call, but I needed to see you." I take a step toward her without telling my feet to move, watching her eyes flare as my hand wraps around her hip.

"You needed to see me?" she repeats, sounding breathless.

"Yeah, I needed to see you," I say, gently rubbing my thumb over the exposed skin of her stomach where her tank has ridden up. "Were you sleeping?"

"No, I was waiting for you to call," she says, then ducks her head, taking her eyes from me—something she does often, something I honestly find adorable but frustrating as hell.

"Don't hide from me." I pull her into me until we're pressed together from hip to chest, then wrap my free hand around her jaw, forcing her to look at me. "I want you to care," I say, then drop my voice. "I want you to think about me as much as I think about you."

"You think about me?"

"More than is healthy," I tell her honestly, since from the moment she literally ran into me she's been a constant thought in the back of my mind.

"Oh." She swallows, melting into me. Jesus, this woman is going to do me in. I don't know what to do with her kind of sweet, but I do know I'd a be fool not to try to figure it out.

"Come on." I take her hand and lead her to the door, where I turn out the light before tugging her back across her living room.

"Um . . . Levi, what are you doing?" she asks nervously as we walk through her bedroom door.

"We're going to bed."

"We're going to bed," she repeats on a whisper, sounding even more nervous than she did seconds ago.

"Yeah, baby, we're going to bed."

"You're . . . you're going to sleep in my bed with me?" she asks, and I flip on the light, needing to see her face.

"Is that okay?"

"I have my period," she blurts, then covers her mouth as her cheeks darken.

Fighting back a smile that I know she won't appreciate, I duck my face closer to hers so she's forced to look at me. "Baby, I just want to hold you, and like I told you before, we are not having sex until I know you fully understand exactly what that means," I say, and she blinks.

"What it means?"

"What it means," I confirm. "Get in, babe," I mutter while lifting my chin toward the bed. There is nothing I want more than to feel her wet heat strangling my cock, to hear her moaning my name as she comes with her nails digging into my back. There is nothing I want more than her under me, but until I break down her walls and know she understands me having her in that way will make her completely mine, I won't take us there.

"My bed's only a double. I don't know if you'll fit," she informs me, and I watch her ass as she climbs across the bed, scooting over as far as she can possibly go without falling off the edge.

"Oh, I'll definitely fit," I mutter to myself, kicking off my sneakers and stripping off clothes, watching her bite her lip as her eyes scan over my chest and abs. Hitting the light, I get into bed, then listen to her squeak as I grab her wrist and drag her across until she's half on top of me with her arm over my gut. She lets out a whoosh of breath against my pec as I wrap my hand around the back of her knee and pull up until she's straddling my hip.

"Are you going to be comfortable like this?" she asks, holding herself stiff against me.

"Oh yeah." I run my fingers down the smooth skin of her thigh, loving the way her breath comes out in small pants every time I touch her. "How was your visit with your parents?" I ask, and her muscles tense as she tries to pull away, but there is no way I'm letting her go— not when I've got her exactly where I want her.

Giving up with a growl of frustration a second later, she finally answers. "It's always good to see them, but . . ." She pauses, and I feel her shake her head. "I'm so, so sorry about how crazy everyone acted."

"Baby"—I kiss the top of her head—"I swear once you meet my family, yours will look tame."

"No one could possibly be worse than my mom," she mutters, and I try to fight it, but I can't. "Are you laughing?" she asks in disbelief as my chest shakes with silent laughter.

"A little," I admit through a chuckle.

"My mom is so embarrassing," she groans, and I smile, kissing the top of her head once more.

"Does she always suggest you get knocked up by the guys you're dating?"

"No, you are the first," she sighs, burying her face against my chest, and I grin.

"I'm gonna take it as a compliment," I say, giving her a squeeze.

"It was a compliment." She pauses, then lets out a breath. "A weird one, but a compliment all the same." I laugh, feeling her body relax completely against mine as her cheek moves, letting me know she's smiling.

"Sleep, gorgeous," I whisper, tilting her chin up so I can touch my mouth to hers softly.

"Okay," she agrees, resting her cheek against my chest and pulling the blanket up around us. "Night, Levi," she says quietly, turning her head to kiss my chest. "I'm glad you're here."

"Jesus." I hold her tighter, closing my eyes and wondering how the fuck this happened. It's been forever since I've been even remotely interested in being in a relationship. I haven't wanted to feel obligated to someone, but every second I spend with Fawn makes me want those things with a ferocity I would have thought impossible. I want her to need me, and that fact alone should scare the shit out of me, but it only makes me feel more determined.

"Night, baby," I whisper, listening to her breathing even out as she falls off to sleep against me.

"No, Muffin." Hearing that and feeling Fawn's ass shift against my hard-on and thighs, I open one eye, then the other, finding the room lit with the morning sun coming in through the closed blinds covering the window. "Muffin, I said no," Fawn growls, sounding frustrated, and I watch her up on an elbow with her hand on Muffin's chest, trying to push her off the bed where she's standing with both paws on the mattress.

"Ruff." Muffin barks loudly, attempting to push forward against her palm.

"There's no room you," Fawn cries as Muffin reaches her goal of getting all four paws on the bed and lies down. "I swear, you are the most stubborn dog in the whole world," she huffs, falling to her back, and I pull her against me, kissing her shoulder and feeling her shiver.

"Does she normally sleep in the bed with you?" I ask, and her eyes come to me over her shoulder. Her tongue comes out to touch her bottom lip, making my cock—which has been hard since last night—throb painfully.

"Not always. Some nights she'll sleep on the couch." Nodding, I run my fingers down her creamy-smooth cheek, watching her eyes as they fill with something soft.

"Tonight we'll sleep in my bed. She can have the couch, and I'll shut the bedroom door."

"Your bed?"

"Yeah."

"Tonight?"

"Tonight," I confirm, then lean back as she rolls over to face me.

"That would be three nights in row we've slept in the same bed," she says, holding up three fingers between us.

"I wasn't keeping count, but you're right," I agree, then drop my eyes to her mouth when her bottom lip disappears between her teeth. Something she does when she's overthinking, something she does normally right before she blurts something out that either makes me laugh, pisses me off, or leaves me frustrated.

"I've . . . I . . ." She closes her eyes, then shakes her head. "I've never spent the night with anyone I'm not in a relationship with."

"Okay."

"Okay." She looks up at me. "So I don't think we should be spending the night together until we are in a relationship." Staring at her for a long moment in disbelief, I tilt my head back toward the ceiling and beg for patience.

"What exactly do you think is happening between us?" I ask after a moment, dropping my eyes back down to her.

"We're seeing how things go?" she says quietly with a shrug, and I nod, tucking a piece of hair behind her ear.

"We're seeing how things go, but while we're doing that, you're mine and I'm yours. We are in a relationship, Fawn—you're my woman." I watch her lips part and form a soft O. "Jesus, you have the ability to make me insane."

"What?"

"Baby, you wanna know how many women I've spent the night with?"

"Not really." Her face scrunches up, and her brows pull together tightly. If I wasn't so annoyed, I'd find her expression adorable.

"The answer would be none. I've never spent the night with a woman I'm not in a relationship with—not even after being intimate with her."

"Well, that's rude."

"That's honest. I don't play games, and I don't lead women on." I wrap my arm around her waist, pulling her close, then duck my face until it's an inch from hers. "I'm gonna say it one more time and pray to god this shit finally sinks in. I like you. I like spending time with you. I want this thing with you to work out even though you are frustrating as fuck."

"How was I supposed to know?" she asks, forcing me to my back and glaring down at me. "Obviously you haven't dated recently," she huffs, tossing her leg over my hip and pointing in my face once she's straddling me. "The whole dating scene is a mess. You never know when a guy is really interested; you never know what the hell is going on, and you're constantly left questioning every single thing that happens," she growls, sliding off me and the bed and beginning to pace across her room.

Watching her breasts bounce with each step and the way her hair moves over her shoulders as she tosses her head, I fight my own growl. "So sorry for not assuming that we're in a relationship." Her eyes narrow on mine as she plants her hands on her hips, tossing her head to the side. "And stop checking me out and making me all dizzy when I'm annoyed with you."

"I make you dizzy?" I smile smugly, and she huffs, blowing a piece of hair out of her face. "I can't help it, baby. Swear to god, you're adorable when you're flustered, but when you're pissed, you're fucking exquisite," I tell her honestly, and she tosses her arms in the air.

"You think I'm frustrating?" She points at me. "You're the one who's frustrating." She moves across the room to the closet and pushes it open, grabbing a sweatshirt and pulling it on over her head before bending over and giving me a view of her ass, right before it's covered with a pair of sweats, that has my teeth clenching together.

Watching her start to stomp past me to the bathroom, I grab hold of her wrist and drag her to stand between my spread thighs. "Are you done being mad?" I ask, grabbing her hips. She rolls her eyes.

"I'm not mad, I'm annoyed."

"Why are you annoyed?"

"Because."

"Because why?"

"I don't know, I just am," she huffs, crossing her arms over her chest. I fight back a grin.

"All right, then, where are you going?"

"I have to take Muffin out." She shrugs, then softly moves her fingers through my hair like she's already forgotten she's annoyed with me.

"I'll take her. It's cold out, baby." While she shakes her head, her face softens.

"It's okay. I want to go to Gino's and get a bagel with smoked-salmon cream cheese while I'm out."

"All right, I'll go with you." I stand, forcing her back a step, then wrap my hand around her jaw, tilting her head back. Leaning down, I press a quick kiss to her upturned lips, then tap her bottom. "Go on—we'll have to stop at my place so I can clean up." I send her on her way to the bathroom. Putting on the clothes I wore over last night, I sit down to put on my sneakers, then stand when she comes out of the bathroom a few minutes later.

"Time to get up," she says toward the bed, where Muffin has now sprawled out across the entire surface. Lifting her fur-covered head, she looks at Fawn, tips her head to the side studying her, then lays it back down on her paws with a huff.

"Baby, seriously, she needs some training, at least enough that she'll listen to you. It's not safe. She's as big as you are, and I know for a fact she can drag you around."

"I know, I signed us up for doggie classes after the park incident," she says, taking a seat on the edge of her bed to slip on a pair of sneakers. "Our first class is soon."

"Good. Has she ever done that before?"

"No, but once when I took her out, I literally had to carry her home two blocks because she refused to walk home."

"How big was she then?" I ask, looking at Muffin, who probably weighs as much as Fawn does soaking wet.

"Just about seventy pounds. That's not even the worst part—it was pouring rain, so by the time we got home, I smelled like a wet dog. I didn't even have time to shower before I had to get to work."

"Jesus."

"I know. Thankfully, that only happened once, but it was so bad I don't ever want it to happen again," she says, then looks at Muffin as she stands.

"Come on, girl, let's go outside." With a groan Muffin rolls over and stands on the bed before hopping off and walking to my side, leaning her weight into me. "You know most dogs like going outside?" I tell her, giving her head a rub.

"Yeah, but she's not like most dogs, if you haven't noticed. I'm pretty sure she's a human trapped in a dog's body," she says to my back as I leave the bedroom and head for the kitchen.

"She is stubborn. Then again, so is her owner." I smile over my shoulder at Fawn as I grab Muffin's leash from the counter.

"Ha-ha-ha." She rolls her eyes, and I grin, stopping at the door and wrapping my fist in her hoodie to pull her closer. I drop my mouth to hers in a quick touch before opening the door. Taking her hand, I lead her across the hall to my place, where I leave her in the living room with Muffin as I head for the bathroom to brush my teeth and take care of business. Stopping in my room on the way back to the living room, I grab a hoodie from my closet and holster my gun from the safe near my bed.

"Ready?" I ask, finding Fawn studying me and the gun holstered under my arm before I put on my hoodie and down vest over it.

"Yep." She stands, and Muffin looks at her, then me, and lets out a huff before getting off the couch, obviously annoyed that she has to go somewhere else.

"Are you expecting trouble while we're out?" she asks softly as I open the door, letting her out ahead of me.

"No, I always carry. Leaving my gun is like leaving my arm behind—impossible."

"Really?" she asks, sounding surprised. "You didn't have a gun on you on Halloween."

"I did."

"You did? I didn't notice." She frowns while I attach Muffin's leash to her collar.

"You were flustered, baby."

I grin, and she mutters, "This is true," stopping behind me while I lock up my apartment.

"How do you feel about guns?" I ask, taking her hand in one of mine while holding Muffin's leash with the other. After seeing the way Muffin was able to drag Fawn across the park, I worry about her walking her on her own.

"I grew up in a house with guns."

"Yeah, but that doesn't mean you aren't afraid of them."

"I guess you're right. When I was fifteen, my dad took me to the shooting range. He wanted me to get comfortable holding and shooting one. I can't say I will ever buy a gun myself, but because of that experience, I'm not fearful of them."

"Your dad's a smart man."

"He is," she agrees with a small smile as we push out of the building and step onto the sidewalk.

"What way are we heading?" I ask, and she looks up at me, smiling.

"The day we met, you asked me when we left the building at the same time what way I was heading. I asked what way you were going so that I could head the opposite direction to get away from you."

"I know." I smile, watching her face soften.

"I knew then that there was something about you," she says quietly, leaning up to kiss the underside of my jaw. "I just didn't know I was going to like you as much as I do."

"Don't say shit like that to me when we're outside, baby."

"What?" She blinks, stepping back, but I don't let her get far. I tug her hand, forcing her back into my space so I can get my arms around her.

"When we're outside"—I duck my head and nip her ear—"I can't kiss you like I want to."

"Oh." She nibbles her bottom lip, then smiles. "I'll keep that in mind."

"Thanks, gorgeous." I lean back. "Now, what way are we heading?"

"To the left." Wrapping my arm around her shoulders, we head down the sidewalk side by side. As soon as we reach the bagel shop, I pull a twenty from my wallet.

"I'll wait out here with Muffin. Can you get me a plain bagel with cream cheese and a coffee?"

"Yes, but I have money." She frowns at the twenty in my hand, and I shake my head. "I'm paying."

"No, you're not," I deny with a shake of my head, and she takes a step toward the door.

"I am."

"Fawn," I growl, and she shrugs.

"You can't stop me."

"Dammit," I hiss as she walks into the shop, leaving me no choice but to stay out front with Muffin.

Coming out a few minutes later with a paper bag and two cups of coffee, she hands me one, lowering her voice. "Don't be mad."

"Baby, if we're out, I pay for you and me, not the other way around."

"Is that some kind of rule?"

"Yes."

"Why? That's stupid. I can pay for our breakfast."

"I'm a man and—"

"This isn't 1950," she cuts me off. "If we are in a relationship, paying for things goes both ways."

"I don't know what kind of men you have dated in the past—and I don't want to know about the men you've dated," I add quickly when it looks like she's about to tell me about them. I know that would piss me off. "I'm the kind of man who takes care of a woman when I'm with her."

"Whatever. Can we go?"

"Yeah, we can go once you tell me you won't do that again."

"Fine," she mutters with a roll of her eyes. Giving up for now, I take her hand and head across the street to the dog park, where we find a bench to sit on inside the closed-off area and unleash Muffin to play.

"Miss Reed." I hear a shout and turn my head to watch a girl, probably ten or eleven, running up to us in an oversize coat with her curly hair bouncing around her smiling face.

"Hey, honey," Fawn says, surprised, as she stands and greets the girl with a hug. "What are you doing here?"

"We came to the park to hang out for a while," the girl says with a shy shrug, then looks over her shoulder when a man yells her name. "Sorry, I have to go."

"Is your mom here with you?" Fawn asks softly.

The girl nods, then adds, "Yes, and Juan."

"Oh," Fawn says, looking across the park. "Tell your mom I said hello."

"I will," she agrees before taking off at a run across the grass toward a woman who's not dressed for the cold but wearing a skimpy dress and short leather jacket and a man wearing a dark suit and wool overcoat. Studying the guy, I realize why he looks familiar. Juan Varges is the main suspect in the murder of the prostitute that happened Halloween night. He's also a well-known pimp and all-around piece of shit.

"Fuck." My eyes meet his across the distance. I lift my chin toward him, letting him know I see him. He smirks, then lifts his chin in return before taking the girl's shoulder and turning her away from us.

"Who's the girl?" I ask Fawn's back as she stares off across the park, watching the couple and child as they walk away.

"Tamara—she's one of my students."

"Is that her dad?"

"No, her mom's new boyfriend," she whispers, and I watch her hands ball into fists at her side. "I don't like him."

"You shouldn't."

"Do you know him?" she asks quietly, turning around to look at me.

"Come here." I pat the bench next to me and wait until she's seated, then wrap my arm around her shoulder. "He's not a good guy. He's also a pimp."

"Oh no," she breathes, looking toward where the couple disappeared. "Please tell me you're joking."

"Baby." I hold her tighter when it looks like she's about to bolt.

"He's around her, he picks her up from school almost every day . . . What if he—"

"Calm," I command, cutting her off when I see she's working herself up. "How long has her mom been with him?"

"I don't know, maybe a couple months." She closes her eyes, dropping her forehead to my shoulder. *Fuck.* I press a kiss to the top of her head, fighting the urge to tell her that I'm investigating him. I can't—I don't want her involved any more than she already is, and if she accidentally slips up and mentions it to someone, it could blow my whole case. "It will be okay."

I rub her shoulder in an attempt to comfort her while raging inside. Men like Juan Varges believe they are above the law. They have the means and the power to control the people around them and will do whatever's necessary to stay out of jail. This case isn't the first one Juan has been a suspect in. One other woman from his stable has been murdered in the last year that we know of. And I say *know of* because most women who work in the sex industry are forgotten by their families. So if they go missing, no one realizes it until it's too late.

"Can we go?" she asks, and my arm tightens.

"Yeah, baby." I stand, bringing her with me. Taking her hand, I lead her to a garbage can near the edge of the sidewalk and dump our trash before walking toward the dog area where Muffin is being chased by a small Yorkie. Putting my fingers in my mouth, I whistle, then shout, "Muffin." Her head swings my way, and her tongue lolls out of her mouth before she starts to trot in our direction.

"Did you have fun, girl?" Fawn asks, opening the gate and attaching the leash to Muffin's collar before handing it to me. She bends down and sticks her hand through one of the slats in the fence to pet the Yorkie that followed Muffin across the play area. "Toby, you've gotten so big, look at you," she coos to the small dog as he licks her fingers.

"Fawn," a man calls behind us, and she stands and turns with me to face a guy with messy hair and glasses. He's wearing a pair of jeans, a tee that has paint on the front of it, and a black jacket. Watching his eyes scan her as he gets close to us, I fight the urge to growl *mine*.

"Hey, Hank." She smiles warmly, leaning up to give him a one-armed hug, since there is no fucking way I'm letting go of her hand. "How have you been?"

"Good, and you?" he asks, dropping his eyes to her hand in mine before he lifts his gaze my way.

"Hank, this is my . . ."

"Her man." I stick out my free hand in his direction, and he takes it, squeezing a little too tight for someone who's just a friend. "Levi," I mutter, letting him go.

"I didn't know you were dating someone. I thought you said you were taking a break from dating?" Hank says, studying Fawn in a way that says she obviously told him that and he was disappointed by the news.

"Oh." She laughs, shaking her head. "I was . . . I mean, Levi and I, we live next door to each other, and this just kind of happened." She raises our hands, laughing.

"Hmm." His eyes slide to me briefly. "Did you get the invitation I e-mailed you last week?" She nods.

"Yeah, I'm going to see if Mac and Libby want to come to your showing with me."

"Good." He pushes his glasses up the bridge of his nose, then runs his hand through his shaggy hair. "I'd love to see you there."

"Hank is an artist, and he has a showcase in SoHo after Thanksgiving," she explains, tilting her head back to look at me. "He's really very talented."

"Really. Maybe I'll go with you to check it out," I say, wondering where the fuck that statement came from. I'd rather pull my teeth out one by one than go to an art show.

"It's invite only," Hank huffs, shoving his hands in the front pockets of his jeans.

Fawn frowns, then mutters, "Oh." Smiling at that, I drop her hand and tuck her under my arm. My woman seriously has no fucking idea when a man is interested. "Well, we were just getting ready to leave. It was nice to see you, Hank."

"You, too." He steps forward like he's going to give her a hug, but Muffin steps in front of her to block the move. Hank's eyes drop to the big wolfhound, and he visibly swallows. "I'll see you at the showing."

"Yeah, see you then," she agrees, as I give Muffin a scratch for being so good.

"Nice meeting you, Hank. I'm sure I'll see you around." I lift my chin to him, and his eyes narrow.

"Yeah, see ya," he mutters, walking to the gate and opening it, then bending down to pick up the Yorkie Muffin was playing with.

"So you and Hank?" I ask as we head toward the park exit with Muffin walking in front of us.

"Me and Hank?" she asks, and I drop my eyes to meet hers.

"Yeah, have you ever dated that guy?"

"Um, no." She shakes her head, scrunching up her face. "He's just a friend—well, we kind of know each other from the dog park."

"Has he asked you out?"

"No. I mean, he's asked me to coffee before, but that's all, we've never dated."

"He's into you."

"No, he's not."

"Baby, I'm a man, and as a man, I can tell you that guy is interested in you and was definitely upset that you're no longer available."

"Really?" She bites her lip, studying me.

"Yeah, baby, really," I say softly, and she frowns.

"I had no idea," she mumbles.

"You wouldn't know, because you've got no idea how beautiful you are," I state, rubbing my thumb over the pulse of her wrist, feeling it speed up.

"I . . ."

"You're gorgeous, and this sweet, unassuming thing you've got going on is a breath of fresh air to men like me and Hank, who are surrounded by women who've got nothing more to offer than a pretty face."

"Um . . ." She drops her gaze from mine, and I smile. Most women who look like Fawn does would be using that beauty to get their way, but not her. No, she doesn't even understand the power she has or when a man is interested in her. For me that shit is priceless and the exact thing that has drawn me to her from the beginning.

"Just so you know, you and Hank will never happen," I inform her and feel her eyes on me, so I drop mine to look at her. "You're mine, and I don't share. He missed his chance when he didn't step up to the plate like a man and straight up ask you out."

"I . . . I was never interested in him."

"Good to know, seeing how he's going to try to convince you otherwise when you go to his showing."

"What?" she asks as we head down the block toward our building.

"He made it pretty clear that I wasn't invited to his showing—that right there tells me he plans on using that time alone with you as a way in."

"I'm not . . ." She pauses, shaking her head again. "I don't even like him like that. I don't even really know him."

"That's good, considering you're already in a relationship." I smile, dropping her hand to press in the code for the door and holding it open for her to enter before me.

"Remember when I told you this morning that you were frustrating?" she asks, stomping up the stairs, and my smile turns into a grin. "Well, that still stands, but you're also annoying." I'm chuckling at that as we stop outside her door and unhook Muffin's leash while she unlocks the door and pushes it open. Going in behind her, I head to the kitchen to put down some fresh water for Muffin while she walks back into her bedroom, coming out a few minutes later with a bag of laundry that's almost as big as she is and a jug of detergent.

"I'm gonna run down and put this in the machine. I'll be right back," she says, muffled behind the bag, and I shake my head.

"If you really think I'm going to let you carry that shit down four flights of stairs, you don't know me at all. Drop it, babe. I'll take it down for you while you feed Muffin."

"No," she huffs moving to the door, not seeing that I've stepped in front of her because the damn bag in her arms is at least five inches over the top of her head.

Taking it from her with ease, I watch her eyes narrow as I grab the jug from her hand. "I'll be right back."

"Levi, you are not doing my laundry," she semishouts, trying to take the bag from me.

"And you're not carrying a bag of laundry as big as you are to the basement."

"I don't carry it down the stairs," she cries, tossing her hands in the air. "I carry it to the top of the stairs, then let it roll down to the bottom."

Staring at her in disbelief, I tilt my head back toward the ceiling, praying she's not being serious right now but having no doubt that she's done that exact thing each time she's done her laundry. "What do you do if someone's coming up the stairs when your laundry is rolling down?" I ask, and she presses her lips together before planting her hands on her hips.

"That's never happened. I always make sure no one's around."

"I hate to point this out to you, but you are one of the most accident-prone women I have ever met in my life."

"I'm not accident-prone," she yells, and I lean in.

"You ran into me, literally ran into me, when you were running with your goddamn eyes closed," I growl, and she bites her bottom lip.

"Fine," she huffs. "You can carry it down for me, but I'm doing my own fricking laundry."

"Fine," I agree, hefting the bag up onto my shoulder before opening the door. Carrying the bag down the steps, I listen to her light footsteps on the steps behind me as we head for the basement, then mutter a curse under my breath when I see how fucking dark the room is where the washers and dryers are kept. The shit looks like something you'd see in a scary movie. I've never been down here, because I have my laundry washed and folded through a service.

"They need to get better lighting down here."

"It's fine; it's always been like this," she grumbles as I drop her bag on a yellow folding table near the door.

"It's not safe."

"The building is secure, Levi. Stop thinking like a cop for five minutes," she says, opening the bag, pulling out an armful of laundry, and carrying it to one of the machines.

"I am a cop. Telling me to stop thinking like a cop is like asking a doctor not to save lives. This building is secure, but that doesn't mean criminals don't live here, or that people don't give out the code to the door."

"I give up," she huffs, putting quarters into the slots in the top of the machine and starting it up before dumping in a cup of detergent.

"I'll tell the super to put new lights in," I say, looking at the one yellow bulb hanging in the middle of the room.

"Haven't you ever been down here before?" she asks, looking over at me as she fills a second machine with laundry.

"Nope."

"So where do you wash your clothes?"

"I send my laundry out. I don't have the time or the inclination to do it myself."

"They have that kind of thing?" she asks, and I smile.

"Babe, you live in Manhattan, one of the biggest cities in the world. They have laundry services."

"Oh." Her nose scrunches up adorably. "I don't know how I'd feel about someone besides me washing my clothes. What if they're a weirdo?"

"You don't think that someone could come down here and pull your panties out of the dryer to sniff them?"

"Don't say that," she cries, looking horrified. "Now I'm going to have to sit down here while my laundry's in the machine, because I'm not going to be able to stop thinking that someone is down here doing that."

"You'll worry about that but not about the fact that you could kill someone or yourself getting your laundry down here? Or the lighting in this room?" I shake my head, and her eyes narrow.

"I've been doing my laundry down here for over two years and nothing has ever happened, so I'm pretty sure I'm good, and besides that, until you came along, I had never been accident-prone. So maybe my sudden clumsiness is all your fault."

"You did say I make you dizzy." I grin, and she rolls her eyes.

"You are so full of yourself," she huffs, picking up her jug of detergent and heading for the door. Following her up the first flight of steps, I watch her ass, then give in and toss her over my shoulder.

"What are you doing?" she squeaks as I jog up the steps.

"We're getting to the good part of the day."

"The good part?" she asks, and I pull her down until she's in front of me and her legs are wrapped around my hips.

"Yeah, the part where we spend a couple hours making out."

"Oh," she breathes as I push open the door of her apartment, taking her mouth while I carry her across to the couch. We spend most of the day there, only stopping to eat and go downstairs to change over laundry.

Chapter 9

Way Too Fast

Fawn

Knocking on Levi's door, I chew on my bottom lip in nervousness. When I left him this morning to catch my train, I hadn't planned on seeing him again until after the weekend. But once I got to my parents' house out on Long Island and walked through the door, all I could do was think about him being home alone tomorrow on Thanksgiving. My mom, who knew exactly why I was in such a strange mood, pulled me aside and suggested I leave and spend the holiday with Levi. I didn't debate for a second. I kissed my family goodbye and got back on the train to come home. Only now I'm wondering if I should have. Yes, the last two weeks with Levi have been amazing—magical, really. But we are still very new, and spending holidays together is a big, giant step forward, even if we have spent every night in the same bed and under the same roof unless he had to work.

Hearing the locks click, I come out of my head and pull my shoulders back, feeling my stomach fill with nervous butterflies.

"Baby." His eyes scan over me slowly from head to toe, like he's checking to make sure I'm okay. "What's going on? Is everything all right?"

"Yeah, I . . ." I pause, wondering what I should say, exactly, then figure the truth is probably the best place to start. "I couldn't stand the idea of you being home alone tomor—" My words come to an abrupt end as he nabs my hand and pulls me into his apartment, slamming the door, pushing me back against it. My purse falls to the floor. "Levi—" My hands go to his bare chest as he moves closer, pressing his body against mine.

"You—" He pauses, searching my face, and I watch his eyes darken to a deeper, richer amber color. "You came back to spend Thanksgiving with me?" he asks quietly, and I feel my face soften as my hands move up his chest to his shoulders while his hand wraps around the back of my head and his fingers slide up into my hair.

"Yes, I came back to spend Thanksgiving with you."

"We have no food for tomorrow," he says, dropping his mouth to my neck, licking up the column of my throat as his free hand slides up the front of my shirt, over my stomach, stopping to rest on the underside of my breast.

"Th . . . that's okay," I pant, pressing my head back into the door as his lips, tongue, and teeth work along my neck. "We can eat out," I moan as he pulls down the cup of my bra and slides his thumb over my nipple.

"No," he denies, shaking his head. "I don't want to eat out." He licks up to my ear, making the space between my legs pulse. "I want to eat you."

"Oh," I breathe, closing my eyes. We've done a lot—I mean, *a lot*—of fooling around over the last two weeks, but he's never gone too far and has always stopped before things could get out of hand, insisting I need to understand what giving myself to him means.

"You're mine, Fawn, aren't you?"

"Yes." I don't even hesitate or try to deny it. I'm his, all his. He pulls back to look at me, and I stare into his eyes, which have become so familiar and so important.

"There's no going back. I won't let you go," he says with a finality that should scare me as his hand tangles more tightly in my hair, like he's afraid his words will cause me to disappear.

"Good," I say, meaning that sentiment with everything in me. I don't want him to let me go. Ever. I know this is fast, but I also know the thought of being without him makes me panic.

"Christ." He drops his forehead to mine, resting it there for a moment before moving his hands to my ass. "Hop up," he commands, lifting me until my legs encircle his hips. Carrying me across his apartment, he takes me into his room and kicks the door closed. "Lose the jacket and the shirt, baby," he says softly, keeping me in his arms. Working quickly I slip off my jacket, then pull my long-sleeved shirt off over my head, leaving me in a sheer dark-burgundy—almost black—lace bra. As soon as I drop the shirt to the ground, his mouth lands against mine and we're moving again. Putting one knee, then the other on the bed, Levi walks us across the mattress, then lays me down with my head resting on the pillow. His mouth never leaves mine as my fingers run through his thick hair and my hips arch into his. Pulling back, he sits up on his knees, and my eyes rake over him. His hair has grown out a little over the last two weeks and now curls around his ears and the back of his neck. His eyes are darker and filled with something warm, something I know is only for me. His jaw is hard and grinding as he looks me over. Dropping my eyes to the expanse of his chest, the cut of his abs, and the deep V that disappears into his sweats—and the outline of his giant erection—my core pulses. He's perfect.

"Fuck, I don't know where the fuck to start." His hand wraps around my neck, then slides down between my breasts, over my stomach and to my jeans, which he unbuttons and unzips, exposing the lace panties that match my bra. Sliding both hands up my waist, he cups my breasts, then pulls down the lace to expose my nipples to his gaze.

"Levi." My hips lift, and I feel the hard ridge of his cock against my pussy through the layers of fabric between us. "Please." He pulls my jeans down over my hips, then runs two fingers over the lace covering me before removing the jeans and tossing them to the ground. Putting me back in the same position I was in moments ago, his fingers slide back down over the lace covering my core.

"God, you're already so fucking wet for me," he groans, bending forward and putting his fist on the bed near my shoulder. I watch as his muscles flex. "I love that. I'm going to enjoy every drop you can give me," he says, kissing me once more, deep and desperate, like he can't get enough of me. Running my hands through his hair, I skate them down the smooth skin of his back as his weight presses me into the mattress and my legs wind tighter around his hips. Pulling his mouth away from mine, he licks, nibbles, and bites down my neck to my breasts, where he proceeds to torment me by licking around my nipples—avoiding giving me what I really need.

"Levi." I take hold of his hair, watching him grin right before he pulls my nipple into his mouth, tugging hard on the stiff bud before letting it go and blowing a cool breath across it. Moaning, I arch into him as his fingers skim down my stomach, making my muscles twist. As he runs his fingers along the edge of my panties, I wait impatiently for what's to come, feeling my body start to shake. The moment his fingers finally slide under the edge of my panties and down between my folds through the wetness he's created, his mouth latches onto my neglected nipple and he sucks hard. My back leaves the bed, and my hands leave his hair to latch onto his shoulders. Digging my nails in, I hold on tight. Feeling one thick finger enter me, I arch farther into his touch and circle my hips, moaning loudly.

"Oh," I whisper as he hits my G-spot. Then I moan down his throat as he kisses me and thrusts his tongue into my mouth, moving it in sync with the one finger that soon turns into two.

Pulling from my mouth, he kisses me softly, then moves down my body, leaving wet, openmouthed kisses along the way. "I want you to watch," he says, and I open my eyes that I didn't know were closed and look down the length of my body. I watch him as he opens his mouth over the lace covering my core and sucks hard. My heels dig into the bed and my hips lift as I grab onto his hair, needing something to keep me from floating away.

"Yes," I moan, lifting my hips, offering myself up to him. He pulls my panties to the side; the feel of his wet tongue on me without anything between us makes the moment that much more erotic.

"Christ, you taste like heaven," he growls against me, making me pant. Feeling him licking and circling my clit as his fingers work ruthlessly inside me, I know it won't be much longer before I fall apart.

"Levi," I cry, overwhelmed by the things he's doing to me. Moving one hand up my stomach, he takes my nipple between his thumb and middle finger, twists, and pulls. "I'm—"

"I'll catch you, baby, let go," he says, and I do. I let go and fall over the edge, my body buzzing and stars dancing behind my closed eyelids. I've never experienced anything like it in my life, and I know only he can make me feel like this. Only he has the power to take me to the edge of bliss and send me over with the promise to catch me when I land. Slowly the muscles of my thighs that had tightened loosen, and my body relaxes back against the bed. He licks me once more, slowly, before moving back and pulling my panties down my legs, tossing them behind him before forcing my legs apart and settling his hips between mine.

"Let's get this off you," he says. Reaching behind me, he unhooks my bra and gently removes it from my shoulders. Then he leans down, placing a kiss to the tips of each of my breasts, to allow his weight to settle against me. Wrapping myself around him, I pull his face down to mine and kiss him, hoping that he knows what he means to me. Feeling his cock nudge my entrance, I lift my hips, listening to him growl.

"Please," I beg, and his muscles tense and flex.

"I can't do this," he says, suddenly pulling away, and my heart begins to crack open.

"Wh—" I start to ask what the hell he means, but then he rolls us until I'm straddling him.

"I'm lost in you, baby." He takes my face between his large palms. "So fucking unbelievably lost in you, Fawn, and I don't trust myself right now. I don't want to hurt you, so I'm going to let you set the pace." I finally catch his meaning and feel his hard length nestled between my wet folds. Dropping forward, I rest my palms against his chest, watching his eyes darken with lust as they move over my hair, face, and breasts. "Fuck." His head tips back, and his fingers dig into my hips as I move along his hard length. Watching the muscles in his neck and the way his jaw grows tight, I roll my hips, feeling myself become even more turned on. I love this power, I love that I'm in control—it's an aphrodisiac of its own kind.

"Fawn," he growls, tipping his eyes to mine, and there is no missing the warning in his tone. Biting my bottom lip, I move my hand between us and wrap it around his length, amazed that my fingers don't come close to meeting. Holding him, I line myself up, rubbing the tip against my clit. My head falls back, and my free hand moves to my breast without thought. "Fawn." He grabs my hips, and my eyes drop to his, feeling heavy with desire. Shaking his head, his teeth snap together as I slide the tip of him inside and slowly slide down his length, feeling him stretch and fill me. He's so thick and long that there is a bite of pain with every inch of him I take inside me.

"Oh god." My head falls back once more as I seat myself on him and his thumb sweeps over my clit.

"Look at me." My gaze meets his as my body starts to buzz again when I see how hard he's trying to hold back.

Moving against him, slow at first, I quicken my pace as his thumb circles faster. I'm close, already so close again. Moaning loudly I rock against him, watching his eyes flare and his muscles bunch. "Levi." My body bucks as he sits up, pulling my legs to wrap around his back, locking us together. Holding me tightly against him, his mouth takes mine in a soft, gentle kiss that has my toes curling. I have never felt more connected to another human in my life—I've never felt closer to anyone than I do to him right now. Tears start to build in my throat as we rock together, touch, and kiss. Holding him as tightly as he's holding me, I come unexpectedly, listening to him groan as I do.

"Shh," he hushes me when his fingers find my clit once more, and I begin to whimper. My body is overstimulated; every nerve ending feels like it's exposed. Laying me back on the bed, he stays planted inside me as he wraps my legs around his waist, then pulls out slowly.

"Levi." I lift my head, burying my face against his neck as he thrusts in, hitting something deep inside me I didn't even know was there. My nails dig into his back as my heels fall down to his ass. This is too much, way too much, feeling him inside me, his weight pressing me into the bed, his scent seeping into my pores—all of my senses are overwhelmed with everything that is him.

"Fawn." His fingers skate up my side, along the edge of my breast, over my collarbone before he takes hold of my jaw, forcing my head back. "Kiss me, baby." He thrusts in, and I watch his muscles bunch as I run my fingers into the back of his hair and force him closer to me. Licking across his lower lip before kissing him, I watch his eyes flare. His thrusts become faster, more erratic.

"Oh," I cry as he pulls his mouth from mine and drops his face to my chest, where he pulls my breast deep into his mouth. Biting my bottom lip to keep myself from screaming out, I cling to him with every part of me as I come, once more tightening around him. Letting go of my breast, his mouth covers mine, and he groans down my throat as I pulse around him. Panting heavily, we share the same breath, and I can feel his heart beating hard against my chest with my own. "That was—"

"Amazing," he finishes for me, and I kiss his jaw, thinking *amazing* is the understatement of the century. What just happed was beautiful and life changing. Without losing our connection, he rolls us until we're face-to-face on our sides, then his hand wraps around the back of my skull and he tucks my head under his chin, wrapping his other arm around my back. "Thank you for coming back to spend Thanksgiving with me," he says quietly, and those stupid tears I felt earlier come back. Swallowing them down I nod my head, too afraid he will hear them in my voice if I try to speak.

"Tired?"

"Yes," I whisper against his skin, cuddling deeper into his chest, feeling my eyes grow heavy. I mumble, "Three orgasms will do that to a girl." Listening to him laugh makes me smile.

"Christ," he groans, and I blink my eyes open, not knowing when I fell asleep. I hear a paw hit the door. I'm such a bad dog mom—I didn't even greet my girl when I came in, not that Levi gave me a chance to, but still. "She probably needs to go out. You wanna stay here or come out with me?" he asks, and I tip my head back to look at him.

"I'll stay, if that's okay," I say, feeling too exhausted to get up and get dressed to go outside. "All right, baby." His eyes search mine for a long time before he closes his eyes and shakes his head. I want to ask him what he's thinking, but before I can, he leans down to kiss my forehead, and then my lips. Rolling me to my back, he pulls out of me slowly, making me mewl in protest, and my arms tighten around him. I don't want to let him go, and he must know what I'm thinking, because he smirks. Bending his head he presses a soft kiss to my lips. "I'll be right back."

"Okay," I agree, releasing him. Watching him stand, grab his sweats off the floor, and put them on, I sit up and move until I'm leaning back against the headboard. I pull the sheet up around me and tuck it under my arms. These last two weeks I've watched him get dressed just like I'm doing now, I've run with him in the mornings, lazed with him in bed, eaten breakfast and dinner with him, whispered in the dark about the future—but even with all of that, nothing could have prepared me for what I'm feeling right now. I knew it would happen eventually, but I didn't expect to feel the way I do right now. This is way too fast, I know it is, but I also know there is no denying that I'm falling in love with him.

"You okay, baby?" he asks, and my eyes focus on his.

"Uh . . . yeah." I nod, wondering if he can see what I'm feeling right now, and I bite my lip.

"You sure?" God, he's so nice, so perfect.

"Yeah." I nod again. "I'm sure. Just wondering if we will be able to find a turkey tomorrow," I say to cover what I'm really thinking.

"We can go out early. This is Manhattan—somewhere will have a turkey."

"Do you know how to cook one?" I ask, and he grins smugly. "Never mind, of course you would know how to cook a turkey." I roll my eyes, watching his smile until it disappears behind a shirt he pulls down over his head. Hearing Muffin's paw hit the door again and her huff of aggravation, I start to get up to let her in but lean back once more as he goes to the door and twists the knob.

As soon as the door is open, Muffin unexpectedly pushes past him to get to me and hops up onto the bed. "Hey, girl," I greet her as she pushes her face into my chest. Rubbing her head, I scratch her behind her ears, then smile as she drops to the bed to lie down with her head in my lap. "Maybe she didn't need to go out after all," I say, looking up at Levi.

"She's going, even if I have to carry her," he mutters, putting a hoodie on over his shirt. Smiling at that, I debate getting up and putting something on just so I can watch if that really does happen. "Why are you smiling?"

"Just picturing you carrying Muffin down the block after she's refuses to budge." I laugh, and he shakes his head.

"She's doing better since her classes have started." He's right—last week I took her to one obedience class by myself, and Levi came with me to another one. She did well, but I think it was more about the constant feeding of treats than anything else. "It may take some time, but she'll get there," he says, walking toward the bed. Leaning over Muffin, he wraps his hand around the side of my face, then leans in and kisses me before pulling back to look down at Muffin. He rubs the top of her head. "Come on, girl." She lifts her head off my lap to look at him, and I expect her to lie right back down, but she surprises me by standing and jumping down off the bed and trotting out of the room.

"Be right back." He leans over, kissing me again, then stands and walks out of the room. I hear the front door open and close. Rolling over, I get up and head for the bathroom, picking up my panties off the floor as I go. Turning on the light near the door, I walk to the sink and look at myself in the mirror. My blonde hair is out of control, the curls that I thought I tamed this morning are now wild. My eyes are sparkling and my lips swollen. Turning on the warm water, I clean up quickly, then put on my panties and head for the bedroom. Not wanting to wear the clothes I came home in, I grab one of Levi's shirts from a drawer and slip it on over my head before pulling my hair out of the neck, feeling the fabric brush against my thighs as I drop my arms.

Padding to the kitchen to get a glass of water, I stop in the living room on the way back to the bed when something catches my attention out of the corner of my eye. Moving across the room without thinking, I feel my stomach melt. Sitting on the coffee table is Levi's open laptop, with the sleep screen sliding through picture after picture—some with him and his family, others with him and me. I didn't even know he had taken so many pictures of us together. Taking a seat on the couch, I turn the computer to face me and watch the pictures slide by until I hear the doorknob turning. Jumping off the couch, feeling like I'm going to be caught doing something I shouldn't be, I run for the bedroom, stubbing my toe on the edge of the bed right before I fall into it. Turning over quickly, I sit back and pull the blanket over my lap.

"Back, babe," he calls from the living room, and I take a breath, trying to fight back the pain in my toe.

"That didn't take long," I squeak through the pain.

"No," he says, walking into the bedroom, ripping off his sweatshirt, and tossing it into his closet. "She handled her business as soon as we made it across the street to the park," he says, then turns to look at me, frowning. "Are you okay?"

"Fine . . . Why?" I say casually, like my toe isn't throbbing so badly that I wonder if it isn't broken.

"You look a little flushed."

"Hmm, weird. I don't know, maybe it's hot in here," I say, trying to shrug off his concern.

"What's wrong?" he asks again, and tears from the pain start to fill my eyes.

"Nothing."

"You're getting ready to cry," he points out, and I pull in a breath through my nose to fight the tears back.

"I think I broke my toe." I squeeze my eyes closed.

"What?" He frowns, studying me.

"I think I broke my toe," I repeat, and he takes a step closer to the bed.

"I was gone maybe fifteen minutes. How did you break your toe in that time?"

"I stubbed it when I was jumping into bed," I admit, opening my eyes as he pulls the blanket off me. I yank my foot away from him when it looks like he's going to prod at it, and his eyes meet mine.

"Let me look at it, baby."

"Don't touch it," I say through a panted breath. The idea of him touching it is enough to make me scream out in pain.

"I won't touch it," he agrees, and I slowly slide my foot back toward him. Picking it up he lifts my leg off the bed and carefully twists it this way and that while looking at my second toe.

"It hurts bad."

"You'll be okay."

"Do I need to go to the hospital?"

"No, just ice every twenty minutes and a couple of pain pills," he says, carefully placing a kiss to the top of my foot before setting it down on the bed.

"Are you sure?"

"I'm sure. I'll get some ice and aspirin," he says, propping my foot up on a pillow. "Why were you jumping into bed?"

"It's just something I do sometimes." I shrug, and his eyes narrow. "Fine, I was looking at your computer . . . the pictures on your slide show," I add quickly, not wanting him to think I was going through his computer. "I heard you coming in and I . . . I didn't want you to think I was snooping through your stuff."

"I'm not sure it's snooping when I leave the thing out and open, but I am sure you're accident-prone and should probably keep that in mind when doing crazy shit."

"I wasn't doing crazy shit," I defend as Muffin wanders into the room and lays her head on the side of the bed near my hip.

"I'm not going to argue with you about it. I'll be back."

"I'm not arguing," I mutter under my breath. He shakes his head and leaves the room, coming back a few minutes later with a glass of water, two red-and-blue pills, and a bag of ice. He hands me the pills and water; I take them quickly while he goes to the bathroom and comes back out with a towel that he wraps the ice in before placing it on my foot. "Thank you," I whisper as he kisses my forehead before stands back up.

"Any time." He smiles as I lean my head back against the headboard and watch him pull off his shirt and kick off his sneakers. "Go lie down, girl," he tells Muffin, who has walked over and leaned into him. Dropping my gaze to her, I watch her walk across the wood floors and lie down on a dog bed in the corner of the room that I hadn't noticed before. The thing looks expensive—it's thick, maybe seven inches deep, and more than big enough for her, with black corduroy material along the outside edge and plush, soft-looking gray material on the top. "You got Muffin a bed," I say, watching her turn in circles before plopping down with a groan.

"Yeah, she's not sleeping in bed with us, and I know there are times she wants to be in here, so I'm compromising with her."

"You're compromising with her," I repeat in awe. He got my dog a bed for his place, he has pictures of us together as the screen saver on his computer, he told me that he wasn't letting me go. Studying him, I wonder if he might not be falling a little in love with me, too.

Chapter 10

SURPRISE . . . NOT SO MUCH

LEVI

Waking suddenly to heavy pounding coming from the front door of my apartment, I vow to shoot the motherfucker who's ruining my morning. My first morning with Fawn after making her mine, the first morning of having her naked in my bed, the first morning I can slide into her. "Fuck," I snarl as that thought leaves my head and the pounding gets louder. Throwing the blanket off, I get out of bed, wondering how the hell Fawn is sleeping through this shit, then, looking down at her sleeping form, I smile. Her wild hair is spread out across my pillow, her hand tucked under her cheek; the sheet only covers one creamy thigh. The other leg is crooked at the knee. I might or might not be the cause of her exhaustion. I couldn't keep my hands off her last night. Every time I woke up, I took her, just to remind myself that she was real, that she was with me, and that she was mine.

Finding a pair of boxers, I put them on, then slip on my sweats, watching Muffin finally decide to get up. "Stay," I tell her, pointing at the bed, and she sits. Glancing at the clock, I see that it's not even eight yet. Shutting the bedroom door behind me, I head across the living room, unlock the door, and swing it open without checking the peephole, ready to kill whoever it is on the other side. "Wh—" My words come to a halt as I stare at Fawn's mom, dad, sisters, and a dozen other people behind them that I do not fucking know.

"Surprise!" Katie cries happily, leaning up to grab my stunned face and pull it down toward her so she can kiss my cheek. "Happy Thanksgiving, Levi." She pats my jaw before she pushes past me and walks inside my place.

"Just go with it," Aiden, carrying an armful of bags, mutters, shaking his head and following his wife into my apartment.

"Happy Thanksgiving." Libby laughs at the look on my face while holding a casserole dish against her stomach as she moves past me.

"Don't worry, it won't be too bad," Mac says, leaning up to kiss my cheek. "Welcome to the family," she says, and my chest fills with something I don't have time to dissect right now as a man, woman, and two boys come forward.

"Carl Reed, Fawn's uncle; my wife, Anna; and my boys, Mike and Tim. Nice to meet you." Carl pats my shoulder as he walks past me with his wife and sons following, all carrying grocery bags.

What the fuck is going on?

"Amy and Gene." A woman who looks a lot like Katie smiles as she asks where she should put the dish she's carrying.

"I don't know," I mutter to her back, then turn to face another group of people.

"Thomas and Marcie. Our kids, Teea and Brandon." Thomas smiles.

Teea stares up at me with wide eyes, and Brandon lifts his chin, asking, "Do you have any video games?"

"Yeah, Xbox." I smile, and he grins.

"Cool." He follows his parents into the house, and I look up at the last two people in the hall.

"I'm Ethan, Fawn's cousin, and this is my fiancée, Enessa. Nice to meet you."

"Yeah, nice to meet you." I check the hall to make sure there is no one else coming before closing the door.

Looking at everyone in my living room and kitchen, I don't even stop to speak to anyone. I head to the bedroom and shut the door. Seeing Fawn is still asleep, I walk to the bed and climb in behind her, pulling her back against me. "Baby."

"No, no more, I need sleep. You have to let me sleep," she whines, and I grin as she bats me away with her eyes closed.

"You may want to get up," I inform her, getting up on my elbow. I look down at her and run my fingers up the length of her neck to her jaw.

"No.

"Yeah," I say softly, and she shakes her head, keeping her eyes closed.

"No, I want to sleep. Who cares about the turkey we can have leftover Thai food?" She presses her ass back into me, making me groan and my cock harden against her.

"I don't think we need to worry about getting a turkey, since about twenty people just showed up here with food."

"What?" Her nose scrunches up.

"Your family is here."

"What?" she repeats, turning to face me and finally blinking her eyes open. She frowns. "What are you talking about?"

"Your family is currently sitting in my living room." Blinking again she shakes her head, causing the mass of curls surrounding her face to move. She's beautiful, and I hate that I can't do what I really want to do right now—which is make her come and listen to the sweet sounds she makes when she's on edge.

"Are you kidding?"

"Wish I was, but no." She closes her eyes.

"My family is here?" she asks, her tone full of disbelief.

"Yeah, babe, . . ." I pause, then add, "All of them."

"Oh god," she groans, rubbing her face with her hands. "I should have known. I should have known my mom would do this . . . 'Go spend Thanksgiving with Levi, it will be fine.' Blah, blah, blah . . ." She pulls her hands away and turns to look at me, raising a brow. "So do you still think your family will make mine look tame?"

"God, you're cute." I change the subject, watching her eyes soften. Her family really is nuts. I know my family is crazy, but compared to hers they seem normal.

"I guess I should get—"

"Levi," Katie calls. We both look at the door. "I don't want to interrupt. I know you're probably busy . . ." She pauses. "But I searched everywhere, and I can't find any flour."

"Mom," Fawn shouts, sitting up on her elbows causing the sheet to drop and rest below them, "there's flour at my house. Grab my apartment key out of my purse on the island and all of you go over there."

"Oh, morning, honey," she says, and even though I can't see it, I have no doubt Fawn's mother is smiling. "Don't rush. Take your time."

"I swear I was adopted," Fawn groans, falling to her back, then turning to look at me. "I'm so sorry about this."

"Don't apologize." My hand moves to her stomach, and I drop my eyes there as it slides over her smooth, creamy skin toward her breast. Watching her nipple harden, I smile. She's so sensitive that I barely have to touch her for her body to react.

"Levi."

"Yeah?"

"We have to get up," she whispers as I drag one finger along the underside of her breast and up to circle her tight nipple.

"I know." I lean over to lick her other nipple, feeling it harden against my tongue. Her hands move to my hair and lock me in place as her knees bend and her thighs tighten together.

"Please," she breathes as my fingers move back down her body over her stomach.

"You have to open for me, baby."

"My family," she says, but her legs relax just enough to let me in.

"I'm half-tempted not to let you come," I say, and her eyes spring open. "I'm half-tempted to stop so you'll know exactly what I'm going to be feeling all day with your family here."

"But you won't do that, right?" she asks as my fingers slide between her folds, finding her dripping wet already. I rub my middle and pointer fingers up and down along the outside edge of her clit, giving her just enough that her body begins to light up but not what she really needs.

"I don't know, what do you think I should do?"

"I think you shouldn't tease me."

"I would never tease you, gorgeous. I may make you wait to come, but I promise I will always get you off." I pull her nipple into my mouth while thrusting two fingers deep inside her. Her body arches off the bed, and she whimpers. I know she's trying to keep quiet—I know she can hear people in the other room, so she knows if she's too loud they will be able to hear her. Quickening the pace of my fingers, I nip the tip of her nipple, hearing her gasp as her pussy starts to flutter. *Fuck me.* I lean back, gritting my teeth, watching her face as she gets closer to coming. It takes everything in me not to slide between her legs and take her as her pussy tightens and her juices soak my hand.

"Levi," she pants, and her legs start to shake as her hands wrap around my arm.

"Let it go." I lean forward and cover her mouth with mine as she orgasms, digging her nails into my arm and moaning against my tongue. Pulling back as the flutter of her pussy slows, I pull my fingers out of her, watching a smile light up her face as I suck my fingers clean.

"Honey, where are the pie pans I got you for Christmas two years ago?" Katie asks through the door, and Fawn's smile falls away as her cheeks turn a shade of pink that has nothing to do with the orgasm I just gave her. "Never mind, don't rush," she says quickly. "I'll just have Libby look for them."

"Give me twenty minutes, Mom, and I'll be out to help you," she yells, then looks at me. "What do you think the probability of us sneaking out of here without being caught is?" I grin.

"None, babe."

"That's what I thought." She sighs, sitting up. "I better get up and get dressed." Putting my elbow on the bed, I watch her stand and put her hands on her hips as she looks toward the door. "I need to find a way to sneak home to get some clean clothes."

"You've got stuff here," I say, and her eyes come back to me.

"I don't really want to put on the clothes I had on yesterday."

"You have clean stuff in the second drawer." I nod to the dresser.

"What?"

"You have a tendency to leave your shit all over my floor, so the last time I had the laundry sent out, I put your stuff in with mine."

"Then you put it away in your dresser?" she asks, and I study the look in her eyes as her bottom lip goes between her teeth. She looks nervous, and that doesn't sit well with me. I know this thing between us has been happening fast, but I'm not going to be the one to slow us down—not when it feels so right. If I learned one thing from being a cop, it's to always follow my gut, and my gut is telling me she's my future—a future I'm very much looking forward to.

"Baby." I sit up and move to the edge of the bed so I can take her waist and pull her toward me. "You've been in my bed every night for the last two weeks. Some of my shit is hanging in your closet," I remind her quietly, and she nods, running her fingers through my hair. "You okay with having a drawer here?"

Her eyes meet mine, and she smiles softly. "Yeah, I'm good with it."

"Good, now go get ready."

"Okay," she agrees, but she doesn't move. She gives me a smile I haven't seen from her before, then drops her mouth to mine in a soft touch. Before I'm ready to let her go, she pulls her mouth from mine and walks to the dresser, opening the second drawer that I cleaned out for her last week. Staring inside for a moment, she shakes her head and pulls out a few items before closing it and turning to look at me briefly. Then without another word, she heads for the bathroom. Standing, I move around the bed and follow her so I can clean up. As soon as I walk into the steam-filled room I watch her disappear into the shower and hold back a growl of frustration. I should be getting into the shower with her—we should be having our first morning of wake-up sex, then shower sex—but with everyone here, those plans will have to be moved to tomorrow. Unless everyone is planning on staying the night—then I'll be screwed again.

After brushing my teeth, I wash my face, find a shirt to put on, and head back to the bathroom.

"I'm gonna take Muffin out," I say, and the water goes off right before she pulls the shower curtain open.

"Do you want to wait for me? She doesn't really like the guys in my family, and I don't want her to freak out on one of them."

"You shouldn't be on your foot too much," I say as she grabs the towel hanging on the wall.

"It doesn't really hurt anymore. I think I just bruised it, I'm oka—"

"Fuck," I clip out, dropping my eyes down her body. I watch the drops of water sliding down her skin. "This is torture." She laughs, pushing me a step back when I move into her space.

"You're torturing yourself."

"I didn't get enough of you last night." I sigh regretfully, and her big eyes come to me.

"You didn't get enough of me last night?" She looks me over and swallows. "You had me more times than I can count."

"It will never be enough. Being inside you is . . . Fuck, there are no words for what it's like being inside you," I explain, shaking my head, as she steps over the edge of the tub. "All I know is it's my new favorite place to be."

"Stop." She pokes my chest, pushing me back when I unknowingly move to her again. "You're making me dizzy, and I need to get ready. My whole family is out there, so I need to prepare myself for what's about to happen," she says, moving to stand in front of the sink.

"What's about to happen?" I ask, placing myself against her back, wrapping my hands around her waist, and dropping my chin to the top of her head.

"I don't know." Her eyes meet mine in the mirror. "All I know is that it will probably be embarrassing."

"I'll be with you," I say, then mutter a curse as my cell phone rings.

"You should get that," she says quietly, studying me in the mirror.

"Yeah." I kiss her shoulder and let her go. Going to the bedroom, I find my cell on the dresser and expect it to be work, but it's my mom.

"Mom," I answer, putting the phone to my ear.

"Happy Thanksgiving, honey."

"Thanks, Mom. Have you been cooking all morning?" I know she probably has. Since I was little, my mom has been making a feast at Thanksgiving, getting up at six to put in a turkey and get things ready before everyone shows up.

"No, actually, I'm standing outside your apartment building . . . Surprise." She yells the last word, and I scrub my hand down my jaw in disbelief as I look into the bathroom and watch Fawn put her hair up on top of her head. I told my mom about Fawn two weeks ago, and she couldn't wait to meet her. I just didn't expect that meeting to include Fawn's entire family.

"You're standing outside my building," I ask, just to confirm.

"Yes. Well, we all are . . . we didn't want you to be alone on Thanksgiving, so we figured we'd drive in and cook at your place. That way, even if you get called out, you can eat when you come back." *Fuck me, this shit is not going to go well.*

"Fawn's whole family showed up this morning with that same plan," I say. When it goes quiet, I pull the phone away from my ear to check that the call didn't drop. "Mom."

"Fawn is with you? I thought she was going to be with her family today," she says, repeating something I told her last week when she asked what Fawn would be doing on the holiday.

"She didn't want me to be alone," I say quietly and listen to her pull in a sharp breath.

"Oh my," she says, and I know she understands the significance of Fawn coming to spend Thanksgiving with me instead of staying with her family.

"Mom, let me let you go. I'll be down in a minute to let you in."

"Sure, honey," she agrees, and I pull the phone away, end the call, and shove it into my pocket as I walk back into the bathroom.

"Change of plans, baby."

"You have to leave?" she asks, sounding disappointed as she pulls a shirt on over her head—this one is red and has the word *Bazinga* scrolled across the front in large yellow lettering.

"Nope, my family is all downstairs."

"What?" Her face pales, and her eyes shoot past me to the door. "Your family is here?"

"Yeah, I need to go let them in."

"Your family is all here? As in outside our building?" she repeats, sounding panicked.

"Yeah, ba—"

"But . . . but my family is all here," she cuts me off with wide eyes.

"They are . . ."

"Oh my god. This is going to be a disaster. Your family is going to hate me because my family is going to do something crazy."

"It's all good, calm down."

"Calm down," she breathes, staring at me. "Do you not remember when my mom suggested I get knocked up to keep you . . ." She pauses, throwing out her hand and pointing at me. "In front of you?"

"Take a breath." I grab her hand and pull her to me, then take her face between my palms. "It's going to be fine . . . promise. I'll be right back."

"This is the worst day of my life," she pouts, closing her eyes. "We should just break up, because obviously fate doesn't want us together."

"Christ, you're cute." I laugh, kissing her pouting bottom lip quickly. "I'll be back."

"If you don't find me when you get back, look out the window, because I've jumped to my death." Shaking my head at that, I leave her in the bathroom and head out of the room, finding a few people still in the apartment, including Mac, who's in the kitchen making a pot of coffee. "Do me a favor—go to your sister."

"Is she okay?" she asks, looking from me to my bedroom door.

"She's having a panic attack because my family just showed up—they're downstairs."

"Seriously, your family is here?" she asks with wide eyes that look just like her sisters'.

"Seriously"—I nod, heading for the door—"I'll be back."

"Sure," she agrees, turning on the coffeepot before heading for my room, looking slightly amused and a little bit worried.

Swinging the front door open, I move to the stairs and jog down, pushing out of the building as soon as I get to the door. The sight that greets me makes me smile. My mom, dad, and brothers, plus their wives and kids, are all here. As happy as I am to see my family, I know this day is going to be a long one, and it's the first time since meeting Fawn that I'm praying to get called into work. But if I do, I'm taking her with me.

"Mom." I smile as my mom comes forward, wrapping her arms around me.

"Look at you . . ." She shakes her head. "So handsome." She kisses my cheek, then lets me go.

"Dad." I grin at my old man, and he holds out his arms and I walk toward him, hugging him tightly.

He pounds my back two times, muttering, "Son," before letting me go.

"Uncle Levi," my niece Madeline says, bouncing at my feet and holding her arms out to me.

"How's my girl?" I ask, picking her up and swinging her around, listening to her giggle.

"Good." She smiles, wrapping her arms around my neck and laying her head on my shoulder.

"So Fawn and her family are here?" my brother Lucas asks as his wife, Eva, comes forward to take their daughter, Madeline, from me.

"Yep, and she's freaking out."

"I bet," Allison, my brother Cooper's wife, says shaking her head at Cooper, who is holding their sleeping ten-month-old son, Jacob, in his arms. "I would totally freak if this kind of thing happened to me."

"You always freak out." Allison's sister, Ruby, snorts, taking nine-month-old Emma from her husband, my brother Cole, as she starts to cry.

"Just keep that in mind when you meet Fawn. She's a little over-whelmed with all of this."

"It will be all right, she'll see," Mom says, and I nod, knowing she hasn't met Fawn's family yet, so she has no idea what she's saying.

"We need to get the stuff from the car. Do you want to take Emma up for me?" Ruby asks, not giving me much of a choice as she hands the baby over. When my adorable niece's bottom lip starts to tremble, I look at her mother's retreating back for help.

"She'll be okay, it's just a stage," Allison says stepping into the building. "Come on, Madeline," she calls, and Madeline takes off at a run toward her. "Let's go check out Uncle Levi's apartment."

"Okay," she agrees, and I look at my mom.

"The code for the door is six, seven, three, eight—just punch it in and come on up."

"Okay." She smiles, then gets close, taking hold of my biceps to stop me from going in. "How serious is this thing between you and Fawn?"

"Serious, Mom," I say quietly, and she nods, closing her eyes. "But Mom, play it cool. She's a little skittish, so don't freak her out."

"I won't freak her out. I don't even know how to freak someone out." She rolls her eyes at me, then looks at Emma. "Take her up, it's too cold for her to be out here."

"Do you remember the code?"

"Yeah, I remember," she says over her shoulder as she heads toward where my brothers, dad, and sisters-in-law are all unpacking stuff from the cars they drove here.

"Mama," Emma says, and I look down at her as she pounds her tiny fist against my chest. "Mama, Mama, Mama."

"She's coming, honey." I kiss her soft forehead as I head up the stairs.

"This is the best day ever. Fawn just told me your family came to surprise you, too," Katie says, greeting me at the landing between Fawn's apartment and mine. Her eyes drop to Emma and light up. "Who's this little angel?"

"This is my niece Emma," I say, and Emma looks at her with baby curiosity.

"Hi, Emma." She takes her hand, shaking it. "Oh my, isn't she pretty." She pulls her eyes from Emma to look at me. "Now, I don't want to put any pressure on you, but the sooner you can give me one of these, the happier I'll be." When Emma reaches her tiny arms out toward Fawn's mom, she scoops her up.

"I'll keep that in mind," I mutter, feeling my lips twitch.

"Mom, what did I say about embarrassing me?" Fawn questions, coming over to stand next to her mom, and I realize that she's changed out of her T-shirt into a long-sleeved dark-blue button-up top with pleats at the waist that show off her figure, dark jeans, and low-heeled boots. She looks beautiful—but then again, she always does; it doesn't matter what she wears.

"I'm not embarrassing you, I'm just saying . . . I'd like one day, maybe sooner rather than later, to be a grandma."

"Mom." Fawn narrows her eyes.

"Stop raining on my parade," Katie says, hugging Emma, who is focused on Fawn.

"Utt . . . utt," Emma says, and Fawn's eyes go to her and fill with a sweet softness as she reaches out to take Emma's extended hand.

"That means she wants you," says Allison, who's carrying Jacob.

"Baby, this is Allison, my brother Cooper's wife. Allison, this is Fawn and her mom, Katie."

"Nice to meet you both," Allison says quietly before nodding down to Jacob, who is still asleep in her arms. "This is my son, Jacob."

"Nice to meet you two." Fawn smiles, then drops her gaze to Madeline when she comes over to me, holding her arms up.

"I'm Madeline. Are you Uncle Levi's girlfriend?" Fawn laughs.

"I am, and it's so nice to meet you, Madeline," she says as her eyes soften.

"You're pretty," Madeline states, and everyone laughs.

"Thank you." Fawn smiles, then looks back at Emma when the baby gets ahold of her sleeve and tugs to get her attention. Taking Emma from Katie, Fawn tucks the baby against her chest and looks down at her, smiling as Emma starts to babble.

"Yes, we definitely need a few of these little angels around," Katie says, looking her daughter and Emma with hope in her eyes.

"Mom," Fawn warns.

"An old woman can wish, can't she?"

"Don't worry, Levi's mom is just as bad. Jacob is only ten months old, and she's already pestering me about having another one," Allison says, nudging Fawn's shoulder and gaining a smile from her.

"I do not pester—I merely suggest," my mom says, coming up the steps carrying a tray of food that I reach out and take from her.

"Suggest every day," Allison says, and Fawn giggles, making Mom's face go soft.

"Mom, I want you to meet Fawn. Fawn, my mom, Lisa."

"Oh my, aren't you pretty," Mom says, giving Fawn a side hug so she doesn't squish Emma, who is now playing with the chunky necklace around Fawn's neck.

"Um . . ." Fawn smiles shyly. "Thank you, it's nice to meet you. Levi talks about you all the time."

"Good stuff, I hope."

"Always good stuff," she agrees, then steps back. "Lisa, this is my mom, Katie."

"Lisa," Fawn's mom whispers, studying my mom. "Lisa Gurstrich?"

"Katie Michels," Mom says, and they stare at each other. "Oh my lord," Mom cries, rushing to Katie, and they embrace tightly and rock back and forth, hugging. I'm staring at them as I wonder what the fuck is going on.

"Katie and I went to summer camp together for seven years up near Canada," Mom says, looking back at me. "We went every summer until we turned sixteen and couldn't go anymore. Oh my, it's a small world."

"Yes, and now, look—our babies are seeing each other," Katie says happily, pulling my mom in to hug her once more. "I've searched and searched for you on Facebook," she whispers, and I watch my mom's arms tighten.

"Me, too. I can't believe this," Mom says, looking like she's about to cry. Pulling my eyes from our moms, I look at Fawn, who is watching them hug with a look of disbelief on her face. My girl has had a crazy morning, and it seems it's just getting crazier by the second.

My cell rings, and I pull it out of my pocket as Fawn's eyes fly to me and fill with worry. I have no doubt that she's scared I'll be called in and she's going to be left to deal with all of this alone. Looking at the caller ID, I see it's Cole calling.

"Yeah." I put the phone to my ear, shaking my head at Fawn; her body relaxes.

"What's the code?" he asks, sounding out of breath.

"Mom, you locked everyone out."

"Oh." She jumps away from Katie. "I needed to come up and meet Fawn quickly." She grins, leaning over to kiss Fawn's cheek before pushing past me and heading down the steps with Katie following her.

"Mom's coming," I mutter into the phone and hang up.

"Let's get the babies out of the hall," Allison suggests, and we all head into my apartment, which is currently empty of Fawn's family. Heading for the kitchen, needing a cup of coffee, I watch Fawn walk across the living room toward the couch with Emma.

"Do you want coffee, babe?" I ask, and she smiles at me over her shoulder.

"Yes, please."

"Wow, this is really happening . . . You're really in a relationship," Allison mutters from my side, and I turn to look at her, seeing a smirk on her face.

"Don't start."

"I don't know what you're talking about." She grins as she pulls a bottle out and heads for the couch to take a seat next to Fawn. My family has been giving me a hard time for the last couple of years about finding someone to settle down with, but I've always ignored them. After I ended things with Heather, I refused to settle for another woman who didn't really give a shit about me, what I wanted, or what I needed. Until Fawn came along, I thought it would be next to impossible to find that woman, so I know my family is surprised.

"I have the perfect plan," Katie says as she comes through the front door with my family following her. "We can all have Thanksgiving together, since we are all here."

"Mom," Fawn says from the couch, but Katie ignores her and looks at my mom, who is nodding like a loon.

"I think it's a great idea. The more the merrier," my mom agrees, huddling in the kitchen and whispering with Katie.

"It will be fine, baby," I state, handing Fawn her cup of coffee as Ruby comes over to take Emma from her. "Baby, I'd like you to meet Emma's mom, Ruby, and her dad, my brother Cole," I introduce them as Fawn stands to greet each of them with a hug.

"It's nice to meet you." Fawn smiles, and I tuck her under my arm.

"You're the pizza girl," Ruby says, and I look at Fawn, wondering what she's talking about.

"Um, yeah." She blushes. "Thank you for the birthday cake—it was delicious."

"You're welcome. I'm glad you liked it." Ruby grins, then steps aside, whispering to Cole as my dad pushes his way in front of Lucas and Eva.

"Dad, Fawn. Fawn, my dad, David," I say as Dad picks her up off the ground in a bear hug.

"Nice to meet you, girl," Dad says, and Fawn laughs.

"Nice to meet you, too, sir."

"Don't *sir* me. That title is better for my boss's boss," Dad says, then looks at me. "You did good, boyo." Shaking my head at him, I grin, then watch him move to the kitchen when my mom calls him over.

"Baby, my brother Lucas and his wife, Eva. Their daughter is Madeline," I say, and Fawn hugs Eva, who does not return the hug.

Eva lets out a huff as Lucas pulls Fawn into a hug next, muttering, "They like to save the best for last," before letting her go, gaining a glare from his wife, which he ignores.

"Nice to meet you guys." Fawn smiles as I wrap my hand around her waist.

"Now, seriously, what the hell are you doing with this uptight asshole?" Lucas asks, looking between the two of us.

"He's not so bad," Fawn says looking up at me.

I dip my head and place a kiss to her forehead, then pull away when Libby comes through the front door, stating loudly, "I vote that only one apartment has the game playing and the other one is free rein."

"I want to watch the parade," Madeline says, taking a seat on the couch—she's holding a cookie that she got from god knows where.

"We're only a few blocks from the parade. We should go see it in person," Libby says, and Madeline's face lights up.

"I'd like to get out of here for a while," Eva says, looking at Libby. Eva wanting to get out of here isn't a surprise—she's not the most friendly person, and I seriously wonder what the hell my brother is still doing married to her.

"I'll go with the girls," Lucas says, then adds, "or with anyone else who wants to come along."

"Do you want to go, baby?" I ask Fawn, and she shakes her head no.

"Not really unless you want to. I went last year, and it was a little too much for me."

"That's cool, we can stay."

"You can go," she says softly, and I shake my head no.

"I'm going to go next door and see who else wants to come out with us," Libby says as my cell starts to ring.

Giving Fawn a quick kiss, I pull my phone out of my pocket, seeing it's my partner, Wesley. "I gotta take this, baby," I say quietly, and she nods as I put the phone to my ear and move to my bedroom.

"What's up?" I ask as soon as the door is shut behind me.

"Just seeing if you wanted to get a bite to eat later. I know you're on your own today."

"Actually, my whole family—and Fawn's—just showed up with bags upon bags of food," I say. Wesley's been giving me shit about Fawn for the last few weeks, asking if I needed any help with her since I was having a hard time pinning her down.

"Lucky bastard," he grumbles, and I grin.

"Why don't you come over here for dinner?"

"Nah, I don't want to impose."

"You're not imposing. We'll have plenty of food, and I'd like you to meet Fawn."

"All right, I'll be there."

"That wasn't hard," I mutter and hear him laugh before he hangs up. Shoving my cell back in my pocket, I leave the room, finding Fawn in the kitchen.

"Do you have to leave?" she asks as soon as she sees me.

"No, but my partner, Wesley, is gonna stop by for dinner."

"Where is his family today?" she asks quietly, and I move into her, wrapping my hand around her hip, then sliding it around her back to pull her closer.

"Seattle. He moved here a little over a year ago, so he's on his own."

"Oh," she says softly, moving her fingers up to run along my jaw. "In that case, I'm glad everyone showed up with food. I'd hate for him to be alone, too."

"You'll like him," I state softly when I see that her eyes have filled with worry, and she nods, then looks past me. "You doing okay with all of this?"

"Yeah, unless you get called into work, I'll be okay."

"If I get called in, I'm taking you with me," I say, and she laughs, dropping her forehead to my chest. I wrap my arms around her and place my lips to her hair, breathing in the scent of berries that always seems to surround her.

"Fawn, are you ready to cook your first turkey?" Katie asks, breaking into the moment. Fawn pulls away to look at her mom, who's poking her head in the door.

"Do I have a choice?" she asks, and her mom rolls her eyes. "Apparently not. I guess we're playing Russian roulette with everyone's lives today," she mutters, and I laugh, throwing my head back, then drop my mouth to hers and whisper against her lips.

"You got this, baby. If you need me, I'll be here watching the game," I say, and she frowns at my smile.

"This is the first time in my life I wish I could say I wanted to watch football," she grumbles right before I kiss her once more, then let her go, wondering how the hell it's possible that I'm already falling in love with her. She throws a smile at me over her shoulder before she leaves, making me realize it's just her.

Chapter 11

WHERE ARE THE GIBLETS? WHAT THE HELL ARE GIBLETS?

FAWN

"Who's going to cut the turkey?" Mom asks, looking between Levi's mom and me. I shrug, taking a sip of beer, which I normally hate, but I need alcohol to get through today and there is no wine in the house.

"I think Levi should cut it since he's the man of the house," Lisa says, smiling at me, and I fight the urge to roll my eyes at her the way I would if my mom had just said the same thing. My reaction to her isn't a surprise—after spending the day with Levi's mom and mine I've realized why they were such great friends. They have the same personality, neither of them understands the meaning of boundaries, and they are both crazy as hell. I mean, they're even wearing similar outrageous Thanksgiving-themed sweaters with sparkles and bedazzles.

"Oh, I love it, Levi and Fawn's first Thanksgiving together. This is just too perfect." My mom claps as she looks at me, smiling.

"Mom," I warn—not that she's paying me any mind. No, she's been like this all day. Which means she's in make-believe mom heaven, where Levi and I are past the point of dating and onto the baby-making part of our relationship and I'm planning on giving her ten grandkids.

"This is just so exciting," Lisa gushes, looking at me. "You are so much better than Levi's ex-fiancée. Ugh, I hated that girl."

Um, what? I feel my eyes get wide, and my heart skips a beat as I stare at her.

"Levi was engaged?" My mom voices my question, and I wait with my fist clenched for the answer as I study Lisa, who is suddenly looking anywhere but at me.

"It was years ago," she says, waving it off like it's not a big deal when it most definitely is. Or in my head it is. In reality it shouldn't even matter, since I didn't even know him then and am just getting to know him now. "Let's not think about that right now."

"Right," I agree quietly, knowing that's all I'm going to be able to think about for the rest of the day.

"Now where are the giblets?" she asks, looking around.

"I don't know, what do they look like?" I look around myself, wondering what the heck giblets are.

"They were in a bag inside the turkey," she says, and my head flies in her direction.

"There was something inside the turkey?" I ask, and both sets of mom eyes land on me.

"You didn't find them when you were stuffing the turkey?" Mom asks, and I shake my head no.

"Oh dear," Lisa whispers, and I look through the clear glass door on the oven at the turkey inside—a turkey I stuffed myself, a turkey I've been basting off and on all day—and know instantly I messed up. Big. "Don't worry, it's fine." She waves once more, and I can tell she's fighting back a smile.

"You've been cooking the turkey with the bag of giblets inside it," Mom says, fighting back her own smile.

"This isn't funny." I shake my head at the two of them as they smile at each other.

"It's a little bit funny, sweetheart."

I glare at them as they start to laugh. "I've ruined Thanksgiving. I can barely make mac and cheese, and you two thought I should be the one in charge of cooking the turkey."

"Don't worry, Levi can cook," Lisa says through her laughter. "You won't starve with my son around."

"I tried to teach my girls to cook, but they never wanted to learn." Mom smiles, and I look at the ceiling. She never tried to teach us to cook—she secretly liked us depending on her for sustenance.

"I'll just take out the stuffing and get the bag out of it. Maybe it won't be so bad," I mutter to myself when the two women who were supposed to be teaching me to cook the damn turkey start to laugh again. "I don't even know why you think this is so funny," I growl, digging through a drawer for a spoon to scoop out the stuffing.

"What's going on?" Levi startles me as he comes into the kitchen, and I feel my face heat. I wonder if his ex-fiancée did all the dumb things I can't seem to stop doing. I doubt she did—she was probably perfect in every way.

"Nothing. Your Fawn is just funny," Lisa says softly as Levi gets close to me, wraps his hand around my waist, and places a soft kiss to my forehead.

"What'd she do?" he questions, with a smile on his face that says, *She's always doing stupid shit, so what did she do this time?*

"Nothing," I cut in before they can tell him about my latest disaster. "Do you need another beer?" The guys have been over at his place most of the day watching the game, only coming over now and again to get food and beer that they stocked in my fridge while everyone else was watching the parade and walking around in Times Square, since Madeline has never been to the city before.

"Nah, just coming to check on my girl. You've been out of my sight too long," he says quietly, and my stomach fills with butterflies. He really is always making me dizzy, and I don't know what to do with that or him, which makes me start to panic a little.

"What time is Wesley getting here?" Lisa asks, and Levi thankfully pulls his eyes from me to look at his mom.

"Any time now."

"Good. We're going to need you guys to start getting everything set up. I know you have those foldout tables in your storage, so go on over and tell your dad and brothers to help you get them," she says as she pulls him away from me and starts to shove him out of the kitchen.

"Trying to get rid of me?" he jokes. His eyes lock on mine and narrow slightly, like he sees something he doesn't like. Pulling my gaze from his, I pretend to look through the drawers for something.

"Yes," Lisa huffs right before I hear the door close.

"You okay, honey?" Mom asks, and I close the drawer and smile at her.

"Yep, totally okay, just gonna scoop out the turkey and hope I can salvage it," I say, then go about doing just that while secretly wondering why the hell a guy like Levi is with a girl like me. I don't have long to think about it. Levi returns and introduces me to Wesley, then they start to set up the tables, and before I know, it we're sitting down to eat.

"This turkey is delicious," Wesley says, and I take my eyes off my plate, where I have been pushing around my food for the last twenty minutes, to look at him. He really is a nice guy—and he's hot. Superhot. Not as good-looking as Levi, but he's definitely not hard on the eyes, with sun-kissed golden skin, dark hair, blue eyes, and full lips that would look feminine if it wasn't for his sharp jaw.

"Thanks," I say, giving him a smile that he returns. Dinner is awkward, but not for my family or anyone else, really. No, it's just awkward for me, because almost since the moment everyone came back from watching the parade, Lucas's wife, Eva, has been talking about Levi's ex-fiancée, Heather, who is apparently amazing—and moving into the city in a few weeks to work for some magazine. I thought when I met Eva this morning that she was nice, but it turns out I was wrong—very wrong. She's catty and a total bitch, and I seriously don't get why Lucas is with her when he seems so down-to-earth and sweet. Plus, the way he is with his daughter is adorable.

"Should I give Heather your new number?" Eva asks, and I feel Levi tense next to me as my own body goes rigid.

"Why on earth would Levi want to talk to her?" Cole asks. Ruby puts her hand on top of his on the table.

"Just drop it," Lucas says quietly, and Eva looks at him.

"What? I was just wondering. She's going to be new to the city, just like he was, and it would be nice if she had someone to show her around," she says, and Levi's hand that has been on my thigh since the moment we sat down tightens, like he's afraid I'm going to get up and take off. *Which I might.*

"I don't want to speak to her. I don't want anything to do with her," Levi states in a low, deep rumble, and I can tell he's trying to keep control over his tone.

"I just . . . You two were good friends before you got together," Eva says, looking at him. I bite my lip because his hold on me has tightened almost painfully.

"Eva, now is not the time for this discussion," Lisa, who is glaring at Eva, states. Pulling my eyes from them, I look around at my family, who are spaced throughout the tables, and feel my face heat when I realize they all have their eyes on me with varying looks of anger and pity. I don't know what to do in this situation, but I do know that if I open my mouth and say what I want to say to Eva, Levi and his family will probably never speak to me again.

"Fine." She lets out a little huff before picking at the minuscule amount of food she put on her plate. Dropping my eyes to my own plate, I try to eat, but every bite tastes like cardboard and I have to force it down.

"So, Fawn, Levi said you're a teacher. What grade do you teach?" Ruby asks, and I reluctantly look at her.

"Fifth grade. Most of my students are ten and eleven," I say, attempting to smile.

"I wanted to be a teacher, but then Allison and I got into baking, one thing led to another, and our baked goods took off, so I dropped out of college to open a bakery with my sister."

"Well, the cake you made for my birthday was delicious, so I think you made the right move," I say, meaning that, and she smiles softly.

"Thanks."

"So how did you guys end up dating brothers?" I've wanted to ask since the moment I found out she and Allison are sisters, but I regret asking almost immediately, knowing it's none of my business and probably sounds rude. "Sorry, ignore me—my filter doesn't always work."

"It's fine." She laughs. "I met Cole first when he came into the bakery to put in an order for a cake for his mom's birthday, and we exchanged numbers that day," she says.

"She fell in love with me on the spot," Cole says, and she smiles at him.

"I did," she agrees, then she looks at Cooper and Allison. "Cooper came in to pick up the cake since Cole couldn't, and that's when he met Allison."

"I thought he was a jerk," Allison chimes in, and I grin at her. "He was totally arrogant." She shakes her head, then smiles as he leans over to kiss the side of her head.

"So how did you two end up together, then?" Libby asks, looking between the two who are very obviously in love.

"We were forced to be around each other since our siblings were in love, then one thing led to another."

"She was secretly in love with me the whole time and just playing hard to get," Cooper says.

Allison mutters, "That's partly true," with a smile on her face that says it's really very true.

"That's awesome." I smile at them, then look over at Mac and Libby, who are talking quietly. I can't make out what they are saying, since they are down at the other end of the table, but I can tell Mac is annoyed. Mac hasn't been herself since Wesley got here, and I swear there was a moment of recognition when Levi introduced them—not that Mac will tell me if she knows Wesley or not. She's been a closed book lately, which is really damn annoying, especially since she's been all up in my business about Levi, though I did overhear Libby asking her about some guy she was seeing or sleeping with. I'm not sure which, since I was trying to listen through the door when they were talking.

"So Ruby and Allison run a bakery. What about you, Eva? What do you do?" Mom asks, and Eva sits up straight in her chair.

"I don't work, I'm a full-time mom," she says, and I swear I hear either Allison or Ruby snort.

"That's the hardest job in the world," Mom says quietly, and Eva nods, but her eyes narrow when Madeline giggles and Libby laughs. Madeline insisted on sitting next to Libby when we were setting the table, because apparently they hit it off when they were out at the parade and sightseeing. Looking at my sister, I watch her make a face at the little girl that makes her giggle again. Libby has always had a way with kids, especially little girls, because they are all about the color pink, hair, and makeup, just like she is.

"Madeline, you know better than to play at the table," Eva says, and her daughter looks at her with wide eyes. Libby bristles next to her and shoots daggers at her mom.

"Sorry, Mom."

"She's fine," Lucas says, and Eva turns her head to glare at him.

"It's not fine, she knows better."

"Jesus," Lucas growls as his jaw tightens.

"I'm going to go get the desserts and bring them over," I announce, probably a little too loudly as I stand quickly and look around the table.

161

I need to get out of here for a few minutes. I need to get away from everyone before I say something to Eva that I will regret.

"I'll help," Libby says as she pushes away from the table.

"Me, too." Mac stands and without a backward glance I head for Levi's apartment for the pies and cakes Allison and Ruby brought over.

"Oh my god, that chick is just awful," Libby mutters shutting Levi's front door as I walk across his apartment to his bedroom, where Muffin has been most of the day. She's done much better with the men around, but I haven't wanted to risk her getting out by accident.

"This whole day is awful," I say under my breath. My family showed up, Levi's family showed up, I almost ruined the turkey, I found out the guy I'm falling in love with had a fiancée at one time, I found out the ex-fiancée is moving to the city, and to top it all off, Eva is a bitch. I want to go home and crawl into bed with a book, but unfortunately that isn't possible, seeing how everyone is sitting in my apartment.

"Are you okay?" Mac asks as I take a seat on the couch with Muffin, wondering if anyone would notice if I disappeared to take her for a walk—for a couple of hours.

"Yep, fabulous."

"Liar." She shakes her head as she takes a seat next to me. "Talk to me, what's going on?"

"You want to talk? Let's talk about why it looked like you know Wesley," I say, raising a brow and she looks away from me.

"You're right, we don't need to talk."

"I give up." I shake my head at her while I stand.

"Where are you going?" she questions, watching me attach Muffin's leash to her collar.

"I'm taking Muffin out for a walk. Can you and Libby take the desserts over to my apartment and tell everyone I'll be back in a bit?"

"Sure," Mac agrees softly. I look to Libby, who has a fork in her hand and is digging into one of the pies.

"Yeah," Libby says, chewing and swallowing. "But do you think Levi's going to be happy about you just taking off?"

"Levi's not going to care," I say, then realize I don't have a coat and I'm sure it's cold out. Determined to leave, I head for Levi's hall closet and grab his hoodie, putting it on along with his down vest.

"Do you want me to go with you?" Mac asks, and I shake my head.

"No, I just need a few minutes alone."

"All right," she agrees as I head for the door. Leaving them at Levi's apartment, I take the stairs with Muffin leading the way. As soon as I push through the front door, I come face-to-face with Lucas, who is standing on the sidewalk, smoking a cigarette.

"You taking off?" he asks me, and I try to smile but know it doesn't quite meet my eyes.

"No, just taking Muffin for a walk. She's been locked up most of the day," I explain, wanting to hurry away from him, but I know that would be rude, so I stay put.

"Look, I'm sorry about Eva . . ." He pauses, running his hand through his hair, and I realize just how much he looks like his brother when he's agitated. "She doesn't always know when to stop." One could say that. One could also say she's just a bitch, but what the hell do I know.

"It's fine," I say, shrugging it off. "I'll be—" I start to tell him I'll be back and step away, but he cuts me off, stopping me in my tracks.

"Heather and Levi were never meant to be together, so please know that you have nothing to worry about when it comes to her."

"I'm not worried," I lie, and his lips twitch into a smile.

"He cares for you, more than I've ever seen him care about anyone, so don't let Eva put shit in your head. She and Heather were friends, and she's got it in her head that Heather is meant to be with Levi. But I promise you, that is not the case. They don't belong together. They—"

"Please stop," I say softly, cutting him off before he can say more. "Levi and I haven't had a chance to talk about her or them, and I'd rather wait until he's ready to tell me . . . No offense."

"None taken." Lucas smiles at me, then takes a drag from his cigarette before tossing it into the street. I want to tell him he should quit smoking and not litter, but I keep quiet, knowing that he probably doesn't want to hear me nag him about his bad habits—one of them being his wife. "Do you want me to go with you?" he asks, giving Muffin a head rub when she moves close to sniff his hand.

"No, I'm sure you want to get back inside. I'll be back in a few." I like Lucas—or what I know of him—but the idea of spending more time with anyone right now is about as appealing as getting my nails pulled out one at a time.

"You sure?"

"Yes, thank you for the offer. That's very nice of you." He nods, then looks at the door, and I can tell he doesn't want to go back inside. God, why can't I be one of those women who is a bitch and just doesn't care about how people feel? "Actually, I think I could use the company, and Levi doesn't really like me walking Muffin alone since she has a tendency to take off. And with her size and mine, it's hard for me to control her."

"You sure?" he asks, studying me, and I put on another fake smile.

"Yep." I nod, then start across the street to the park, making sure to look for traffic as I cross the road. Seeing him walking alongside me out of the corner of my eye, I head down the tree-lined path. "Madeline is very sweet," I say, trying to fill the awkward silence that has settled between us as I keep my pace slow, in no rush to get back to the drama at my place.

"She's the best thing that has ever happened to me," he says quietly, and I smile at that, because even without hearing him say those words, I know he loves his daughter—you can see it in his eyes when he looks at her. "I'm getting a divorce."

My step stutters and I almost trip as I swing my head in his direction. "I'm sorry," I say, not sure how to react to that news, but very sure high-fiving him would not be appropriate.

"Don't be, I'm not . . ." He shakes his head. "I don't even know why I just told you that when I haven't even told my family about my plans," he says. I stop to let Muffin sniff around a tree off the path and look at him. "Have you ever felt like you've been living, but not really living at all?" he asks quietly. I nod. "I've been living a lie for the last five years of my life. Since the moment Eva got pregnant, I've been doing the right thing for everyone else. I've been doing what's best for everyone but myself."

"I get that . . ." I don't know how he feels, but I understand what he's saying and I'm sure feeling that way isn't easy on a person.

"Sorry for putting this all out there. I don't know, maybe I just needed to tell someone else to make it more real or some shit."

"It's okay." I smile softly, resting my hand on his biceps. "Sometimes you just need someone to talk to who isn't involved and doesn't have an opinion."

"Yeah." He pulls in a deep breath, then lets it out. "It's for the best, especially for my daughter," Lucas says in a tone that is full of regret and sorrow. Without thinking, I wrap my arms around him, needing to offer him some kind of comfort. It takes a second, but his arms wrap around me, and he hugs me back. "Thanks," he whispers, and I nod, then start to pull back when Muffin tugs the leash in my grasp and runs around us, basically tying me and Lucas together.

"Muffin," I shout, then scream her name as she runs around us again, drawing us even closer and tighter together.

"Muffin, heel." Oh, thank god, *Levi*. I close my eyes, then open them back up and peek around Lucas's shoulder and watch Levi walking toward us.

"This is—"

"Awkward but not surprising," Levi cuts me off as he comes over to take Muffin's leash and untangle me from his brother. Feeling my face heat in embarrassment, I pull myself off Lucas as soon as I can then take a step back and run my hands down my thighs. This day keeps getting better by the minute.

"You okay, baby?" Levi asks, and I don't even look up at him.

"Yep, totally cool," I say as Muffin comes over to me, wagging her tail and looking between Levi and me, like, *Look who I found. Isn't it so exciting*, making me glare at her.

"I'm gonna head back," Lucas says, and I nod as he lifts his chin toward Levi before shoving his hands in his pockets and walking off.

"You didn't tell me you were going to take Muffin out," Levi says as soon as Lucas is gone. My eyes go to him.

"I didn't think I needed to, and it wasn't something I planned. I just needed to take a break for a few minutes," I say in a rush.

"You're pissed," he states, studying me, and I shake my head. I don't feel pissed, I just feel annoyed and on edge, and I really can't wait for this stupid day to be over with.

"I'm not pissed. Like I said, I just needed a few minutes alone."

"You weren't alone, you were with Lucas," he says, and I would swear there is an edge of jealousy in his tone—but that would be ridiculous, so I push that thought aside.

"I could tell he didn't want to go back inside, so I invited him to walk Muffin with me."

"Why didn't you tell me you were heading out?" he repeats, and I begin to get annoyed.

"I already told you why. I needed to think."

"To think about me and Heather?" he asks, and I narrow my eyes on him.

"Is there a you and Heather?" I ask. His lips twitch, which makes me want to kick him in the shin.

"Definitely not."

"You were engaged to her, though, weren't you?" His eyes narrow a little.

"How do you know that?"

"Your mom told me. Well, she didn't tell me the woman's name, but I put two and two together at dinner when Eva kept bringing Heather up."

"Christ." He shakes his head running his fingers through his hair. "That's something for me to talk to you about when I'm ready."

"Okay, so when would that be?" I question, and his eyes lock on mine.

"I don't know, twenty years from now . . ."

"What?"

"Baby, my ex was part crazy, part bitch. She's not exactly someone I spend a lot of time thinking about."

"But you were engaged to her?"

"Yeah, when I was young and my dick did the thinking for me, I was engaged to her." He pulls me close with his fingers in the front pocket of my jeans. "I know what Eva said upset you."

"She didn't upset me," I lie, and his eyes narrow. "She just annoyed me. She's not a very nice person."

"No, she's not, but she's the result of thinking with your dick and an unplanned pregnancy." That was a little harsh—probably true, but still harsh.

"Lucas is asking her for a divorce," I say, then close my eyes, wondering why the hell I just told him that when it's not my news to share.

"Did he tell you that?"

"Forget I said anything. I don't think he's ready to tell everyone yet."

"How long were you two on a walk before I caught up with you?"

"I don't know, five minutes." I shrug, and his eyes soften.

"Hmm." He shakes his head and I wonder exactly what that *hmm* means, but I don't want to ask him about it.

"I wish we were alone. This day has been a disaster."

"It's been good," he says, and I widen my eyes in disbelief.

"Are we on different planets right now?"

"Baby, think about it. Our families met, our moms—who just happened to be old friends—reunited, I didn't get called into work, and I spent the day with my woman. Yeah, there was a little bit of drama, but all in all, it's been a good day."

"You missed the part where I didn't know about the giblets in the turkey and had to unstuff the damn thing, then restuff it," I grumble.

"What?" He smiles, tucking a piece of hair behind my ear.

"Why are you with me?" I ask instead of answering his question, then cut him off when it looks like he's going to open his mouth to speak. "I can't cook, I dress like a nerd, I'm clumsy and always doing dumb stuff, plus my family is crazy. Why are you with me?" I repeat and he drops his forehead to rest against mine.

"Do you know how hard it is to find a woman who isn't all about herself? To find a woman who isn't superficial and self-centered?" he asks quietly.

I whisper, "No."

"I do know how hard it is. And I also know that the kind of beauty you hold is so rare most men would be lucky to even catch a glimpse of it."

"So because you think I'm pretty—"

"No," he cuts me off, taking my face between his palms. "It's not because you're gorgeous, which you are, it's because the parts of you that make you *you* are beautiful. That's why I'm with you. I'm with you because you're real, you care, and you don't know how to put on a front or be mean. I'm with you because you're the kind of woman who goes to a shelter to volunteer when most wouldn't even think about wasting their time. Because you worry about a little girl that looks at you like you have the ability to change her life. Because you are the kind of person who won't judge a guy you don't know when he tells you he's getting a divorce. I'm with you because the idea of not being with you isn't something I want to consider."

Oh.

My.

His words cause my breath to freeze in my lungs and tears to burn the back of my eyes.

"You really like me," I say after a moment, and his lips twitch into a smile.

"I more than like you, gorgeous, but yeah, I really like you."

I'm such an idiot. I close my eyes and drop my face to his chest. "I'm sorry about just leaving . . . You're right, I was worried about what Eva was saying and worried that you would want to get back together with your ex. I . . . I worry that you're going to realize I'm not worth the hassle."

"You're definitely worth it."

How does he know just what I need to hear?

"Thank you," I say, pulling my face back to look at him.

"Baby, caring for you isn't a hardship."

"Don't make me cry."

"I don't want you to cry, I just want to know that we're good and that when our families take off, we'll still be good. Today has been crazy, and I know you're stressed."

"I'm good, but I will be better once everyone leaves. Meeting your family has been great, but our families together . . ." I shake my head. "That's a little much for me."

"Well, before we head back, I want you to prepare yourself. Our moms are already planning our wedding."

"What?" I blink up at him, and he grins.

"They were arguing over where we would get married when I took off, so keep in mind that when that day comes, we're getting married at the courthouse and telling no one about it until it's done."

"What?" I breathe. His eyes lock on mine and fill with something that is so beautiful it makes every part of me feel warm.

"That's not for now," he says softly, rubbing his fingers down my cheek. "That's for when the time's right, but we are not having a wedding."

"What if I want a wedding?" I ask, wondering where the hell that question came from.

"Do you want a big wedding?"

"I don't know, I've never really thought about it before."

"You've never thought about getting married?" he asks in a tone filled with disbelief.

"Well, once I saw a Harry Potter–themed wedding on YouTube and thought that would be cool," I say, and his eyes close right before he drops his forehead to rest on mine once more.

"We are not having a Harry Potter–themed wedding."

"Why not?"

"Because we're not."

"But . . ."

"It's not happening, babe." He stops me with a quick peck to my lips.

"What if it's important to me?" I say, not ready to let the idea of a Harry Potter–themed wedding go now that the idea is in my head.

"Is it important?"

"Well . . ." I chew the inside of my cheek as my stomach dances with butterflies at the thought of being Levi's wife. "I guess not really. But if the day comes that we do get married, we're not doing it at the courthouse, because my mom and yours would somehow find out. So we will just have to go to Vegas."

He smiles right before he takes my mouth in a kiss that has me wishing we weren't in a public park but alone in his bed. When he pulls away, his lips touch my forehead, then he takes my hand and leads me back to the building, where thankfully everyone is getting ready to take off so they can beat the Thanksgiving Day traffic.

"Are we sleeping at my place?" Levi asks as I shut my apartment door after saying goodbye to his family and promising to see them again soon.

"Yep, my bed's too small," I mutter, and he leans down, kissing my nose.

"I bet I could make it work for what I have planned," he says, sending a tingle dancing over my skin.

"Oh," I breathe, right before I'm up in his arms and he's carrying me into my room, kicking the door closed behind us. Dropping me to the bed, he crawls up between my legs and moves his face an inch from mine.

"Now that we're alone, how about I do what I wanted to do to you this morning?"

"Okay," I agree with a whimper as he slides his hands up the front of my shirt while taking my mouth before showing me exactly what I missed out on this morning.

Chapter 12

MISSING

FAWN

"Miss Reed."

Looking up from the papers on my desk that I've been grading since school let out, I spot Tamara in the open doorway of the classroom. Glancing at the clock on the wall, I notice that it's way past the time she normally gets picked up.

"Is everything okay, honey?"

"My . . ." Looking like she's about to cry, Tamara takes a step into the room and pauses, dragging her backpack up higher on her shoulder. "No one has come to pick me up," she says quietly, and I nod.

"That's okay. Come on in and take a seat. Let me just get my stuff packed up." I smile at her, and she walks slowly toward my desk. "We'll just call your mom and let her know that I'll take the train with you. Okay?" Most of my students take the bus home after school, but some, like Tamara, are picked up. On occasion their parents are late, and when that happens I call the parent and take the train with the child to make sure they get home safely.

"You can't call my mom," she says so quietly that I almost don't hear her, and my body freezes as my eyes meet her worried ones.

"Why can't we call her?" I ask, and she looks away, biting her lip. I can sense she doesn't want to say whatever it is she's about to say.

"My mom . . ." She drops her eyes from mine and looks at the ground. "She hasn't been home in two days, and she's not answering her phone."

"Pardon?" I hope I heard her wrong, but I know I didn't.

"My mom . . ." Tamara wrings her hands together and shakes her head, looking up at me. "She went to work two nights ago, and she hasn't been home since then." *Oh my god.* I fight the urge to close my eyes in despair.

"Has this kind of thing ever happened before?" I ask softly, and at first she shakes her head no before nodding yes and biting her lip once more.

"Once or twice she's spent the night out of the house, but she always comes home. Always. She's never been gone this long. I know something happened to her, I just know it," she cries, and I breathe through my nose to fight back my own tears.

"It's okay, honey," I say quietly as I walk around my desk and wrap her in a tight hug. "It will be okay, but we have to go talk to Mrs. Thompson about this, then we need to talk to a friend of mine, okay?"

"I don't want to get her in trouble," she whispers, and I pull back to look her in the eyes.

"I know you don't, honey, but we need to let people know what's going on so they can look for her," I say, wiping away the tears trekking down her cheeks.

"I'm scared." More tears burn the back of my throat at her quiet confession. I have no doubt that she is scared, and if I'm honest with myself, I'm scared, too.

"I'll be with you. Let's go talk to Mrs. Thompson." I leave her to go around the desk to pick up my bag and coat. Gathering everything in one hand, I take Tamara's small hand with my free one and lead her down the hall to the office. As soon as we're there, Sammy looks up from the computer, smiling.

"Miss Samantha, is Mrs. Thompson in?" I ask, and her smile slides away slowly as she looks between Tamara and me.

"Yes."

"Good." I nod at her, then turn to Tamara. "Honey, can you sit out here and wait for me?" She nods. Leading her over to one of the chairs next to Sammy's desk, I watch her take a seat.

"Hey, Tamara," Sammy says, then she opens a drawer full of candy and treats. "Go on and pick something out to eat while you wait for Miss Reed."

"Fawn, what is it?" Mrs. Thompson asks, reading the look on my face as soon as I step inside her office and shut the door.

"Tamara's mom hasn't been home for two days," I say quietly as I drop my stuff in the chair across from her desk. "She said that she's never been gone this long."

"Let's try to reach her at the numbers on her contact list and go from there," the principal says, looking concerned. For the next few minutes she tries to call Tamara's mom, never once getting an answer. "I'm going to call Tamara's grandmother, fill her in on what's happening, and see if she's available to pick Tamara up," she says after she hangs up the phone.

"I'm going to call a friend of mine who's a police officer. He knows Tamara's mother's boyfriend, so I'm hoping he will be able to track down her mom or at least file a missing person report."

"Of course." Mrs. Thompson nods, and I pull my cell phone out of my bag as she types something into the computer before picking the phone back up and putting it to her ear. "Hello, Mrs. Albergastey, this is Mrs. Thompson. I'm the principal of PS 189," she says as I turn away from her with my cell to my ear.

"Hey, baby, you off work already?" Levi asks, and my eyes slide closed.

"No, one of my students—the one you met in the park with me? Her mom is missing and has been for two days. I don't know if I should call someone el—"

"Jesus," he cuts me off. "Are you at the school with her now?" I nod even though he can't see me.

"Yes, I'm here. We're both here."

"I'm on my way. It shouldn't take me more than twenty to get to you."

"Okay, see you then." I shove my cell back in my bag as Mrs. Thompson hangs up the phone on her desk.

"Tamara's grandmother is on her way. I explained that we were having an officer come to the school to file a missing person report."

"When was the last time she spoke to Tamara's mom?"

"She said that she had a falling-out with her daughter and that they haven't spoken in a couple months. She didn't like the new man in her life and refused to talk to her until she dumped him."

Pulling in a breath, I let it out slowly. "I don't have a good feeling about this," I state, and Mrs. Thompson nods.

"Me either, but there is always hope, my dear." Yes, and for Tamara, I will hope.

"I'm going to go sit with Tamara and wait for everyone to get here."

"Good. I'm going to put in a call to the social worker and let her know what's going on. Thankfully, Mrs. Albergastey is on the approved pickup list, so Tamara won't be spending any time in child protection." Yes, thank god for that. I would never want that for her, and if it came down to it, I would find a way to get her placed with me.

Leaving Mrs. Thompson on the phone in her office, I head out and, sitting next to Tamara, take her hand in mine. "Your grandmother is on the way," I tell her quietly. Her head turns my way, and her eyes lock with mine.

"She's coming?" she asks, seeming surprised. I nod.

"Yes, she should be here soon, along with Levi, the guy I was with in the park. He's a police officer, and he's going to come talk to you."

"Is he your boyfriend?"

"Yes, he's my boyfriend."

"Is he nice?" she asks, searching my face, and I smile gently, giving her fingers a squeeze.

"He's very nice, one of the nicest people I've ever met."

"You deserve to have someone nice," she says, dropping her eyes from mine, so I squeeze her fingers again, needing her to look at me when I say what I'm about to say.

"Everyone deserves to have someone nice honey, everyone," I state, and she swallows, looking away. I don't understand why most women nowadays don't think they are worthy of having someone who treats them right, someone who respects them and cares for them.

Hearing the front door of the school open, I watch through the glass as Levi comes in with Wesley. They both flash their badges at the security guard at the door. Standing, I step into the hall, and Levi's worried eyes lock on mine.

"That didn't take you long," I state, since it's only been about ten minutes since we spoke.

"We don't have time to waste. You said her mom's been missing for two days?"

"Yeah, that's what she said. She's right in here. We're waiting for her grandmother to arrive," I inform him as he stands close—so close that I can feel the tips of his fingers brush over mine. "Hi, Wesley." I smile, and he dips his chin toward me.

"Fawn. I wish these were better circumstances."

"Me, too," I agree, noticing then that he and Levi have on almost the same uniform of dark jeans, boots, and dark shirts with their blue NYPD jackets, which are hiding the fact they are both carrying. "I'll introduce you to Tamara, then we will go in and talk to Mrs. Thompson, the principal," I say over my shoulder as I lead them both into the office.

As soon as we step inside, I get close to Tamara and rest my hand reassuringly on her shoulder. "Tamara, this is Levi and Wesley. Guys, this is Tamara." I ask Sammy, "Can you do me a favor and just let Mrs. Thompson know that we are all here?" She nods, looking between the two men who seem to be taking up all the space in the office, then she gets up and heads for Mrs. Thompson's door.

"She said to go on in," Sammy says, and I take Tamara's hand in mine. The guys follow us into the office.

"Gentlemen." Mrs. Thompson stands and introduces herself to both Wesley and Levi, then she looks at Tamara. "Your grandmother is on the way. Would you like to wait for her to arrive before telling the officers what you know?" she asks, and Tamara looks at me.

"It's okay, honey, if you want to wait, we can wait," I say gently, and she shakes her head no.

"I . . . I can tell them what I know now," she says, and I nod at her, then lead her over to the couch in the corner of the office and take a seat next to her.

"Whenever you're ready, sweetheart," Levi says after grabbing a chair from in front of Mrs. Thompson's desk and pulling it over to take a seat. Wesley does the same, only he pulls out a pad of paper and a pen.

"My mom didn't come home from work two days ago," she says, and I watch her hands ball into fists. "She's normally home when I get up for school, but she wasn't on Tuesday."

"Has she ever done that before?" Wesley asks, and her jaw tightens.

"Yes, but only once or twice." She swallows, then adds, "But she always tells our neighbor if she's going to be out, and she will come over and check on me and make sure I'm up to go to school." Wesley nods.

"When was the last time you saw her?" Levi asks gently.

"Monday night at around eleven, when she was getting ready to leave for work."

"Where does she work?" Wesley asks, and Tamara drops her eyes to her lap.

"Mr. D's in Queens," she whispers, and I wrap my arm around her shoulders.

"Did someone pick her up for work?" Levi asks. Tamara nods, keeping her eyes cast down.

"Yes, her boyfriend, Juan, picked her up from the apartment."

"Have you seen or spoken to him since then?" Levi asks. Tamara lifts her eyes, and her chin wobbles.

"I . . . I called him today when no one was here to pick me up, but he said him and my mom weren't together anymore and not to bother him again." *Oh my god.* My eyes meet Levi's rage-filled ones for a brief second, right before a knock on the office door drags my attention from him.

"Tamara, honey," a woman says as she comes into the room. She looks so much like Tamara that I know immediately she must be her grandmother.

"Grandma." Tamara rushes toward the older woman, burying her face against her chest while wrapping her arms around her. "I didn't think you would really come."

"Of course I'd come, you know that, honey. All you have to do is call, and I will always be there for you," she says, and Tamara pulls back to look at her.

"Mom's missing," she says, beginning to cry.

"I know, I wish you would have called me sooner," Tamara's grandmother scolds her softly, holding her tighter.

"You and Mom were fighting, I . . . I didn't think you would care," Tamara says, pulling back to look at her.

"Of course I care, child." She shakes her head at her, then pulls her back in for another hug, and I see the tears in her eyes as she does.

"Mrs. Albergastey, this is Officer Levi Fremont and Officer Wesley Jameson. They are with the NYPD. Tamara has been filling them in on what's happened," Mrs. Thompson says, and Mrs. Albergastey looks at both men, who are now standing.

"Please tell me you will find my daughter."

"We will try," Levi says looking at her, then Tamara. "I think we have all we need from you for right now, Tamara, but I'm going to give my number to your grandmother. If you think of anything else at all, call my cell, and Mrs. Albergastey, if you think of anything, you can do the same."

"It's that man . . . ," she huffs, shaking her head at Levi. "That man Juan that she's been seeing, I told her that he's no good, but my daughter is stubborn and refused to listen to reason. He did something to her, I know he did."

I feel my heart lodge in my throat. I hope she's wrong. I hope—as bad as it is—that she just needed to get away and took off for a couple of days. I hope that nothing happened to her.

"We will do our best to find your daughter, Mrs. Albergastey," Wesley says, then his eyes move to Mrs. Thompson. "Where can I get a list of addresses and phone numbers for Tamara's mother?" he asks, and Mrs. Thompson looks at me.

"I'll be back in a moment. I'm going to have Samantha print the information out."

"Sure," I agree, watching her leave the room with Wesley.

"Will you find my mom?" Tamara asks, and I look at Levi. I can tell he's torn between lying to her to give her what she needs and telling the truth.

"We will do our best," he states, and she nods, moving her eyes to me.

"How will I get my schoolwork and stuff?"

"I . . ."

"I will stay with you in the city until this is sorted, honey. That way you won't have to miss class," Mrs. Albergastey tells her, and her body relaxes right before she comes over to give me a hug.

"Thank you, Miss Reed."

"Any time, and if you need me, you can call Levi's number, okay?" I whisper, and she nods against my chest. Catching her grandmother watching us, I let her go, then stick my hand out toward her. "I'm sorry for not introducing myself earlier. I'm Miss Reed, Tamara's teacher."

"I've heard about you. Tamara said you are the first person she's met who may love books more than she does," she says, and I find myself smiling as she pulls me in for a hug. "Thank you."

"You're welcome."

"Now, we really should get going. We need to go to my place and pick some stuff up," she says, ushering Tamara toward the door. "And please, the second you know anything, anything at all, you call and tell me," she says to Levi. He nods as I wrap my arms around my waist, watching them leave huddled together.

"You okay?" Levi asks as soon as they're gone, and I shake my head no.

"I'm worried. Do you think her mom's okay?"

"I don't know, baby. But I'll find out."

"Okay," I whisper, and his eyes soften as he takes a step toward me.

"Got the stuff we need, you ready?" Wesley asks, breaking into the moment, but Levi doesn't take his eyes off mine. I can tell that he wants to touch me—I can almost feel the energy flare between us.

"I'll be okay, I'll see you tonight," I say, and his jaw ticks.

"See you tonight. Call me when you get home."

"I will." He nods, then looks to Mrs. Thompson, who's looking between the two of us with curiosity. "It was nice meeting you."

"You, too." She gives him a smile, then he and Wesley leave through the open door.

"I hope they find her," Mrs. Thompson says, and I pull my eyes from Levi's retreating back to look at her.

"I hope so, too."

She shakes her head, then pulls in a breath. "Go on home and try to enjoy your evening."

I won't be enjoying my evening. In fact, I will most likely spend the rest of the night until Levi gets home pacing the apartment, but I don't want to stay around the school any longer than I have to.

"Have a good night, Mrs. Thompson," I say as I head to the door with my stuff, saying a silent prayer as I put on my coat that Levi is able to find Tamara's mother alive and well.

∽

Hearing my cell phone ring, I drop the book I've been reading to my lap and pick the phone up quickly. "Levi?"

"Yeah, baby."

"Is everything okay?" I ask, glancing at the clock, seeing that it is already after two in the morning.

"Yeah, just wanted to tell you to go to sleep."

"How did you know I wasn't asleep when you called?" I smile, rubbing the top of Muffin's head when she drops onto my lap on top of the book resting there.

"Were you?"

"Well, no." I sigh. I hate when he's working late at night, and after today it's even worse.

"You need to sleep, baby."

"I know," I agree, but it's hard to find sleep when he's not in bed with me. "Have you found anything out?"

"Nothing yet. What are you wearing?"

"Your shirt."

I can hear the smile in his voice when he mutters, "My girl misses me."

"Yes, I do, so please be safe and come home soon."

"I will, baby. I've got one more stop, then I'll be home. We sleeping at mine?"

"Yes."

"I'll be there soon. Go to sleep, gorgeous."

"Night, Levi," I murmur, then drop my cell to the bedside table and put my book away before flipping off my light. I lie there awake for another hour until he finally gets home and crawls into bed with me.

Chapter 13

PLAIN OL' IN LOVE

FAWN

Waking to the smell of coffee, I roll to my stomach, lift my head toward the clock, and frown when I see it's only seven. Levi always sleeps late on the weekends, and last night—just like the three nights before—he didn't get in until after midnight, so I know he must be tired. Doing a stretch, I roll out of bed and grab my dad's old flannel shirt from the back of the door. Slipping it on over my tank top and sleep boxers, I head for the bathroom and clean up, then make my way back through the bedroom and open the door. Levi is sitting on his couch, shirtless, wearing a pair of sleep pants with his laptop open in front of him on the coffee table.

"Morning, baby." He grins as I crawl into his lap and cuddle against his chest.

"Morning." I press my lips against his neck, then turn to see what he's doing on his computer, but he minimized whatever he was looking at. "You're up early."

"Couldn't sleep," he says as his fingers run over the top of my bare thigh, causing a tingle to slide through me.

"Have you gotten any new leads?" I ask the same question I've been asking him every day for the last few days.

"Nothing new."

"That's not good. Have you guys been able to question Juan?" I lean back to see his face.

"He's MIA and no one's talking. I have a couple informants that are checking into things, but I'm not sure they will be able to find anything more than I can."

"Do you think that maybe Tamara's mother is on drugs or something?" I ask hopefully. I know that wouldn't be good, but it would be better than her being dead.

"There is always a possibility that she could be b—"

"What?" I cut him off when he breaks off and his body gets tight with tension under mine.

"What I'm about to tell you stays between us, do you understand that?" he asks quietly but firmly. I know I won't like what he tells me very much.

"Yes." I nod, and he adjusts me until I'm straddling him, then takes my face between his large palms.

"Juan is my main suspect in the murders of two other women. Both were from his stable. Both were known to be in relationships with him prior to their deaths." Swallowing down the sudden bile that rises to the back of my throat, I close my eyes. "I'm not saying that's what happened to Tamara's mother, but with her missing and his history, it's likely that she could be one of his victims."

"My poor girl," I whisper, and he brushes a soft kiss over my lips.

"Don't give up hope," he demands, running the pads of his thumbs along the underside of my jaw. "She may turn up—she may be hiding from him. All we know right now is that she's missing."

"I know," I agree as a sinking feeling fills the pit of my stomach. I don't know how Tamara will deal with the loss of her mother if she doesn't turn up. I can't imagine having to go through something like that at her age. I just pray she's strong enough to get through whatever happens.

"Do you feel up to a run?" he asks, and I look out the window. Winter has hit New York, and it's not only cold, but also it snowed yesterday evening, turning everything white except the sidewalks that have been cleared.

"Actually, yeah," I say knowing a run will help me clear my head, which is probably the reason he's suggesting it.

"Up you go." He taps my thigh before helping me stand. "We'll stop for breakfast at the diner on the way back."

"Sounds good to me." I give him a quick kiss when he pulls me in, and then head for his room, where most of my clothes have ended up in the last week. Actually, I don't even remember the last time I was over at my place. We have just kind of fallen into a routine of staying at his apartment.

After putting on running gear, we head out, leaving Muffin behind—not that she's upset about it. She didn't even want to go out to use the bathroom, which wasn't surprising, but Levi forced her to while I was getting ready.

I don't listen to music like I normally do; I just run in pace with Levi, listening to his controlled breathing. By the time we are done, I'm starving and freezing, so I'm a little more excited than usual to go eat. As we make our way toward the diner hand in hand, my stomach growls, and Levi smiles down at me.

"Hungry?"

"Very." I smile back as he pushes open the door to the restaurant. Finding an empty booth, I slide in, and just like always, he slides in next to me.

"What can I get you two?" a waitress asks, and I look up at her while blowing on the tips of my ice-cold fingers.

"Two coffees, please," Levi says.

As she walks off, she nods, muttering, "Got it."

"Still cold?" he asks, grabbing my hands and holding them between his warm ones.

"Yes, I knew it would be cold, but I didn't think it would be that cold out," I say, feeling a little dizzy as he puts the tips of my fingers against his mouth, blowing on them.

"I know something that could warm you up." He winks, and my stomach dips.

"I bet you do." I laugh, and he smiles and kisses me softly, then moves away when the waitress sets two cups of coffee in front of us.

"Do you know what you'd like to order?" she questions, pulling out a pad of paper and a pen.

"She'll have the chocolate chip pancakes, and I'll have the hungry man's breakfast," Levi tells her. She jots down our orders on her pad, then takes off again.

"How did you know that's what I wanted?"

"Babe, you order the same thing every time we come here, unless it's after eleven. Then you get a turkey club."

"I'm kinda boring."

"You're perfect," he says, turning to look at me, and I notice his eyes are soft. "You're perfect for me," he continues, then leans in, resting his forehead to mine. "I love waking up to you and coming home to you at night." *Oh god.*

"I love that, too," I agree quietly as my stomach fills with butterflies.

"How would you feel about moving in with me?"

My mouth goes dry, and I blink at him, wondering if I just heard him correctly. "Pardon?"

"It doesn't make sense for you to pay rent for a place you're never at." That's true, but moving in together is not a step forward—it's a giant leap.

"I . . . Don't you think it's way too soon for that?" I ask, and he searches my face for a long moment.

"If I thought it was, I wouldn't be bringing it up," he says, leaning back and touching the side of my face softly with the tips of his fingers. "When is your lease up?"

"In February," I say quietly as my heart begins to pick up tempo at the idea of living with him.

"We can wait until then to decide if that makes you feel more comfortable."

"I . . . This is all just very fast." I shake my head while moving my hand between the two of us.

"Yeah, you're right, this is all fast, but tell me you're not happy and that this doesn't feel right." I would be lying if I said it didn't feel right, if I said being with him didn't make me happy. I'm pretty sure I'm past the falling-in-love part and now just plain ol' in love with Levi—not that he knows it. We have spent every night together unless he's working, but even then he always crawls into bed with me at some point during the night, and when we have days off, we've spent them together, hanging at home or traipsing around the city going to the movies and out to eat. I've even gotten him to go to a couple of museums, even though he said he hates that kind of stuff. But are we ready to live together? That I just don't know.

"I'm happy, so, so happy, but I really think I would feel better if we waited until my lease is up to make that kind of decision," I say regretfully, and his eyes soften as he leans closer.

"That's fine with me, and it's not going to change anything, so stop tearing at your lip," he says, pulling down on my chin and forcing me to release my lip. I hadn't even realized I was chewing on it. "I want to make sure you're ready, too. I don't want to push you into something you're not ready for."

"Are you . . ." I swallow and pull in a breath. "Are you ready to live with me?" He leans in close enough that I can smell the mint and coffee on his breath.

"I've been ready, gorgeous, but this isn't about me being ready. It's about you feeling secure enough with me that you know you can trust me."

I already know I can trust him. I also know the thing that is holding me back from jumping into his arms and screaming *Yes, yes, yes, I want to live with you.* He never once mentioned love, and although I have no doubt that he cares about me, being in love with me is something altogether different. "Eat, baby." He leans in, kissing me, after the waitress places our food on the table, and I do eat, wondering why I can't just tell him that I love him.

~

I smile around the toothbrush in my mouth as I study the blatant happiness in my eyes. After Levi and I got back from breakfast, we spent the rest of the day making love and talking. Spitting the foam in my mouth into the sink, I rinse with water, then wipe my face.

"Babe," Levi calls from the living room, and I smile again as I open the drawer under the vanity and dig through his stuff for the lip gloss I left there a few weeks ago.

"I'll be out in a minute," I yell back, dropping the gloss back into the drawer before going to the bedroom to put on my boots.

"Your sis . . . Holy shit," he says, and I look up from the boots that I'm zipping up and find him in the doorway staring at me.

"What's wrong?"

"Where are you going?" he asks, scanning me from the top of my head, down over the black wrap dress I'm wearing, ending on the knee-high black leather boots with pointed toes and three-inch heels on my feet.

"I told you this afternoon, remember? My sisters and I are going to Hank's showing in SoHo." I'm not really surprised he doesn't remember, since I brought it up right after we had sex when we were doing the whole lazy-talk thing I love so much.

"You're wearing a dress."

"Yes, well, it's a fancy showing, so I have to dress up."

"I've never seen you in a dress."

"That's because it's winter, and I normally don't wear dresses in the winter unless I'm going someplace fancy, hence the showing and the dress."

"What did you do to your hair?" he asks, wrapping a strand of my straightened hair around his finger.

"I had a little time, so I decided to straighten it," I explain, then press my hand against his chest when he takes a step closer, so close that I know he's going to try to make me dizzy. I don't have time for that, because I can hear my sisters talking in the living room.

"I'm rethinking you going to this thing."

"What?"

"You look . . . Jesus, you look fucking amazing right now."

Smiling like a loon, I whisper, "Thanks," then push against his chest again when he starts to get even closer. "You can't mess me up or make me dizzy, so you need to stop." I try to sound firm, but the words come out in a low whimper as his body presses the length of mine and his hand squeezes my ass.

"He's not allowed to touch you."

"Who?" I ask, dipping my head to the side as his mouth travels up my neck to my ear.

"That art dude. He's not allowed to touch you, do you understand?"

"Why would I let him touch me?" I say, trying to comprehend what he's saying, but my brain is short-circuiting with the way his mouth and tongue are moving along my neck.

"You wouldn't, but I guarantee he's going to try," Levi says; then I feel his lips tug on my neck, and I pull back, stunned.

"Did . . . did you just try to give me a hickey?" I ask in disbelief, holding my neck, and he looks from me to the open bedroom door.

"Fawn's gonna be a minute," he growls toward the living room, shutting the door on my sisters, who start to laugh.

"Levi," I warn, watching him prowl toward me. I walk backward until I have no place left to go and my back is literally against the wall. "Stop," I plead half-heartedly, watching his eyes drop to his fingers beginning to trail along the front V of my dress, which he brings down along with my bra, baring my breasts to him.

"I've never felt the need to possess someone the way I feel the need to own you," he mutters to me—or to himself—right before his mouth latches on to my breast and he pulls, sucking hard, so hard that I feel it in my core and know I'm going to have his mark on me and be soaking wet before he's done.

"Levi." I latch onto his hair. His fingers skate up under my dress, along my inner thigh, slide my panties to the side, and flick over my clit, making my hips jump.

"Wet. Always so damn wet for me," he says as he runs his nose up my throat, nips my bottom lip, then thrusts his tongue into my mouth as one finger thrusts inside me, sending me to my tiptoes.

"Don't stop," I beg as my core starts to throb in beat with his one finger that turns into two. Just like that, with barely a touch from him, I'm already so close to flying over the edge. "Levi," I mewl in disappointment when his fingers disappear, leaving me on the edge of an orgasm.

"When you come home, I'll take care of you," he says, putting his fingers to his mouth and sucking them clean, then taking a step back.

"That's . . . that . . . that was not nice," I pant, and he grins a grin I've never seen on him before, then ducks his face until we are sharing the same air.

"What's not nice is knowing my woman looks more beautiful than I've ever seen her and she's going to spend time with another man."

"I'm not spending time with another man," I huff as I fix my bra and my dress, completely annoyed with him and his caveman ways. "I'm spending time with my sisters."

"Is he going to be there?"

"Well, yeah, it's his showing, but there are going to be lots of men there." Levi narrows his eyes on me, and then shakes his head as his phone rings.

"Fuck," he clips, looking at the screen before putting it to his ear. "What's up?" he asks, and I watch his eyes close briefly. "Finally. All right, I'll be there," he says, then hangs up.

"Is it Tamara's mom?" I ask hopefully.

"Juan," he says, making me feel worry and relief all in one instant. "Where is he?"

"You know I can't tell you that, baby," he says, stepping toward me and wrapping his arm around my waist. "I don't know when I'll be home," he says quietly. I nod, then lay my head against his chest and wrap my arms around him.

"I'll be here when you get back," I say, wanting so badly to tell him I love him.

"Be good and send me a text when you get to and get back from the showing."

"I will," I agree, feeling his lips on my hair right before he uses the tips of his fingers to tilt my head back so he can kiss my mouth. "Be safe."

"Always," he agrees, taking hold of my face. "You look gorgeous, baby, and you owe me a date where you wear this dress so I can take it off you when we get home."

"Sir, you owe me a date where you give me a reason to wear this dress." I smile, and he shakes his head, kissing me once more before letting me go. He heads for the door.

Turning to look at me with his hand on the knob, his eyes scan over me, making me feel light-headed. "I'll plan something for next weekend," he says, opening the bedroom door and disappearing without another word, making my heart fill with worry. It's hard to see him leave for work whenever he has to go. Being a police officer has never been a safe occupation, but with the added tension between the police and the public right now, I worry about him whenever he wears his badge.

"Either Levi's a five-minute man or you two didn't have sex," Libby states, walking into my room and plopping down onto the bed. I roll my eyes at her, then turn and dig through the closet for my ankle-length coat.

"What?" I ask when I turn to find her staring at me with wide eyes.

"You look . . . you look amazing. Holy shit, what have you done to yourself?"

"I didn't do anything. I just straightened my hair—you've seen it like this before," I say, and she shakes her head.

"No, it's not the hair . . . it's you . . . You look . . . you look really happy."

"I *am* really happy," I say softly, and she blinks at me, then widens her eyes.

"You're in love."

"How can you tell?"

"You just look happy, happier than I've ever seen you. Don't worry, I doubt anyone else will notice."

"Notice what?" Mac asks, coming into the room, and I wait to see if she sees the same thing as Libby. "You're in love," she states, and I feel my heart beat a little harder.

"How can you tell?"

"It's written all over your face."

"Do you think Levi can tell?" Mac sweeps her eyes over me.

"I don't know." She shrugs. "But I do know that the guy who just left a few minutes ago looked pretty fucking happy to me, and if I'm not mistaken, he may also be in love with you."

"Do you really think so?"

"Yeah," she says as her face softens. "You're easy to love, Fawn. I wouldn't be surprised at all if he's in love with you, too." God, I hope he is in love with me, because the idea of him not caring for me the way I care for him is enough to make me feel sick.

"He told me today that he wants us to move in together."

"And you're sitting here questioning if he loves you or not?" Libby says, shaking her head. "No man would want to live with a woman unless he's in love with her. Trust me, if I didn't love Mac, I sure as hell wouldn't live with her."

"Oh, please, you love living with me," Mac says, and Libby rolls her eyes, then looks at her watch. "We should probably go if we're going to make it on time."

"Yes, let's go. I don't want to spend too much time overanalyzing this," I say as Mac's phone starts to ring. Pulling it out, she looks at the screen, rolls her eyes, and shoves it back in her coat pocket.

"Who is that?"

"No one."

"Seriously, are you still on the whole *I'm not telling you anything* gig?" I ask, studying her.

She presses her lips together, then mutters, "Fine. It's Wesley."

"So you *do* know him. Ha." I point at her, and she lets out a loud huff.

"Yes, we know each other."

"And?" I draw it out, and she crosses her arms defensively.

"And nothing. I know him, that's all."

"You're so full of crap. Are you sleeping with him?" I ask, and her cheeks turn a dark shade of pink. "You are, I can tell you are."

"I'm not sleeping with that man."

"Oh yes, you are, I heard you when you came home last night." Libby glares at her, then looks at me. "She was all, 'Stop it. My sister's here. You need to leave before she finds out about us,' blah, blah, blah.

Seriously, either we need a bigger place or I need to get a place of my own."

"I can't believe you just said that," Mac breathes, and Libby crosses her arms over her chest, raising a brow.

"Really, and what is the point of you hiding your relationship with him?"

"I'm not in a relationship with him, I'm just having a little fun."

"Whatever. You two are together all the time, and do not even try to deny it, because I know it's true."

"It's complicated."

"How is it complicated?" I ask softly. Mac looks at me, wringing her hands together.

"It . . . him and me." She tosses her head back toward the ceiling. "God, I don't know. I really like him, but I just don't know. After what happened with Edward, I just don't know if I can put myself out there again."

"I don't want to point out the obvious, but Edward was kind of a dick."

"Not kind of, he was a dick." Libby shakes her head.

"I know, I'm just afraid I'm going to be let down."

"You won't know unless you try, and Wesley seems nice and genuine. I think he deserves a real chance."

"You're right," she agrees, pulling in a deep breath.

"And I, for one, would like to know how you met him." Mac presses her lips together.

"Oh, me, too," Libby says, wiggling her brows.

"I know." I look between the two of them. "How about we skip the showing and go have sushi at our spot?"

"*Yes,*" Libby cries, and I laugh, then say goodbye to Muffin and lead my sisters out of Levi's apartment. We get into a cab and head downtown to our favorite sushi spot, where we eat way too much and drink sake while Mac fills us in on everything that is Wesley.

"I'm so full," Mac groans as we walk out of the restaurant a couple of hours later.

Smiling at her, I pull out my cell phone when it rings, feeling my stomach melt when I see Levi's calling.

"Hey, honey, we—"

"Fawn," says a voice I don't recognize, and my step falters.

"Yes."

"Shit. This is Wesley, I . . . Fuck." He pauses, and I can hear that he's upset, which puts me immediately on guard. "I need you to come to Lenox Hill Hospital," he says. My stomach drops, and my hands start to shake.

"What happened?"

"Levi was shot. He's in surgery now."

"No," I breathe, feeling my sisters get close. "Please tell me you're lying." My eyes close, and I wait for the inevitable to come as I feel my heart split open.

"I'm sorry, sweetheart," he says as Mac slides my phone out of my hand.

Hearing Mac tell him we will be there soon and that we don't need a police escort, I lean into Libby as she leads me to the sidewalk and puts out her hand for a cab.

"It will be okay," Mac soothes, and I nod my head, praying she's right. I don't know what I will do if Levi's not okay. I don't even want to think about what I will do if he's not.

"I . . ." I swallow over the lump in my throat. "I need to tell his family. They need to know what happened."

"I'll take care of it," Libby says as she helps me into the back of the cab. "I'll call Mom and have her get in touch with Levi's mom. Don't worry about that right now."

Pulling in a deep breath through my nose, I let it out and hold on to my sisters' hands as we ride to the hospital. As soon as we arrive, we head inside, where Wesley is waiting for us.

"What have they said?" I ask him as soon as he's close, and he shakes his head.

"Nothing yet. We're still waiting for an update." His eyes go to Mac, and he reaches over, taking her hand.

"Where was he hit?" I ask as he starts to lead us toward a group of elevators.

"Right shoulder. The shot was through and through, but he lost a lot of blood."

"Did they say if he would be okay?" Libby asks as my mouth dries up and my stomach rolls.

"He'll be okay, but he was asking for Fawn when they were rushing him into surgery. He wanted you here," he says.

I nod and step onto the elevator with my sisters flanking me, vowing that when I see Levi again, I will tell him I love him.

Chapter 14

ACTIONS SPEAK LOUDER THAN WORDS. I LOVE YOU.

LEVI

Fighting against the heavy weight holding me hostage, I slowly climb to the surface of consciousness, only to have reality hit me as the smell of antibacterial cleaner and the sound of machines beeping reminds me of what happened. When Wesley called, he told me that our informant found out Juan was hiding at the apartment of one of his longtime girlfriends.

When we arrived on the scene, two officers and SWAT were waiting for us. What Fawn didn't know was that morning we'd finally been able to procure a warrant for Juan's arrest after his SUV turned up in Brooklyn with blood evidence inside. We hadn't gotten the DNA analysis of the blood samples back from the crime lab yet, but we suspected when we did we would find out it belonged to Elia Albergastey, Tamara's mother. When SWAT went into the building to arrest Juan, Wesley and I went with them. It was all good until Juan's girlfriend decided she wasn't willing to let her man be arrested and pulled out a gun from under the couch where she had been sitting quietly up until that point.

After that, all hell broke loose. The officers holding Juan got distracted by the bullets flying and let him have just enough leeway that he was able to grab a weapon from under the entertainment unit. That was when he shot me. After that, everything is a blur.

"I love you." I hear it again, only this time I know it's not a dream. *Fawn.* Jesus, she must be flipping out. I hate that she's seeing me like this, but then her words register and I force my eyes open. "Oh my god, you're awake," she whispers, then reaches out, fumbling for something on the bed.

Soon a voice is calling through the quiet room, "How can I help you?"

"He's awake, you said to call when he's awake," she says quickly while running her fingers down the side of my face, like she's attempting to make sure I'm really here.

"The doctor will be there in a few minutes."

"Thanks," she says, then leans in, carefully placing a kiss against my lips. "How are you feeling?" She closes her eyes, shaking her head. "Never mind, don't answer that. It's a stupid question," she mutters, opening her eyes back up, and I chuckle, then groan in pain when I reach up to touch her. "Don't move, you crazy man, you've been shot. You need to take it easy," she scolds softly.

I ignore her, wrap my hand around the back of her neck, and pull her toward me, ignoring the pain shooting through my shoulder.

"I love you," I say, and she leans back suddenly with wide eyes that search mine.

"What?" she whispers in disbelief.

"I love you, baby."

"You do?"

"Yeah," I say softly, and she drops her forehead to my chest, making me bite back another wince.

"I should have told you I was in love with you when I realized I was," she whispers, and I shake my head. She didn't need to tell me; she's shown me every day.

"I already knew you did," I mutter, and she pulls back to look at me.

"Is it that obvious?" She smiles, running her fingers softly down my face again.

"I don't know if it's obvious, but I see it in the things you do, feel it when we are together. *Love* is just a word unless there is action behind it, that's how I knew."

"And you love me?"

"Yeah, baby."

"When did you realize you loved me?"

"After Thanksgiving."

"And you didn't tell me?" She frowns, making me smile.

"I've shown you every day," I say, then look over her shoulder when the doctor walks into the room clearing his throat.

"While he's checking you over, I'm going to let everyone know you're awake," she says. I don't want to let her out of my sight, but I know I don't have a choice.

"Are my parents here?"

"Not yet. They're on their way. Traffic is insane getting into the city—I guess the president is in town."

"All right, come back to me," I demand, and she nods, kissing my jaw before leaving the room.

Once she's gone I look at the doctor, who's studying the beeping machine at the side of the bed. "What am I looking at here?" I ask him, and he finishes writing, then looks at me.

"You're alive." He shakes his head. "The bullet went straight through, but it hit your subclavian artery on the way, which caused most of the damage. You lost a lot of blood—just a few centimeters more and you could have lost your arm, so I'd say you're a lucky man." Not so lucky, seeing that I had on a bulletproof vest and still managed to get hit. "We rushed you into surgery, stitched everything up, and gave you two separate transfusions. You'll be here for a couple days, but you'll be okay."

Nodding at that, I stay put and let him inspect the wound. While he's doing that, another nurse comes in to let him know the room I will be moved into is ready.

As soon as they both leave, Wesley pokes his head in through the door. "Where's Fawn?" I ask him, and he grins.

"What, you don't want to see me?"

"Not really." I smile at him, and he shakes his head, walking toward the bed.

"She's down greeting your family and hers. They all just arrived, so I told her I'd wait with you." Damn, my parents and Fawn's together do not bode well for me being alone with my girl and healing without drama.

"What happened after I got hit?"

"We got Juan. He's going down, and no one can save him this time. His girl is talking—she's currently trying to save her own ass."

"Thank fuck."

"Yeah," he mutters, then runs a hand over the top of his head. I notice he's still got blood on him—it's most likely mine. "You scared the shit out of me."

"You? Fuck, man, we should have known to check the apartment for weapons, given his history."

"Yeah," he mutters, taking a seat next to the bed. "Fawn was a zombie until the doctor came out and told us you were going to be okay. I don't think I've ever seen a woman so damn scared in my life."

"I would be the same if something had happened to her," I whisper, not even able to stomach the thought. I can't imagine getting a call like the one she got. I can't imagine thinking I might lose her.

"My baby," I hear, and I turn my head toward the door and watch my mom rush across the room toward me. "I . . . Don't ever scare me like that again, do you understand me?" Mom cries, placing her hand against my cheek.

"Sorry, Mom."

"Just don't let it happen again. Why weren't you wearing your vest?"

"I was . . . I—"

"You need a better one, then." She shakes her head as she leans in and kisses my cheek. When she steps back, my dad comes over.

"Son." He shakes his head, reaching out to touch the top of my head. "You doing okay?"

"I'm good. The doctor said I should be out in a couple days."

"Good." He nods, and I can tell he's working at holding back the emotions written all over his face.

"Jesus, man, you sure know how to get attention, don't you?" Lucas says, coming over to stand on the other side of the bed.

"Jealous?"

"A little. I wouldn't mind lying around for a few days having people wait on me hand and foot," he jokes, and I shake my head at him as he leans down, touching his forehead to mine. "But seriously, I'm happy as fuck that you're okay."

"Me, too," I agree, then watch Fawn's parents come over.

"We had to come," Katie says, leaning down to give me a kiss on my cheek. "I'm glad to see you're okay, we've been worried sick."

"Thanks for coming," I say, and she smiles as Aiden touches the top of my head like my dad did moments ago before stepping back without a word. Getting hugs from the rest of my family, I frown when Eva walks into the room with a woman I know. Jesus, this bitch just doesn't fucking stop.

"Levi," Heather says as she comes toward me, and I look at Fawn, who is now standing next to my bed. Her face goes pale, which pisses me the fuck off.

"What the fuck, Eva?" Lucas asks, and she turns her eyes to him.

"She wanted to see him—she could have lost him."

"I can't believe you would do this right now," Mom says glaring at Heather and Eva.

"I just . . . Eva told me what happened and I wanted to . . ."

"That's nice and all, but if you're who I think you are, then you need to leave. If Levi wanted anything to do with you, he would have called you, but he didn't," Libby says, and I hold back a smile. Libby is hard as nails when it comes to her family.

"She's right. I appreciate your concern, but we have nothing to talk about," I state firmly, and Heather looks around the room before looking at me once more.

"We were going to get married. I still care about you," she says, but I know it's a lie. She didn't care about me when we were together, and she sure as fuck doesn't care about me now.

"If you don't leave, I will call security to escort you out," Fawn says as Heather starts toward the bed.

"You can't do that," Eva says. Fawn's eyes go to her.

"I can and I will. You shouldn't have brought her here."

"Who do you think you are?" Eva asks as her face turns red.

"Eva, take Heather and leave," Mom says.

"Seriously?" she asks, looking at Mom, then at Lucas.

"Yes," Lucas says, and she narrows her eyes.

"Whatever, I'm leaving," Heather says. Eva looks around the room, glaring at everyone, before she disappears out the door with Heather.

"Good riddance," Fawn mutters, and I chuckle, then groan again. Her eyes fly down to me. "Are you okay?"

"Kiss me."

"No."

"Kiss me," I repeat, and she sighs, then leans down, pressing a kiss to my lips.

"Love you, baby."

"I love you, too." She rests her hand against the side of my face, kissing me once more, softly, before taking a seat on the chair next to my bed, where she pretty much stays until it's time for me to be released from the hospital.

~

Watching Fawn walk into the living room with the phone to her ear, I set my computer aside, then tag her hand as she tries to pass me. I pull her toward me, forcing her to take a seat. I dodge her hand as she reaches out to smack me away as I try to kiss her. "Yes, I will be there Saturday at noon," she says to whomever she's talking to, and I kiss the side of her neck, smiling as she tries to elbow me, never putting enough force behind the action to actually do damage, since she knows I'm still healing. It's been four days since I was released from the hospital, and even though I still have a lot of healing and physical therapy to do, I feel back to myself.

"Okay, I'll see you Monday, Mrs. Thompson, and thank you for the update," she says, pulling the phone away from her ear and hitting the "End Call" button. "Seriously, you need to stop. You are going to end up hurting yourself," she grouches, glaring at the smile on my face.

"What was the phone call about?" I ask, ignoring her glare. She narrows her eyes when I try to pull her into my lap.

"Mrs. Thompson talked to Tamara's grandmother today. She wanted to let me know that Tamara will be moving. She didn't want me to worry when Tamara wasn't at school when I return to work next week."

"What's going on Saturday?"

"They are having a service for Tamara's mom. Her grandmother asked Mrs. Thompson to let me know so I could go show my support if I wanted to."

"You feel up to that?"

"Yes," she says quietly, then turns sideways on the couch to face me completely. "I'm glad that Tamara's getting some kind of closure. I just hope now she can work on healing."

"Me, too, baby," I agree softly. The DNA from the SUV came back as that of Elia Albergastey, so we knew something happened to Tamara's mom in that vehicle. The CSI team concluded that one person could not lose that much blood and survive without immediate medical help, which left us to conclude, sadly, that Tamara's mother had been murdered.

"What are the moms doing?" I ask, hearing banging in the apartment next door, and she rolls her eyes.

"Who the hell knows? I swear, they are going to make me lose my mind. Whose idea was it to let them help me move, anyway?" she asks, looking at the wall between our apartments when the banging gets even louder.

"Yours." I smile, and her nose scrunches up.

"I don't know what I was thinking."

"You were thinking that you wanted to take care of me, so you needed their help to move you out of your space and into mine," I remind her. The day I got released from the hospital, Lucas asked me if I could help him find a place in the city, and Fawn told him that she knew of the perfect spot, then went on to say that she was moving in with me. I was a little surprised but honestly happy as fuck that she was moving in earlier than February. My family is a little disappointed that Lucas is leaving the town we grew up in, but they understand completely that he needs a change—and since he filed for divorce from Eva two days ago, he needs that change to come with at least a hundred miles attached to it.

No one was happy about Eva showing up at the hospital with Heather, but Lucas was so pissed, he finally broke down and told everyone he was leaving his wife. Not that she really cared. Apparently she had been having an affair for the last year and was all too happy to tell Lucas that she was already planning on moving in with the guy. Thankfully, though, she agreed to give Lucas full custody of Madeline, since her new man isn't exactly interested in raising another man's child.

"That's true—at least one good thing is coming out of their stay," she mutters, bringing me out of my head.

"It hasn't been that bad." I smile, and she glares.

"It hasn't been that bad? Really, are you crazy?" she huffs, making me grin. "Okay, I will admit the first couple of days it wasn't so bad because they were occupied with you, but now I swear, every time I go over there, they are talking about weddings and babies. And your mom is constantly trying to convince me to move to Connecticut so she can help raise her nonexistent grandchild. I think that is the only time they really fight."

"They fight?" I ignore the comments about my mom since I've been hearing it firsthand for the last few days. She keeps saying that I need to think about moving home, where there is less crime. I know what happened shook her, but that kind of shit could happen anywhere, and unfortunately, in my line of work it's a risk you have to take.

"They don't really fight, they just bicker about crap like where we're going to get married, where the baby—that doesn't exist—is going to be baptized, who is going to babysit said baby, who's going to be Nana and who's going to be Grandma. You know, crap like that. I'm pretty sure they are both certifiably nuts." She sighs, looking at the wall again when the banging starts back up.

"I say we just give them a baby."

"Give them a baby?" Her head swings my direction. "Did you hit your head?" She laughs, but I don't. I want that with her. I want her to be my wife, I want her to have my babies, I want everything with her. "You're serious?"

"I'm not saying I want a baby tomorrow, but I do want babies with you. I can only imagine how beautiful you will look pregnant with our child, and I know you will be an amazing mom. You love kids and are great with them."

"You're serious," she repeats with wide eyes, and I carefully pull her over and adjust her on my lap to straddle me.

"I'm crazy about you, and I want all of those things with you. Is that so hard to believe?"

"No . . ." She rests her hands on the underside of my jaw while my fingers skim along the skin under the edge of her T-shirt. "I guess I never really thought about having a husband and a family before now." She smiles, then leans close, brushing her lips over mine. "Please don't mention this conversation to our moms—they are already hard enough to deal with as it is, and if they get wind that one day we want kids, I have no doubt they will toss my birth control out the window."

"I won't tell them." I smile, and she reaches out, touching my shoulder where there is a bandage covering the wound.

"Have I told you today that I love you?" she asks, lightly touching the gauze with her fingers.

"This morning," I murmur, and she looks up at me.

"Well, I still do, just so you know, and maybe even more than I did this morning."

"That's good to know." I smile, roaming my hand up the back of her shirt, enjoying her smooth, warm skin against my palm. Feeling goose bumps break out across her skin, my cock, which has been hard since she sat on me, hardens more. I love that she's so affected by my touch.

"Levi," she breathes, sounding nervous, and I know that nervousness is because she's worried about hurting me.

"I need to be inside you," I tell her, lifting my hips, letting her feel exactly what she does to me.

"We . . ."

"You won't hurt me."

"Are you sure?" she questions, running her palm over my erection, and I bite back a curse. It hasn't been months since I've been inside her, but a few days is way too fucking long to go without her.

"You have to promise to stop me if you're in pain," she murmurs, sliding her hand inside my sweats and taking my cock into her palm, stroking it.

"I'm in pain now," I point out, and she rolls her eyes. Sliding my hand down the back of her sweats, I grab her ass, then move around her hip and slip my fingers between her legs.

"I swear, if I hurt you, I'm never having sex with you again," she says against my mouth as her hips rise and fall and she rides my fingers in sync with her hand pumping my cock.

"Get your clothes off, baby," I urge, needing to be inside her. Standing quickly she rips her shirt off over her head, then kicks off her pants and panties, all the while keeping her eyes glued to my hand that is running over my cock.

"Christ," I groan, dropping my head to the back of the couch as she leans forward, taking me into her mouth. Spreading my legs farther, I make room for her as she kneels in front of me, wrapping her hand around the base of my cock while using her mouth on me. Feeling her nails scrape down my thigh, I lift my head and meet her gaze. Her eyes are as wild as her hair, and she looks beautiful taking me down her throat. "Come here," I command, not willing to come in her mouth, which I know I'm seconds away from doing if she doesn't stop. She sucks me harder and goes deeper. I groan, then bite out, "Fuck," as I tug her hair, pulling her head back.

"I wasn't done," she complains, and my teeth snap together as she licks over the head of my cock. Lifting her and ignoring the pain it causes in my shoulder, I drop her to the couch and spread her legs wide, then bury my face between her thighs. I could live on her taste alone—she's like nothing I've ever had before. Licking and sucking her clit, I listen to her breathing become heavy, then move my hand up her stomach and take hold of one nipple, twisting just enough to make her pussy walls contract around my tongue thrusting inside her.

She moans, her fingers latching onto my hair and holding me in place as she winds her hips, trying to get more, but I'm not going to let her come like this. Fuck no, I need to be inside her. I need to feel her pussy contract around me. I need to feel her tight walls sucking me deeper. Sitting back, I pull her up with my arm around her back and set her on my length, groaning as she clamps down on me.

"Levi," she whimpers as I raise my hips and force her down onto my cock.

"Ride me hard," I demand, and she does, her hips rising and falling rapidly, making me wish I had a mirror so I could watch myself disappear deep inside her. Feeling her walls start to ripple, I know she's close, and I know she's going to pull me over with her when she comes.

"Kiss me," I say, holding on to her tightly. The second her mouth touches mine, I thrust my tongue between her lips and listen to her moan down my throat as she comes hard, so fucking hard that her walls tighten almost painfully around my cock, which sends me over the edge with her. Breathing heavily, she collapses against my chest.

"Did I hurt you?" she asks after a moment, and I shake my head no and relax back into the couch, holding on to the woman who changed everything for me. The woman who has made me want more out of life, the woman I want to spend my life with.

Epilogue

LEVI

Looking at Fawn asleep in my arms, I wonder how the hell I got so god-damn lucky. I never thought for a moment that I would find someone so perfect for me, but somehow I was lucky enough to move in right next door to her. "Merry Christmas." I kiss her ear, then watch a small smile spread across her pretty mouth as she sleepily rolls toward me and tucks herself even closer.

"Merry Christmas." Her sleepy eyes open to meet mine, and I know without a doubt that I will never get tired of waking up to her.

"Are you ready for your first present?" I ask, and her eyes light up.

"Yes. Gimme, gimme, gimme." She claps excitedly, and I laugh.

"A little bit greedy this morning, I can see," I mutter, and she smacks my shoulder.

"Whatever, I just love opening gifts. It could be a lump of coal, and I would still be excited about it." She smiles as I pull out the card I tucked away in the top drawer of my nightstand. "A card, I love cards." She holds it to her chest, and I laugh again. None of this surprises me, since my woman is Christmas obsessed. Everything is decorated—even Muffin has a red-and-green leash and collar with bells on it.

"Are you gonna open it or stare at it?" I question, running my hand up her thigh, and she leans up, kissing me on the edge of my jaw before ripping the card open.

"Vegas?" she breathes as she studies the two plane tickets sitting in her lap. "We're going to Vegas for New Year's?"

"Yes, and while we're there, I want you to do me a favor."

"What?" She pulls her eyes from the plane tickets to look at me, and I take her hand in mine, running my fingers lightly over her smooth skin.

"Be my wife," I say as I slide a ring onto her finger. I thought the ring would be perfect for her—it's simple and understated but still absolutely gorgeous. Everything she is.

"You . . ." She shakes her head. "You want to marry me?" she asks in disbelief, blinking at the ring, then me. How she can still react with surprise is amazing to me.

"Yes . . . I—"

"Oh my god. You want to marry me," she yells so loudly that Muffin, who was asleep, gets up quickly and jumps onto the bed to see what's going on.

"I take it that's a yes." I laugh as she launches herself at me, forcing me to my back and kissing me all over my face and lips.

"Yes, yes, yes . . . oh my god, I'm getting married."

"We're getting married."

"Yes, we're getting married . . . ," she says quietly, then looks at her hand resting against my chest. "This is so beautiful." She pauses to meet my gaze. "I love you."

"I love you, too, gorgeous," I murmur, bringing her face down toward me. I kiss her softly, then mutter, "Fuck me." She sobs, dropping her forehead to my collarbone.

"This is . . . I'm so happy," she cries, tucking her head under my chin and lying against my chest. "How did this happen?"

"You stole my heart and my breath the day you ran into me," I say simply, and she pulls back, wiping away the tears on her cheeks.

"Who would have thought running with your eyes closed would lead to love?" she asks, and I grin at her, then look over at Muffin.

"Out, girl," I command, and she huffs but jumps off the bed and heads out of the room, giving me the privacy I need to get my Christmas present from my girl.

Two years later

LEVI

"Hush," I whisper against the side of my daughter's head as I hold her against my chest. As her weight starts to finally settle against me and her cry dies down, I close my eyes and rest my head back against the headrest of the rocker.

"I would have gotten up with her," Fawn says, and I open my eyes to find her standing in the doorway to the nursery, wearing a tank top that shows off her beautiful breasts and still slightly rounded stomach. I knew she would be gorgeous pregnant, and I was right. The extra weight still looks good on her, and knowing that her body provided life and protection for our child makes her even more beautiful in my eyes.

"You need to sleep, baby," I say softly. At eight months old, Olivia is no longer nursing, but she is teething, which has led to many sleepless nights for her mom and me.

"So do you," she murmurs, coming into the room. My little angel senses her mom is close, and she lifts her head from my shoulder.

"Mama." She reaches out for Fawn, and I smile as she takes the baby from me, placing a kiss to her forehead.

"Were you having a cuddle with Dada?" Fawn asks her, and she looks at me with bright eyes that remind me of her mom.

"Dada." She nods her head, and Fawn laughs.

"Yes, that's your Dada," Fawn agrees with a smile, and I pull her down into my lap. Then we sit there in the dark and rock our girl until she falls back to sleep.

Three years later

FAWN

Watching Olivia drop yet another piece of broccoli onto the floor, I sigh. I know she thinks Muffin is going to help her out by getting rid of the evidence of her uneaten vegetables, but unfortunately for her, Muffin hates broccoli more than she does.

"Olivia." I raise a brow as she pretends to put another piece in her mouth and drops it on the floor.

"Yes, Mama?" She looks at me with wide, innocent eyes that you would swear were the eyes of an angel, that is if you didn't know her. Only her father and I know different—our baby girl is a monster. Yes, she's sweet, loving, cuddly, and so damn adorable that you just want to squeeze her, but she is also a hellion who pushes the limits every chance she gets.

"You know Muffin doesn't like vegetables, honey, so now when you're done eating, you are going to have to clean up the mess you made under your chair," I tell her, and she looks at Muffin, who is sitting at her side—where she is every second of the day—and frowns.

"Muffin, you need to eat your vegetables. They're good for you," she scolds before muttering something under her breath, reminding me of her father.

"How are my girls?" Levi asks, coming into the kitchen and stopping to kiss Olivia before making his way to me. He kisses my forehead and lips, then places his hand on my very large, very pregnant stomach, over our son.

"Daddy, did you know Muffin doesn't like to eat her vegetables?"

"I didn't know that," Levi lies, and I roll my eyes at him.

"She doesn't. I tried to feed her some, but she just didn't like them." She points at the ground, and I bite my lip to keep from laughing at the put-out look on her face.

"Maybe you should eat some to show her how good they are."

"Great idea," she says before going about pretending to eat her vegetables.

Shaking my head at her, I look at Levi and catch him smiling at me. No matter how much time passes, no matter how crazy life gets, there is never a day I regret running into him with my eyes closed.

Two years later

FAWN

"Tamara Albergastey," the speaker calls, and I stand and start to yell and clap as loudly as I can as I watch Tamara head across the stage. Her eyes meet mine for a brief moment, and she grins, then continues walking. I'm so damn proud of her. Not only did she graduate, but she did it at the top of her class.

"I'm so proud." I smile, taking a seat next to Levi, and he wraps his arm around my shoulder and tucks me against his side.

"She's a good kid," he says, and I nod. Olivia and Lucas love her and are both sad that their favorite babysitter is leaving the state to go away for college after the summer.

"I'm going to miss having her over as often as we do now," I confess, and his arm tightens for a moment.

"Boston is close. We can visit her whenever you want," he says, and I lean my head against his shoulder. He might not admit it, but he's going to miss her, too. There are people you meet in your life, people you just know are going to do amazing things, and Tamara is one of them. I'm lucky to know her and even luckier that I have gotten to witness her growing up into the beautiful woman she is becoming.

Acknowledgments

First I have to give thanks to God, because without him none of this would be possible. Second I want to thank my husband. I love you now and always—thank you for believing in me even when I don't believe in myself. To my beautiful son, you bring such joy into my life, and I'm so honored to be your mom. Thank you, Mom, for being here and stepping in when I need you. Thank you to my agent, Susan, for believing in me. I'm so grateful to have you in my corner.

Maria, thank you for taking a chance on me, and Melody, I loved working with you on this book. Thank you for all your help and advice. And thank you to the rest of the Montlake editing team—you are all amazing.

To every blog and reader, thank you for taking the time to read and share my books. There would never be enough ink in the world to acknowledge you all, but I will forever be grateful to each of you.

I started this writing journey after I fell in love with reading, like thousands of authors before me. I wanted to give people a place to escape where the stories were funny, sweet, and hot and left you feeling good. I have loved sharing my stories with you all, loved that I have helped people escape the real world, even for a moment.

I started writing for me and will continue writing for you.

XOXO Aurora